ALMOST LOVE

ALMOST LOVE

Louise O'Neill

riverrun

First published in Great Britain in 2018 by

riverrun

An imprint of

Quercus Editions Limited
Carmelite House
50 Victoria Embankment
London EC4Y 0DZ

An Hachette UK company

A CIP catalogue record for this book is available
from the British Library.

Hardback ISBN 978 1 78429 886 9
Trade Paperback ISBN 978 1 78429 885 2
Ebook ISBN 978 1 78429 887 6

10 9 8 7 6 5

Typeset by CC Book Production

Printed and bound in Great Britain by Clays Ltd, St Ives plc

For Catherine Doyle, who held my hand through it all

NOW

Sarah lay on the bed, watching Oisín as he slept. This is it, she thought as she looked at his face, his slack-jawed, drooling mouth. This is the man I'm going to spend the rest of my life with.

'Baby.' Oisín yawned, rubbing sleep from his eyes. 'Babe, are you awake?'

'Of course I'm awake,' she said. 'I've been awake for hours because *someone* came home demented drunk at four o'clock last night.'

'Sorry,' he said, nestling into her, stroking her stomach. 'You know I didn't do it on purpose.'

'No, Oisín.' She pushed his hand away. 'I'm not in the mood.'

'You're never in the mood anymore,' he said under his breath.

1

'What did you just say to me?' Sarah asked, even though she had heard him.

'Nothing,' Oisín replied, even though he knew she had heard him.

Sarah sat upright. The curtains were still open, and outside blue skies promised a perfect June day, the sort of day that other couples would want to spend together – reading the newspaper in bed, going for walks in their local park, taking selfies and counting how many Instagram likes their love could collect.

'I'm pissed off with you, Oisín.'

'I know.'

'You said you'd be home straight after work yesterday.'

'I texted you about the leaving party, didn't I? I had to go.'

'I'm surprised Bryant has any stockbrokers left, the amount of leaving parties you "have to" go to.' Before, Oisín would have wanted her there. *It's not as much fun without you,* he used to tell her when he came home early from a night out with the lads. *Nothing is as much fun when you're not there, Sarah.*

'We were supposed to go to the cinema,' she said. 'I bought the tickets and everything, like we agreed.'

He took a deep breath. 'Okay, can we stop? I'm sorry. I didn't mean to let you down. Will you forgive me?'

Sarah folded her arms, reluctant to give in so easily.

Oisín tried again. 'So, what did you get up to yesterday? Did you get into the studio at all?'

2

'I didn't have time.'

'But I thought we said you would—'

'We?'

'Sarah . . .' Oisín swung his legs over the side of the bed so he was facing away from her. 'Sarah, I can't—'

'I met some friends for lunch yesterday so I didn't have time to paint,' she interrupted him before he could finish his sentence.

'What friends?'

'What do you mean, "What friends"?'

'I didn't mean anything by it. It's just that I met Fionn and Robbie in O'Donoghue's last night and they never said anything about seeing you for lunch.'

'Fionn and Robbie were out? Together?'

'That's what I said, isn't it?'

'Whatever. I do have other friends, you know,' Sarah said. (No, I don't.) 'We went to Dun Laoghaire. To Harry's.' (No, we didn't.)

'That's nice,' Oisín said as he got out of bed. 'I hope you had fun.'

He stood with his back to Sarah as he stretched, razor shoulder blades biting through the flesh. Oisín was so thin; he couldn't seem to gain weight no matter what he ate. Last year, Sarah didn't mind. She couldn't get close enough to Oisín then, as if she wanted to unzip his skin and settle inside his body, make a nest for herself there. (*I carry your heart with me*, Oisín had recited to her, touching his fingertips to her chest. *I carry it in my heart.*) No one had ever told Sarah that being in a relationship could feel like coming home, that love didn't have to mean feeling scared all the time. But now, as she watched Oisín pull off his underwear, throwing it in the general direction of the laundry basket – because putting it *in* the basket, like she had asked him to do a million times, would be far too difficult, clearly – she began counting the knuckles of his vertebrae. She imagined doing that every morning for the rest of her life, itemising each bone, and she could feel her throat closing over.

After his shower, Oisín grabbed his laptop bag and leaned over the bed to kiss Sarah goodbye.

'Where are you off to, then?' she asked.

'I have to go into town. I need to get a haircut before the wedding next weekend. Alannah has very specific ideas about how she wants the groomsmen to look.'

'Why do you have to go into town for that? What's wrong with the barber in Dun Laoghaire?'

'I have to go to someone who actually understands what to do with my hair, Sarah; you know that.'

'But it's Saturday,' she said, pouting. She was copying an actress, she thought, from a French art-house film that Fionn had forced her to watch with him, although she couldn't remember which one. 'Saturday is supposed to be *our* day.'

'You just got your summer holidays; every day is a Saturday to you right now.' Oisín ruffled Sarah's hair and she glared at him.

4

'My job is actually really fucking difficult. I'd love to see you try teaching for one day; see how long you'd last.'

'Babe, I didn't mean it like that.'

'No, just fuck off.'

'Sarah, you can't just tell me to fuck off. That's not how people in healthy relationships communicate with each other.'

'Oh, Jesus Christ. Have you been reading Oonagh's self-help books again?'

'For once, just for once, Sarah, can you leave my mother out of this? She's never been anything but lovely to you.'

'Oh, really? Like when she walked in here unannounced without even ringing the doorbell?'

'She thought you had gone home to Dunfinnan for the weekend.'

'But what was she even doing here in the first place? It's like she wants to check up on me every second of every day, make sure that I'm not wrecking her precious house.'

'Sarah—'

'Trekking mud through the hall.'

'*Sarah*—'

'Keeping livestock in the kitchen, I suppose.'

'I'm not having this conversation with you again,' Oisín said as he left the room. 'My mother likes you. You need to get over this.'

Sarah waited for him to come back, to say he loved her and he hated fighting with her and he couldn't enjoy his day unless he knew that she had forgiven him. She waited until she couldn't wait anymore.

She dressed, applied her make-up, lining her lips in bright red. *He* used to tell her that she had 'blow-job lips', usually while she wiped her mouth clean, after he came. He liked it when she swallowed, so Sarah did. Sarah always did what that man liked her to do. She walked downstairs, pausing in front of a canvas splashed with reds and purples, a woman's face screaming in the swirling colours. Open-mouthed, her tongue cut out; silenced forever. One of Oonagh's creations, naturally. Everything in here belonged to Oonagh.

Stripped wooden floors, Aztec-print rugs, exposed brick walls, a neon-pink light fixture that made everyone look like they had rosacea but she was sure had been hideously expensive. Sarah hated all of it. 'It's a bit obvious,' she had said to Fionn, whispering, '*New money*,' under her breath, and Fionn told her she was a spoilt brat. Maybe Sarah was being a brat, but it was hard living in a house where everywhere she looked was evidence that people *could* make money from art, that being an artist *was* a viable career. If you were good enough.

Sarah reached out to touch another one of Oonagh's paintings, the coagulated oil like clots of blood beneath her fingers. The hopelessness that she so often felt in this house began to return, as if it was embedded in its very walls. She needed to get out of here, she decided. She needed to go to the sea, to taste salt on her tongue. She would be able to breathe there.

6

She locked the front door behind her, smiling at Mrs Morrison from next door, who was watering her flowers. The Morrisons had a gardener who came every Thursday, Johnny, but Mrs Morrison liked to pretend that she was responsible for his handiwork. 'Natural green fingers,' Sarah heard her tell friends who admired the pink and yellow roses sneaking up a trellis against the stone house when they came to visit.

'Going somewhere nice, Aine?' Mrs Morrison said, peeling off her pristine gardening gloves.

'Why does she keep calling me Aine?' Sarah had asked Oisín when they moved in to the house.

'It doesn't matter,' he replied, pouring her a glass of champagne to celebrate this next step in their relationship. But Sarah couldn't let it go.

'Who is Aine?' she asked again. 'Who is Aine? *Who is she?*'

That had been their first fight.

'I think I'll go see Oonagh and William,' Sarah said, surprising herself. 'It's such a nice day.'

'Isn't that lovely?' Mrs Morrison said. 'Giving up your Saturday to spend some time with your in-laws. I wish my Damian's Paula was half as conscientious about keeping in contact with me.'

Sarah pushed out the creaking gate as she *hmmm*ed her disapproval of Mrs Morrison's daughter-in-law, a lovely woman who left the Morrisons' every second weekend with a haunted expression on her face.

On the DART, she sat by the window, watching the sun flinch as it hit the flat sea. The train passed Blackrock, Dun Laoghaire, Glenageary.

Killiney, she told herself. Killiney. I'm going to see Oonagh and William.

She would get off the DART at Killiney station and walk to Oonagh and William's mansion, with its turrets hewn out of stone, the facade designed to resemble a medieval castle. Ostentatious, and not to Oonagh's taste – she had admitted as much to Sarah. 'I loved the house in Booterstown,' Oonagh had said over brunch in Avoca, which she insisted on paying for. 'I didn't want to leave. But William . . . Anyway,' she said, picking up the dessert menu, 'marriage is about compromise.' Sarah had wanted to ask her why it always seemed to be the woman who was expected to compromise.

The train stopped at Dalkey and, almost unbeknownst to herself, Sarah stood up. She waited for the other passengers to disembark before her: a group of teenage girls in high-waisted jeans, an elderly woman after them, her mouth wizened, like Nana Kathleen's when she took her false teeth out.

When Sarah reached Sandycove, she sat on the wall at the side of the tiny beach and checked the time on her phone. He would be going for his Saturday-morning walk soon. He was a creature of habit, she knew; he didn't like anything or anyone to disturb his daily routine.

Two skinny-limbed children were building a sandcastle, screaming with tears when an older kid ran across them, scattering their creation to the wind. Their mother lay back down on her striped beach towel, keeping her sunglasses on so that she could comfortably ignore the children while gesturing at the man with her to go help. The father, in his swimming shorts, sheer from too much washing, went hand in hand with the knee-high boy and girl towards the water, and the screech of 'Too cold! Too cold!' began as waves splashed against toes. It made Sarah think of her own first time at the seaside. She was young then, and her mother was still there.

'We're going to the beach today,' Helen had told her that day. 'Are you excited, my lovely Sarah?'

Sarah remembered a light cotton dress, sandwiches buttered in the kitchen, a long car journey with the windows rolled down, sweat beading at the back of her neck and dribbling down her spine.

'We're here,' her father said eventually, carrying the icebox and two collapsed beach chairs, Sarah's mother holding her by the hand.

Sarah remembered standing at the shoreline, the view fractured by rainbow-coloured windbreakers and half-falling-down umbrellas. People shrieked as the rickety rollercoaster at the edge of the beach swooped low and she inhaled salt and seaweed and coconut-scented suncream.

'Do you want to go for a dip?' her mother asked her, and Sarah said no. All she wanted to do was stand there and look.

Being by the sea always made Sarah feel small, insignificant in a way that was comforting somehow. It made her think that none of this would matter, in the end.

Time passed. Ten minutes? Half an hour? And then a shadow fell across her. And she knew it was him.

'Sarah?'

She looked up at him. 'Hey,' she said, and something in her broke, yet again. How did he still have the power to do that, after all this time?

'I thought it was you, but I wasn't sure. What are you doing here?'

'What?' She pretended to look confused.

'Not exactly your neck of the woods, is it?'

'I'm living in Booterstown now.'

'When did you leave Portobello?' he asked.

'I was living in Stoneybatter before, actually.'

'Oh, right.'

'It doesn't matter,' she said quickly. 'Listen, we should catch up. Do you want to grab a coffee?'

He checked his watch. 'Sure,' he said. 'I have some time.'

As they walked down Breffni Road, he said, 'I haven't seen you in ages. I can't even remember the last time we met.'

It had been three years. *We can't break up, Sarah,* he had said to her, three years ago, when she decided to stand still and to ask him for more. She had pretended for so long to be sterile, clean, to have no needs of her own except to please him. She couldn't do it anymore. *But we can't break up,* he had said to her while she tried not to cry. He didn't like women who cried; it was messy, undignified. *We can't break up because we were never in a real relationship in the first place.* They had only seen each other one more time after that, a stolen evening in an expensive hotel. But Sarah didn't want to think about that night and how it had ended. What he said. How he had looked at her.

'Yeah, it's been a while,' Sarah said now.

'You look great,' he said.

He had always commented on her appearance, but it wasn't in a weird way, she used to tell Fionn. Being admired by him didn't feel like when other men would look at her, teeth bared as if they wanted to devour her. *Smile, love,* men would shout as she passed them on the street. *You'd be so much prettier if you smiled,* as if a performance of joy was the price Sarah had to pay for existing in a female body in a public space.

'You look well too,' she said.

'Thanks,' he replied. 'I'm feeling uncharacteristically relaxed. Just back from Paris with Flo and Harry.' He held the door to the cafe open for her. Oonagh would have hated that, Sarah thought. *Chivalry is an outdated concept that only perpetuates patriarchal myths,* she'd said at one of the insufferable dinner parties William threw regularly. The beautifully arranged dining table at the Killiney house, linen napkins and silver cutlery, a single orchid in a short tumbler at each seat. The walls were laden with photos of Oonagh and William in their twenties and thirties, impossibly young and glamorous: Oonagh holding a placard above her head, demanding divorce

11

or abortion rights, waving at the camera as she and a group of equally rebellious women set off on the train to Belfast to procure illegal condoms. *That's why I've made sure that the men in this house know that housework isn't a woman's job,* Oonagh had said as Oisín stood up to clear plates. *All the men.* She'd winked at William and he reached across the table to kiss her.

'Paris,' Sarah repeated. The coffee shop was small, wooden tables with jam jars full of wild flowers. The waitress gave them menus when they sat down. She was attractive, blonde hair and excellent teeth, and Sarah looked at him to see what his reaction would be.

'I don't need a menu,' he told her. 'I'll have an Americano.'

'Are you sure?' the waitress replied. 'Our gluten-free brownies are fab.'

'I'm sure they are.' He leaned back in his seat, looking at her more closely. 'But, sadly . . . What's your name?'

'Luna.'

'Luna? That's an unusual name. But very pretty. I must say, it suits you,' he said, and the waitress blushed. 'But sadly, Luna, I'll have to refuse.' He looked at Sarah. 'What'll you have, Sarah?'

'A chai latte.'

'And a chai latte for my friend.' He handed the menus back. 'Thank you, Luna.'

After she left, he lowered his voice. 'What kind of name is Luna?'

'Maybe her mother was into Harry Potter.'

He didn't answer, and checked his phone instead. That was rude, Sarah thought. Oisín would never do that. Oisín's manners were impeccable; his mother wouldn't have stood for anything less.

'So. How was Paris?'

'Paris is Paris,' he said. 'Harry enjoyed it though, and that's the main thing.'

'It's cool the three of you went on holiday together.'

'Oh, we're terribly modern.'

'Was Daniel all right with Florence going away with you?'

His jaw tightened. 'No idea.'

'Well, I'm glad it went okay – for Harry's sake.'

'I'm glad too. Although I will say seven days is too long to go without getting laid.'

Sarah wasn't sure if she had heard him correctly, but then he smirked at her, confirming her suspicions. She knew that, later that evening, she would be able to articulate exactly why this had hurt her feelings, but for now, the perfect response was somehow just outside her grasp.

'I'm sure you can survive seven days,' she said, wishing her drink would arrive so she'd have something to do with her hands.

'I think we both know that's not true,' he said. His eyes met hers and, for one moment, it was as if nothing had changed.

'Here you go,' the waitress said. She banged Sarah's chai on the table, the milky liquid splashing onto the saucer. 'Sorry,' she said to Sarah, before gently placing his coffee down.

'Is that everything?' the waitress asked him.

'Perfect, thanks, Luna.' He didn't look at her this time, too busy scrolling through his camera roll.

Luna faltered, her smile fading, and Sarah almost felt sorry for her.

'Here,' he said, holding his phone out to Sarah.

She could tell instantly it was one of Fionn's paintings. If Sarah had spent her life trying to make the sea true on the page, then Fionn had attempted to do the same with the sky: swashes of inky blacks and midnight blues. His paintings were intense to look at, as if you were being swallowed whole, the paint swirling in your mouth and crawling up your nose until you thought you might suffocate in the world he had created.

'Sure, there he is,' Sarah said, but she looked away from the photo as soon as possible.

'Isn't it incredible? This fantastic place called Galerie Thaddaeus Ropac had a piece of his in an exhibition of up-and-coming artists. If you're ever in Paris, you should check it out.'

'If I'm ever in Paris?'

'Yeah. You'd love this gallery. Sofia Coppola was a guest curator a few years ago.'

'Did you go to Père Lachaise again?'

'What?'

'Père Lachaise?' Sarah asked again, but his face was blank. 'Did you buy anything by Fionn?' she tried. 'Or is it still only the one piece you have?'

14

'I bought this one,' he replied. 'It was cheap as chips, really, especially compared to the Oonagh MacManus I bought the day before. I was afraid Flo was going to demand extra child maintenance when she saw the price of it.' He took another sip of coffee. 'What do you think of MacManus? I know some people say it's just hype, that she's more ideology than actual talent, but her work never decreases in value, does it?'

'That's weird that you would mention Oonagh.'

'Why so?'

'I'm dating her son,' she said, watching him carefully.

'The black kid in that terrible band?'

'The Principles aren't terrible; they're really popular.'

'They're popular in Ireland,' he said. 'Playing Vicar Street and small pubs down the country. They're not going to set the world on fire, are they?'

'I don't know,' Sarah said. 'Anyway, that's Domhnall. I'm with Oisín, his older brother.'

'Very good.' He caught the waitress's eye and made a scribbling motion in the air: *Bill, please.* 'That's why you're here, is it?'

'What?'

'Are you here to see the Wilsons?' he asked. 'She's an attractive woman, isn't she? Still has it, even at her age. I met her when we sold them that house in Killiney.' He shuddered. 'What a monstrosity. It's like something an itinerant would buy after they won the lotto.'

That's not funny, she would have said to anyone else, but

15

he would have laughed at her. So Sarah stayed quiet and giggled, a high-pitched noise that announced what an *easy* girl she was – an easy, lovely girl. Sarah had always done that with him and she had always hated herself for it afterwards.

The waitress brought the bill and he insisted on paying.

'Don't be going on with that feminist nonsense, Sarah,' he said, ushering her outside into the sunshine, his hand in the small of her back, and she fought the urge to lean against him and murmur her thanks. She wasn't allowed to do that anymore.

'Well, look who it is.' A short, balding man was walking towards them, overdressed for the heat in a royal-blue suit.

'Michael Gleeson, how the hell are you?' He moved away from Sarah to shake the other man's hand.

'I'm good, I'm good,' Michael said, wiping sweat off his brow. 'How was Paris? Florence told Yvonne that you went shopping. Naughty, naughty.'

'I did. They'll sell on well, particularly the MacManus. How's Noah?'

'Ah, he's grand.'

The two men talked about Harry and Noah, how relieved they were that Transition Year was over and the boys were finished with work experience and mini-companies and trips to Kolkata to feed starving children in slums. Yvonne was sick of having to chauffeur Noah around to rugby training and to the disco and she couldn't wait until Noah had his full driving licence, but then you worry about boy racers, don't you? Almost makes you wish you had a girl.

16

Finally, all talk of Noah's rugby-kicking technique exhausted, Michael nodded his head at Sarah. 'And who's this?' He didn't remember her, Sarah realised, even though she had taught Noah for two years at St Finbarr's before she left.

'This is Sarah Fitzpatrick,' he told Michael. 'She's a friend of mine and an artist. You should keep an eye out for her.'

I'm not an artist, Sarah thought. Artists create art. Sarah's art was trapped in her fingertips, like dirt gathering beneath her nails.

'Just a friend?' Michael winked at him.

'Behave yourself, Gleeson,' he replied. 'Sarah is involved with Oonagh MacManus's son.'

'Oonagh MacManus?' Michael said. 'I've been trying to get in contact with her for months but her agent is so bloody over-protective. Will you give her this, the next time you see her?' He handed Sarah a business card, silver font on green. 'My gallery is on Kildare Street.'

'I know where it is,' Sarah said, and she could hear how coarse her accent was, how *country*, Dunfinnan strangling her vowels. 'Kevin's place is only a few doors down.'

'Kevin Walsh? How'd you know him?'

'I'm friends with his boyfriend.'

'Ah, Robbie, of course,' Michael said. 'Does that mean you know Fionn McCarthy as well?'

'Sarah and Fionn went to Dublin Art College together,' he interrupted, and Michael whistled.

'You know all the important people, Miss Sarah Fitzpatrick,' he said. His phone beeped and he pulled it out of his pocket, grimacing as he read the text. 'I'd better go; the wife is looking for me,' Michael said. 'You're a lucky man; no ball and chain for you, is there?'

He laughed. 'Good to see you, Michael. Tell Yvonne I send my regards.'

'I will, of course,' Michael said. 'And nice to meet you, Sarah. Stay out of trouble.'

He waited until Michael was out of sight before he took a step towards her. 'Stay out of trouble? You?' he said. 'Never.'

He was getting old, Sarah realised, the creases around his eyes cut deep, his teeth almost yellow in his thin-lipped smile. He was forty-seven now, and he looked every year of it. What was Sarah doing here?

The wind blew her hair over her face and he brushed it away. 'You dyed it.' His voice was surprised, as if he had only noticed now.

'Yes.' Blonde. I dyed it blonde, like you preferred.

'It suits you,' he said. 'But, listen, I have to go. Duty calls. Do you need a lift to the Wilsons' place?'

'I'm grand,' she said. 'Thanks, anyway.'

'Be good, Sarah,' he said, walking away from her. She waited for him to turn around and look at her, one last time. But he didn't.

Matthew, she thought.

Matthew. Matthew. Matthew.

THEN

Dread was creeping through me, using my veins as a map to spread through my entire body. I blinked once, twice, the room seeming to melt until I felt like I was caught in a Dalí painting. *A fan of Freud*, I could almost hear a lecturer at college say, *this piece underpins all of Salvador's attempts to render his hallucinatory dreams real. Themes of death, decay, eroticism. Dalí believed he could simulate craziness while maintaining his sanity.*

I am going to be sick.

'Is it possible to die of a hangover?' I whispered to Stephen. We were in the staffroom, listening to Mrs Burke, the principal, explain the protocol for this evening yet again.

'I thought your New Year's resolution was to drink less? That didn't last very long.'

'Oh, shut up.'

'Is there a problem, Sarah?' Mrs Burke asked me.

'No, Mrs Burke,' I said.

'Good,' she said. 'These might only be the first-year parent–teacher meetings, but I hope you realise that we always expect a certain standard of professionalism here at St Finbarr's.'

I used to think that leaving school meant never having to do what a teacher told me ever again. I used to think a lot of things. When she'd finished her lecture, I pushed myself off the plastic chair, every muscle in my body aching.

'I know,' I said to Stephen, who was packing his notebook and teacher's diary into his briefcase. 'Self-inflicted, you have no sympathy for me, blah, blah, blah.'

'Good luck this evening,' he said. 'All those mothers, giving out because their sons are head over heels in love with the new art teacher and can't concentrate on their studies.'

'Please, they only fancy me because they know it's completely out of the question. You lot are all the same. '

'Oh, are we now?' Stephen said, trying not to laugh.

'Yes,' I said. 'Men always want what you can't have.'

Stephen held the door open for me, nodding at a few parents who were hovering outside the assembly hall. These students might only be first years, but their parents paid incredible fees and demanded equally incredible results, and woe betide the teacher who failed to provide them. In the hall, tables with rusting legs had been set up in a semicircle, most of them already occupied. I had been assigned a desk by the door, two empty seats in front of me. There were always two in case both parents decided to come, but it was usually women who filed through the doors. *Do any of the dads ever come?* I had said to Stephen after my first PT meeting, for sixth years in October, and he had looked puzzled, as if he had never thought about it before.

I should have been getting off the bus now, putting my key in the door of the terraced house on Oxmantown Road.

'We can't live here,' I had told Fionn when he first found the place two years before. He was giving me the grand tour: the peeling wallpaper, the rotting carpet in red and black check, the filthy kitchen. 'This isn't *Angela's Ashes*,' I said.

He brought me into the final room, an airless, windowless box. 'The rent is cheap, Sarah,' he'd said, 'and we can use this space as a studio. Can't you see it?' And I told him I could.

The lads would be watching TV now, empty pizza boxes strewn at their feet. 'Here,' Fionn would say, if I was at home, handing me the bong and a lighter. I would take both and I would feel better, forgetting about the students and Mrs Burke and the eternally dissatisfied parents. I would forget about Dunfinnan and my father. I would forget who I was. Sometimes, that moment of forgetting was the best part of my day.

'Hello,' the first mother to approach me said. 'I'm Max Aherne's mother.'

'Hi, Mrs Aherne,' I said. 'I'm Sarah Fitzpatrick, the art teacher.'

21

'Oh, yes; you're the girl who took over from Mrs Moloney, aren't you?'

'That's me,' I said, opening my diary and gesturing at the seat in front of me. 'Do you want to sit down? I'd like to talk about Max's results in the Christmas test.'

Mother after mother after mother. *Oh, my Ollie is such a sensitive boy,* and, *I don't see the point of art if they're not going to pursue a career in it,* and, *Poor Beckett says that you're very hard on him.* I tried to express what I hoped was a suitable amount of distress for upsetting 'poor Beckett', a monster of a thirteen-year-old who was either going to end up in jail or running for president.

'Are you all right?' a mother asked me when I twitched involuntarily. I glanced at my notes. Adam Higgins: thin, paints a lot of *World of Warcraft* fan art. I suspected he was on the spectrum, but it hadn't been confirmed yet, which was unusual. They loved a good diagnosis at St Finbarr's.

'I'm grand, Mrs Higgins,' I told her. 'That time of the month.'

'I can't go out,' I had told Fionn the night before. 'We're only just back from Christmas break and I have parent–teacher meetings tomorrow. I have to be on my best behaviour.'

'Come on,' he said. 'Just the one.'

Just the one and just the one and just the one. In Mulligan's, talking about our time at DAC, Fionn wistful.

'We could just paint back then,' he said. 'No worrying

22

about what was "commercial" or what gallery owners would like. The freedom of it, like.'

I smiled, pretending that I agreed, but for some reason I couldn't stop thinking about the orientation day in first year. I didn't know Fionn then, I didn't know anyone, so I ducked into a nearby pub afterwards to grab lunch by myself. And I saw them: Olivia and Matilda.

'Hey,' I said as I approached their table. 'You're in first year at DAC too, aren't you? I saw you at orientation earlier. Can I sit with you?'

'Sure,' they chorused, moving coats and bags and books out of the way to make room.

'What school did you go to?' Matilda asked me, Olivia squealing with excitement when I told them.

'No way!' she said. 'My grandmother was from just outside there. That's hilarious. I haven't been to Dunfinnan in years. Did you know Kitty Purcell? She died about five years ago.'

'No,' I said. 'Sorry.' Then I sat there and listened to them talk about art in terms I had never heard before.

'I love Ana Mendieta?' Olivia said. 'And, like, Judith Bernstein? But I'm obsessed with Carolee Schneemann. *Interior Scroll* was a really *important* moment for me as an artist.'

'Totally,' Matilda said. 'I mean, the way she questions the crippling lack of interest in women's art in what is supposedly a post-feminist utopia?'

They turned to me. 'What do you think of Schneemann?' they asked.

There was an awkward silence when I admitted I had never heard of her.

'She is a bit obscure, I suppose,' Olivia said.

And I had smiled, getting to my feet. 'I'll see you around,' I said.

'Hello.'

My head snapped up when I heard a male voice. The man standing in front of me was at least six foot five, with the kind of shoulders that I was more accustomed to seeing on cattle farmers in Dunfinnan than on businessmen in expensive suits.

'Hello,' he said again as he sat down. He was so large that he looked as if he was sitting on a child's play seat. 'I'm Matthew Brennan.'

Brennan. I scanned my teacher's diary, but I couldn't find any child in my first-year class with that surname.

'I'm sorry,' I told him. 'I think you might be looking for someone else. I'm the art teacher.'

'Yes, I know,' he said. 'My son is in your class.' The chair creaked in an alarming fashion. 'Harry.'

'There's only one Harry in my class, but he's Harry Kavanagh.'

Matthew Brennan stiffened. 'I think you'll find his name is Harry Kavanagh-Brennan.'

I didn't have to look at my notes to picture Harry: tall, gangly, very talented. He was also very famous.

'I have Harold Kavanagh's grandson in my class,' I had

told my father after my first day at St Finbarr's last September. It was late, almost 9 p.m., and I knew Dad would be sitting in front of the television in his worn-out socks and tracksuit pants, a microwavable meal in his lap. I could picture the sitting room, the diamond-patterned lino, the dying embers in the stove. He would have been waiting for my phone call, putting the TV on mute as soon as my name flashed up on his old Nokia. 'That's former President Harold Kavanagh,' I said.

'Oh, former President Harold *Kavanagh*,' my father replied. 'My goodness, Sarah, you have been blessed.'

'Very funny,' I said. 'Anyway, the grandson is called Harold too, but he goes by Harry. He seems like a sweet kid, totally normal,' I said, and my father had snorted.

'Sure, why wouldn't he be, Sarah?'

'I'm sorry about that,' I said to Matthew Brennan, grabbing a biro from my pencil case. 'I'll get that fixed on my records.' I made a note in my diary. 'My name is Sarah Fitzpatrick.'

'Sarah? That's a pretty name,' he said. 'But I must say, it suits you.'

'Wow, thanks,' I said. 'Sarah is a super-unusual name all right.' I looked over his shoulder. 'Mrs Kavanagh-Brennan not with us tonight?'

'She's not "Mrs" anything anymore,' he said. 'And we decided we would take turns coming to these meetings.' He pushed his jaw out, like a belligerent teenager. 'He's my son too, you know.'

25

'Fair enough. And speaking of your son,' I said, 'let's talk about Harry.'

'Yes,' he said, leaning his huge frame forward, so that I feared for the chair's very survival. 'Let's.'

'He's incredible. He's the best student in any of my classes, bar none.'

Matthew Brennan smiled. 'That's nice to hear. You're the only teacher to say anything positive about him tonight. The rest have said he doesn't concentrate, and he's failing maths and lacks any kind of aptitude for languages. I told them I hated maths too when I was at school and it didn't seem to do me much harm, did it?'

'Well, he certainly has an aptitude for art,' I said. 'I know he's young, but I think he should be considering art school.'

Matthew nodded. 'I agree.'

I had suggested art school to a very select number of parents previously and this was the first time it hadn't been met with outright derision. I guessed, with the Kavanagh money behind him, it didn't matter what Harry did. His mother would buy him a beautiful studio and she would urge him to follow his dreams. *Don't sell out, Harry,* she would tell him. And he wouldn't have to. He wouldn't even have to sell.

'Did you go to art school?' Matthew asked me.

'I can assure you, Mr Brennan, I'm perfectly qualified.'

'I have no doubt that you are, Miss Fitzpatrick. I was just curious. Where did you go?'

'I went to the Dublin Art College for my undergrad.'

'And then?'

'And I stayed at DAC for my postgrad in education. I graduated last year.'

'Are your parents artistic?'

'My mother is dead,' I said, without thinking. Shit. 'Mr Brennan, I really think we should—'

'I'm sorry to hear that.'

'It was years ago; I hardly ever think about it anymore.'

'What age were you?' he asked.

'I was ten.'

'That's very young.'

'Yes. Now, if we could just—'

'I was five when my mother died,' he said. 'It never gets any easier, does it?'

'Hmm,' I said, tapping my pen on the table, trying to figure out how I could get rid of this man as fast as possible.

He tilted his head to one side. 'I hope you won't mind me saying this, but you don't look very well.'

'Let's have some proper fun,' Fionn had said last night. A bathroom cubicle, a group of women giggling when they saw us go in together, no doubt imagining trousers around ankles and me bending over the cistern while Fionn fucked me from behind. But it was a key offered out, a dusting of powder. The smell of soap.

'I've told you before, I hate ketamine,' I said, acid dripping into the back of my throat like a promise, and Fionn had laughed.

'It's only a tiny bump,' he said. 'You'll be grand. I've seen you take way more than that before.'

'I have a twenty-four-hour stomach bug. It's not contagious, don't worry,' I said to Matthew Brennan. 'Now, do you want to go through Harry's school journal? I presume you or Mrs –' I caught myself – 'Harry's mother have signed any notes I sent home?'

'Of course,' he said, and then, abruptly, 'Who is your favourite artist?'

'I fail to see how my favourite artist is relevant to Harry's performance in my class.'

'Come on, Miss Fitzpatrick.'

'It's Ms.'

'Oh, a feminist, are you?'

'No, I just—'

'Humour me,' he interrupted. 'Who is your favourite artist?'

'Fionn McCarthy,' I said, to shut him up.

'I've never heard of him.'

'Not yet,' I said. 'But you will.' I closed my diary. 'Anyway, is that all okay?'

'There are a few other things I would like to discuss.'

'I'm sorry, Mr Brennan—'

'Matthew, please.'

'I'm sorry, Mr Brennan –' I pointed at the line of mothers queuing behind him – 'but I'm afraid we'll have to finish here.'

He stood up. 'It was nice to meet you, Sarah. Thanks for being so kind about Harry. He loves your class.' His face softened when he mentioned his son. 'It means a lot to him. And to me.'

I nodded, beckoning another parent to come forward, crossing Harry off my list. 'Hello,' I told the next mother, 'I'm Sarah Fitzpatrick, the art teacher.'

'Oh my God,' she whispered, pushing back her fringe. 'That was Matthew Brennan. Isn't he so good to come to the parent–teacher meetings? Most fathers wouldn't be bothered, would they? And he must be so *busy*. Fair play to him for making the time.'

'He's fantastic altogether,' I said. 'Now, what's your son's name?'

'Matthew – *Brennan*,' she repeated. 'Don't you know who he is?'

'Mr Brennan is the parent of a student in this school,' I said. 'The same as you.'

'He owns MBA,' she said.

'The estate agency?' I asked, surprised, thinking of the black and silver triangle of the ubiquitous *For Sale* signs littering most of the countryside. Everyone in Ireland had heard of MBA.

'I know,' the mother said, staring after Matthew Brennan. 'He's *beyond* rich.'

The front door was swollen with damp, so I had to force it open; I then had to climb over Aaron's bike, helmet and a collection of waterproof jackets, muddy runners and gym bags spilling their guts out onto the wet floor.

'It's like an obstacle course getting in here,' I said in the living room.

Robbie looked up from his laptop to shrug an apology at me.

'Are you wearing a *hairband*?' I asked.

'Give it two months and all the gays in Dublin will be wearing them,' Aaron said as he passed me, his iPhone buzzing. 'I'll have to tell my buyer to put in an order for a thousand of them tomorrow.' He answered the phone. 'Hey, baby, how was your day?' he said as he climbed the stairs, using the creepy voice he reserved for his girlfriend.

'Do you hear that, Rob?' I said. 'Penney's will be stocking your hairband by March. All dem gays will be copying you.' I sat down next to Fionn, throwing my legs over his. There was an exposed spring in the couch, niggling into my spine. I was sure that Matthew Brennan didn't have to put up with cheap furniture that was past its expiry date. It must be nice to be '*beyond* rich'.

'Hard day at the office?' Fionn asked.

'The worst. Why did you make me go out last night?'

'Make you?'

I elbowed the back of the sofa, as if that would somehow help me settle. The *snap, snap, snap* of a failing lighter, a small flicker of heat, a bubbling sound.

'You want some?' Fionn asked, smoke wreathing his face like a halo.

'Nah,' I said.

'You sure?'

My blood was moving too quickly, like it was spitting through my arteries. I felt agitated, restless in a way that was familiar but worrying. That restlessness had only brought trouble in the past. 'Maybe later,' I told him.

In my bedroom, I changed into faded jeans and a bleach-stained sweatshirt. I hadn't worn them for so long, these clothes that I kept for this specific purpose. I hadn't needed to. Taking a deep breath, I opened the door to the studio and stared straight ahead. I didn't look at Fionn's work.

Empty cans of Red Bull. Twisted tubes of paint. An old jam jar of water. Oils on the palette. Crouching over the splattered ground, I moved brush across canvas.

– It never gets easier, does it?

– Triangle, black and silver, and silver and black triangle.

– It never gets easier.

Time disappeared, dissolving into the oils. This had always been another way for me to forget.

'Hey,' Fionn said when I was finished, and I sat back on my heels, fighting the urge to cover it up.

'How long have you been there?' I asked him.

'Long enough.'

'I'm sorry for using your paints. I should have asked first.'

'Sarah.' He knelt down beside me. 'This is good,' he said. 'No blues?' He took a quick look at the palette. 'Or greens?'

'It didn't feel like a sea type of day.'

'I thought every day was a sea type of day for you,' he said,

31

but I didn't reply. I was spent, tired, but I felt perfectly still. It had been some time since I had felt that still.

'Fionn?'

'Yeah?'

'You won't forget me when you're famous, will you?'

'Of course not, Fitz,' he said. 'You're my best friend.'

It was only then that I allowed myself to look at the paintings stacked in the corner of the room, Fionn's brilliance strewn on the floor. He had never been precious about his work. He had no fear because he knew he could always create another one, that there would always be another sky and another sky and another sky that he could reach for, pull down from the heavens and pour on his canvas, each one so utterly different and yet always so recognisably *Fionn*.

'It really is a good painting,' he said.

And I knew he was telling me the truth. He did think it was good.

But it wasn't good enough.

NOW

It was a lovely wedding, Sarah supposed, as weddings went. June behaved itself and it didn't rain, the day dawning overcast but warm. 'We have the wife to thank for that,' Justin Senior told anyone who would listen. 'The Child of Prague has been out in the garden for about two months now; the face is melted off it.' Justin Junior at the altar, his red curls damp with sweat and gel, joking with Oisín.

'JJ wants me to be his best man,' Oisín had told Sarah a year ago, when JJ and Alannah announced their engagement, trying to hide his excitement. 'Can you believe it?'

'Of course I can believe it,' Sarah had said, hugging him. 'You're such a great friend, Oisín.'

After the ceremony, the guests lined up outside the church to tell the bride she looked beautiful and to kiss the groom on the cheek and tell him not to worry, that he looked very handsome too.

'Will you be okay?' Oisín asked Sarah before he left with the wedding party for the official photos on the beach.

'Oisín,' Aifric said, rolling her eyes, 'Sarah is a grown woman. Don't be weird.' She linked arms with Sarah. 'You can come in my car, babes; I haven't seen you in ages.'

'I was going to check where . . .' Sarah tried, but Aifric had snaked an arm around her waist, propelling Sarah forward.

'New car?' Sarah asked when they climbed into the front seats of the Jaguar. It was fire red, sleek lines, low-slung seats: a car that commanded attention. A bit like its owner, really.

How is Aifric Conroy even Irish? Sarah's friends in Dunfinnan used to say when Aifric was pictured at a launch party in *VIP* or *RSVP* magazine. *She's too beautiful.*

'Birthday present from my father,' she told Sarah.

'That was generous of him.'

'Hmm,' Aifric said as she pulled out of the church car park. 'Anyway, tell me more about you. What's been going on? Are you going to Tipperary any time soon?'

'Yeah, I'll probably go down in the next few weeks,' Sarah said, gripping the sides of the car seat. Aifric drove at a pace that suggested she believed in immortality, like neither death nor a speeding ticket could stop her.

'I want you to make more of an effort with Aifric,' Oisín had said this morning when they were getting dressed in the hotel.

34

'She's painful,' Sarah told him, 'and she's never liked me. Probably thinks I'm too much of a culchie for her to bother with.'

Oisín sat on the bed beside her. 'Aifric has her own problems,' he said, 'but will you try, anyway? For me?'

Sarah knew that Oisín understood that when she said 'Aifric is painful', what she really meant was *Aifric is better than me* and *Aifric makes me feel bad about myself*. That understanding made Sarah remember why she had fallen in love with him in the first place. With Oisín, she had finally felt like she could stop pretending.

'Tell your dad hi from me,' Aifric said to Sarah, handing her keys to the valet at the hotel entrance, pointing at her suitcase in the back. The valet, a man in his early twenties, dropped the keys when he saw who it was, stammering his welcome. *Aifric Conroy,* Sarah knew he would tell his friends later, *and she was even hotter in real life, I swear to God.* 'Eddie was so cute at that barbeque in your house last year. He couldn't stop talking about how proud he is of you. You're lucky, Sarah,' Aifric said, pushing Tom Ford sunglasses into her hair.

There was champagne at dinner, beautiful food served in tiny portions. (*Where's the rest of it?* Sarah's father would have asked, poking suspiciously at the foie gras with his fork. *I'll be starving after this, sure.*) Speeches were made.

'Doesn't Oisín look great?' Aifric said, turning to Sarah and smiling too brightly. 'You're so lucky,' she said again. 'He's mad about you.'

35

'What are you getting up to these days, Sarah?' a friend of Oisín's from Blackrock College asked her. 'You're on your school holidays, right?'

What did she get up to these days? Waking up, a dry mouth; Oisín gone to work; burrowing under the duvet, thinking of the day ahead, so long, so many hours to fill.

'I've just been hanging out with friends,' Sarah said, 'you know, visiting art galleries . . .'

Opening kitchen cabinets and telling herself that she should have a kale smoothie or porridge or granola. Be healthy today, Sarah; respect your body. Still in her pyjamas, staring at one of Oonagh's paintings. *My work was better than that,* Sarah said aloud, brave when no one was there to hear her and tell her she was wrong.

'I've been working on some new stuff myself . . .' Sarah said.

Sitting in the dark. Ashes in her chest, thinking of Matthew. The way he had treated her. Hair pulled and flesh slapped and her head thrown back, swearing that she loved it, asking him for more. Sarah was afraid that he might have broken her and she was afraid that she might have been the one who asked to be broken.

'So, yeah,' Sarah said. 'Just taking it easy, really.'

'That sounds amazing; it's great that you're getting the time to work on your own projects,' Aifric said. 'Oonagh was just saying the other day that she thinks your job is perfect for an artist.'

36

'Did she now?' Sarah said. 'When did you meet Oonagh?'

'We went out for lunch last week,' Aifric said, smiling at the waiter who took her plate. 'My mom hasn't been well.'

'I'm sorry to hear that,' Sarah said, wondering why and how her own name came up in conversation between Oonagh MacManus and Aifric Conroy. She stood up. 'I need a toilet break.' *Restroom.* She should have said restroom; that was what Matthew always said.

'You okay?' Oisín asked, walking towards their table when he saw Sarah get up. She fought the urge to tell him to leave her alone, to stop fussing over her; she knew she couldn't do that with everyone watching.

'Aww, you guuuuuys,' one of the Blackrock gang said as Sarah cuddled into Oisín instead, smiling up at him. 'When are you two lovebirds going to give us a day out?'

'When you get married, you have to get William to make a speech. Can you imagine?' Aifric said, clasping her hands together. 'It'll be so beautiful.'

Sarah could imagine it. William in a new Louis Copeland suit, hair greying at the temples, the very picture of the distinguished gentleman. Writing a speech would be easy for him. *Words are my great love,* he told the *Paris Review* when his last book was published. *That's one of the reasons I am so fond of my adopted country: the Irish possess such an affection for language.* Every guest at their wedding would be spellbound by William's eloquence, utterly rapt. Then Sarah's father would stand up afterwards. Eddie would look uncomfortable and he would mumble, his voice barely audible, and the crowd would get fidgety, coughing, looking longingly at the empty bar. Sarah knew that Eddie would spend twice as long as William writing his speech, that he would find it twice as difficult to speak in public, but she knew too that this wouldn't change how she felt. She would be ashamed of her father on her wedding day and she would hate herself for that.

Sarah led Oisín away by the hand, making sure they were out of earshot.

'Are you having a good time, baby?' he asked.

'It's a wedding,' Sarah said. 'It is what it is.'

'What do you mean?'

'You know – bad food and warm cava.'

'What?' He pulled away from her. 'The food was amazing; JJ's dad wouldn't have it any other way. And it was champagne, not cava.'

'Oh, God forbid they serve cava, how déclassé. And then, to add insult to injury, I had to sit with your supermodel ex-girlfriend.'

'Aifric and I broke up *twelve* years ago, Sarah, and she's always been nice to you, hasn't she?'

'Of course Aifric has always been nice to me, super-nice; Aifric is just perfect. Saint fucking Aifric.'

'Jesus, Sarah,' Oisín said, suddenly sober. 'What do you want from me?'

She didn't have an answer to that.

'I have to get back to the top table,' he said.

38

Sarah watched him walk away from her before she remembered that other people might be paying attention, whispering about the state of Sarah and Oisín's relationship. *Not long for this world, I reckon,* she imagined Oisín's UCD mates saying to each other. She quickly ducked into the nearest bathroom. Sitting on the toilet, she took her phone from her bag. Don't do it, Sarah; this is pathetic. But she couldn't help herself. *Florence Kavanagh,* she typed in. It was always Florence she googled. It was always Florence's face she ended up staring at in toilet cubicles and deserted bus stops and at night when she couldn't sleep, Oisín snoring in bed beside her. Florence's cut-glass cheekbones. Florence's ice-blonde hair. Florence was what Matthew wanted and so Florence continued to be the yardstick against which Sarah measured herself.

What do you *want, Sarah?* she heard Oisín's voice saying as she stared at herself in the bathroom mirror.

'I want you to be nicer to your boyfriend,' Sarah mouthed at her reflection. 'I want you to forget about Matthew Brennan. I want you to grow up and move on.'

It seemed so simple when she said it like that.

Sarah knew that she should find Oisín, apologise for being cruel to him, but where would she even begin? It had been a year of small cruelties, subtle digs and put-downs, months of rolling away from him in bed because Oisín insisted on looking into her eyes and telling her that he loved her. Their sex life was gentle, tender, and a part of Sarah wanted Oisín to be more forceful, to do what Matthew had done and use her body for his own. Sarah wanted to be able to drift away and pretend like this wasn't her boyfriend, this wasn't her body. This wasn't her life. She wanted to pretend that none of this was happening to her.

She slipped down the corridor outside the bathrooms, a narrow alcove lined with photographs of Irish authors (*All male, of course,* Oonagh would have complained. *Female artists are never given the respect they deserve*). She would go to bed, she decided. She would take off her make-up and get into her pyjamas. She would not look at her phone. She would take a diazepam and she would sleep.

'It's not the same anymore.'

Sarah stopped. There were a few voices in this world that would snap her in two with recognition, no matter how distracted she was. Her Nana Kathleen had been one, her father, then Fionn. Her mother, for a time. And now Oisín. Matthew's had never been one of them. He had never given her enough time to learn his voice. Sarah saw there was a room tucked away here, the walls lined with bookshelves. JJ and Oisín were sitting on the leather couch, bottles of beer in hand.

'I thought it would be different when—'

'I know, Ois.'

'It's like nothing I ever do is right.'

'I know,' JJ said again.

'I'm tired,' Oisín said. 'I don't know how much longer I

40

can do this.' He covered his eyes with one hand. 'Fuck, I'm sorry to dump all of this on you, today of all days.'

'Man, don't be stupid. It's obvious to all of us that . . .'

Sarah left before JJ could finish. It might not have been how it sounded, she thought to herself, the possibility of what she had heard (*might* have heard, Sarah) too overwhelming to deal with right now. She pressed the button for the elevator, smiling at the elderly couple who got in the lift with her. Yes, yes, what a gorgeous day; yes, you're right, I'm on the groom's side, and didn't the bride look fabulous, and the food was great; it's hard to get food right for that many people, but I guess you'd have to expect that from the O'Mahoneys, they know their food; to be fair, Jay's Tavern does have a Michelin star and you don't get Michelin stars if you don't know your food. Sarah got off on the third floor, telling them to enjoy the rest of their night. Card in door. Not working. Trying it again, the red light flashing. Sarah jammed the card into the door again and again, until, finally, it worked.

She walked up the spiral staircase inside their suite and grabbed the small make-up bag on the bedside locker. She took her contraceptive pill and a diazepam, plugging her phone in to recharge. She swiped through her apps, telling herself this would be the last time she did this, the very last time. Matthew Brennan had checked his WhatsApp at 00.14, she saw. Was he out with friends? Dinner at L'Ecrivain, drinks afterwards, Matthew nursing a single glass of whiskey as the others' eyes turned bleary. And there would be women. There were always women.

She felt the badness rise in her, a hungry thing. She had failed. She should have kept her mouth shut and her legs open, she should have taken whatever crumbs Matthew had been willing to give her and been happy with that. She had wanted too much and she had lost him and now she would lose Oisín.

Sarah looked at the four-poster canopy bed, the white linen draping to touch the floor, the cavernous wardrobe that looked as if Narnia might be waiting if you ever found your way to the back of it. Oisín's clothes were thrown on the floor, expensive sunglasses on top because who cared if Sarah accidentally stood on them and broke them? *They're only things,* Oisín would say. *I can get another pair.* Sarah used to find that endearing, Oisín's blind acceptance of his wealth. Not even endearing, she had found it intoxicating. Matthew had had money, of course, but she didn't have access to it; she wasn't Matthew's girlfriend, or his partner. She was nothing to him. With Oisín, Sarah had begun to understand that there would always be enough. She had felt safe.

But she wasn't safe because it wasn't her money. She wasn't the one paying for the ocean-view suite in this five-star resort. She wasn't the one whose parents gave them a house in Booterstown to live in, rent-free.

'Isn't it cool?' she had said to Eddie before she moved in, showing him photos on her phone.

'Very nice,' he said. 'And very generous of Oisín's parents to let you two live there, but I hope you're paying your own way, Sarah.'

And she had tried, in the beginning. She would pay for half of dinner at Blowfish or Jay's Tavern or whatever restaurant 'the lads' said was the new cool place, but after a while she didn't even make a half-hearted reach for her wallet. She couldn't afford it and Oisín didn't mind. He liked to be generous with his money – or with Oonagh's money, to be precise.

Sarah pushed the heavy curtains back, cream embossed with the faintest imprint of lilac flowers. *Beautiful,* her Nana Kathleen would have said, caressing the fabric, *but fierce impractical.* Sarah wished that she didn't always think about how much things might have cost or whether or not they were good value for money.

'Jesus,' she'd said to Oisín when she had first seen the ivory-white carpet in their living room. 'How on earth are we going to keep that clean?'

'Don't worry,' he said. 'Magda comes twice a week. She'll take care of it.'

Sarah smiled, but she had felt embarrassed that she didn't automatically realise that of course there would be a Magda, that there was *always* a Magda for people like Oisín.

She opened the patio doors out onto the balcony. There were column candles in glass urns, rolling the air into vanilla and musk. She sat on one of the wooden rocking chairs on the terrace, pulling the cashmere blanket up to her neck. The diazepam was softening her limbs, making her mouth tender. She would sleep, she told herself again. She would sleep and, when she woke up, everything would be fine. She would love Oisín and she would forget Matthew. Easy.

Sarah stared blankly at the black sea, at the moonlight lacing its glimmer through the waves. She wished Fionn was here. He would hold her hand in the silence, and Sarah would feel calm. But Fionn wasn't here. Sarah had fucked that up too.

She tried to stand, but her body was limp. She wanted to be nearer to the water, to wind seaweed through her hair like ribbons. She would be a mermaid, she would be a siren calling men to their graves. She would live forever in the depths of the ocean's belly.

She would forget. She would forget all of this.

THEN

'Miss? Miss?'

'Yes, Aodhán,' I said. 'What is it now?'

'You have a hole in your tights,' he said, hinging his chair on its back legs while clinging onto the desk for balance. He grinned, revealing spinach stuck in his braces from lunch.

'Yes, Aodhán. I'm aware of that, thank you.' You little asshole. 'Now, could you please stop—' The final bell rang. 'Okay, boys. Please leave your work on your desk, but put all the chalk pastels and any other supplies you were using back in the supply cupboard. And remember, I expect that coursework to be completed when you come back after the midterm.'

The scrape of chairs against the tiled floors; boys grabbing the back of each other's jumpers, tripping one another up; screams of laughter when one of them fell to the ground. I stayed in my seat until they left, an indistinguishable mob of sloppily untucked shirts and oddly vulnerable-looking necks exposed by buzzcuts. I smiled at the one or two who told me to 'Have a good weekend, miss'. And then there was quiet.

I walked through the room (I should . . .), weaving my way around desks covered in graffiti, *Jamie fingered Rachel* and *Miss O'Brien is hot* etched into the wood with a compass or scribbled with permanent marker (I haven't talked to him in . . .), staring at the pathetic attempts at sunsets and ice-capped mountains and swans floating on glass-still lakes (he's by himself in that house and I . . .), gathering the pieces of paper up and resisting the urge to tear them to shreds. Whatever I might have told their parents, I *did* think talent was more important than the kids' 'creative expression'.

I sat at my desk again, holding my iPhone in my hand. *What would Nana want you to do, Sarah?*

'Hello?'

'Hi, Dad.'

'Sarah? Is that you? Your voice sounds different.'

'How does my voice sound different?'

'I don't know. It's been a while since I've heard from you.'

'I rang you last Friday; that's not a while.'

He coughed into the phone, scraping mucus from the back of his throat. I knew what a good daughter would say: *That's a bad cough you have, Dad. Are you all right? Do you want me to come down to Dunfinnan to mind you?*

'How's work?' he asked. 'I'm proud of you, Sarah; it wasn't

46

easy getting such a good job teaching, and straight out of college as well. You're mighty, do you know that?'

'Thanks, Dad,' I said. 'What are you up to for the weekend?'

'Not much. Mass on Sunday, I suppose.' My father would go to twelve o'clock Mass, like he always did. He stood outside the back entrance of the church, nodding at his friends. They never talked to each other, they just stood there in a respectful silence, only going inside when it was time to get Communion. They left immediately afterwards, the Host barely dissolved on their tongue, their duty done. 'It's a pity you can't come home for any of your break, Sarah. I'd love to see you.'

'I would if I could, Dad, but Fionn needs me right now. The exhibition opens in ten days.'

'Ah, sure I know; I'm delighted for Fionn.' He coughed again. 'Have you been doing any painting yourself these days?'

'No.'

'Right.' He paused. 'Well, tell Fionn I said congratulations. It was very nice of him to send me the invitation to the opening.'

'It was.'

'I could still come, you know. I'd like to be there.'

'But you have the cattle mart the morning after, Dad.' I gripped the phone tightly. 'No point in changing your plans at this stage.'

'Yes,' he said, 'that's true.'

We talked for another few minutes, or rather he talked and I listened.

47

'Ah, you *do* know him, Sarah, he's one of the Mahers, his father died last year and there was fierce trouble between the sons over the will. I told you all about it. Massive funeral. We were queuing outside the funeral home for hours and it was lashing rain . . . You *do* know him. They have the big stone house a half a mile past the old convent . . . See? I told you that you knew him . . . What? Oh, nothing. He was just asking for you, is all. Said he never sees you in Dunfinnan anymore. Apparently his sister is in Dublin too; she's working for an accountancy firm up there. On big money, eighty grand a year, he said, but she comes home every weekend. Which is nice, I thought . . . No, I'm not trying to make you feel guilty . . . I never said that . . . I never said that, did I? You're being silly now . . . Sarah, please don't shout at me . . . I said *don't shout* at me . . . I can't talk to you when you're in one of these moods. I have to go . . . I do . . . I *do* have to go. Bye. Bye . . . No, I'm not angry. Just come home soon, will you? . . . Okay . . . Okay. Bye . . . Bye byebyebye.'

And I sat there, thinking of all the things I should have said to my father.

I don't come home because I still haven't forgiven you, Dad, even though I know it wasn't your fault. I know you didn't mean it. I know you were sick and sad, and Nana Kathleen said you were trying your best, but—

'Sarah, isn't it?'

'Jesus.' I banged my knee off the desk with fright, hissing

48

with the pain. 'You scared the fu—' I stopped myself. 'You scared me.'

'I'm sorry,' the man standing by the door frame said.

'I didn't hear you come in.'

'You were busy,' he said, and I could tell by his tone that he'd heard me talking to my father.

'Well,' I said, trying to regain my professional bearing, 'how can I help you, Mr . . . ? How can I help you?'

'You don't remember me, do you?'

'Of course I do,' I said, trying to buy some time. Tanned. Ridiculously tall. Handsome, I guess, for an old man. Broad shoulders. *Shoulders.* 'Harry's father.'

'Correct. Glad to hear that I'm not entirely forgettable.'

'Right,' I said. 'What can I do to help you, Mr Brennan?'

'I came to collect Harry.'

'Harry wasn't in class today.'

'Yes,' he said. 'I've just been made aware of that.'

He stood there, watching me. Had he come here to hit on me? Besides the fact that I was his son's teacher, I was about a hundred years younger than him. Why did men think that was in any way acceptable?

When I was in college, our lecturers encouraged us to go to exhibitions and gallery shows to 'network' with more established artists. *It's important to make contacts*, they said. Cramped spaces and sitar music and young girls in black, circulating with warm white wine. The artists at the events were generally men in their fifties and sixties and sometimes

49

even their seventies. They would talk about their careers, how their wives didn't understand them and their children resented them for devoting more time to their work than to helping with homework or shouting encouragement from the sidelines at school matches. The art scene is unfair, they would tell me. It's all about who you know. They could see I was talented, they said, and they wanted to make sure that I succeeded.

If I had taken their 'help', would I be a working artist now? Men like Fionn made it on talent, but women like me had to entertain a decrepit predator, their eyes trained firmly on my tits as they talked about how skilled I was with my paintbrush. Or was I just making excuses? Other women I knew made art, art that sold, art that was lauded by critics and buyers alike. It was unlikely that *all* of them had fucked their way to success. Maybe, as ever, the answer was simple: I wasn't good enough. I never had been.

'I was walking past the classroom,' Harry's father said to me, 'and I heard a raised voice. It sounded like you were upset.'

'I'm fine. Just a disagreement with my father.'

'Fathers can be easy to disagree with,' he said, peering at a painting that he had obviously identified as Harry's. 'We were supposed to be going to Boston today.'

'What?' I said.

'Harry and me. We were going to Boston. It's his birthday on Monday and it seemed like the perfect excuse, what with it being the midterm as well. But Flo wants him to stay with her and that's that, apparently.'

'Well,' I said, 'birthdays are important to some mams. They like to make them special.'

'Yes,' he said. 'They do, don't they?'

It was nearly 6 p.m. by the time I finished, waving goodbye to Mrs Burke as I passed her office. She was sitting at her desk, the computer tinting her face green.

'Only leaving now, Sarah?'

'Yes, Mrs Burke; I thought I might reorganise the supply cupboard. I like to keep it nice and tidy,' I said, to impress her.

'Well –' she looked at the paperwork on her desk – 'you *were* late in this morning.' Damn, I was hoping she hadn't noticed. 'I'm sure you had some catching up to do.'

Night had fallen outside, thirsty for any patch of light and sucking it dry. I didn't feel like battling the February winds to the DART station, so I joined the pushing queue onto the bus instead. I stood, clinging on to a tiny section of a steel pole, pressed in between two office workers in sensible shoes and beige trenches. The bus smelled of sweat undercut by an orange that an elderly woman was eating, dropping the peel to the floor. No one else said anything, earbuds in and staring at the ground or their iPhones or their Kindles.

'Honey, I'm home,' I said back at the house. I threw my coat over the banister. 'Fionn?' I ran up the stairs, inhaling paints and methylated spirits as I stood by the door to the studio.

'Hey,' I said.

He didn't reply.

'Fionn,' I said again. 'Fionn?'

'What?' he snapped. The canvas looked as if black wax had melted all over it, sucking you into the unrelenting darkness. 'I'm trying to work.'

'I can see that. It's intense,' I said. 'But that kind of stuff doesn't sell, does it?'

'Nah. Too "uncompromising" to be commercial, according to Kevin.'

'Isn't it a waste of time, then?'

'It's good for the soul. One for me,' he said, then pointed at the stack of paintings behind him, 'ten for them.'

'Listen, do you want some smoke?'

'I'm flat out, here,' he said, bending over to scrape at the paint with his fingernail. 'Ten days to show time.'

'Cool,' I said. 'Good luck with it.' I left, going into my bedroom and closing the door behind me. Stupid, I told myself. That was a stupid thing to do.

I looked at the murals that Fionn painted last year, touching my hand to the wall. *We'll never get our deposit back,* Aaron had said, fretting so much I had to promise him that I would lock the door anytime the landlord came to visit.

Fionn had decided to turn my room into the sea, so that my bed would feel like a raft in the middle of the ocean. 'You can float away anytime you want, that way,' he said, once again demonstrating an understanding of who I was that no one else ever seemed to be able to match.

It had taken him weeks to complete the mural. I would stand and watch, mentally reciting the names of the paints he used: Cobalt Blue, Windsor Green, French Ultramarine, Oxide of Chromium, Cerulean.

'No,' I said when Fionn handed me a paintbrush and asked me to join in. 'No, you do it. You're so much better than I am.'

When he was finished, he guided me into the bedroom with his hands over my eyes. 'What do you think?' he had asked, and I tried not to cry out when I saw it, at how easily he had rolled water around his paintbrush. I could never capture the truth of the sea, not the way that I wanted to, and I knew then that I would die wanting to try, and I would die being too afraid to even begin.

'It's perfect, Fionn,' I told him. 'Thank you. Thank you so much.'

But today the walls felt as if they were squeezing around my narrow bed. Panic had its hands around my neck, resting its fingertips at the base of my throat, like it did when I was a child.

'He'll be home soon,' I used to whisper in the dark. 'He'll be home soon. Hold your breath and count to one hundred. He'll be home when you wake up for school in the morning and everything will be okay.'

Why won't you come home, Sarah?

Why won't you come home?

NOW

Sarah leaned over the kitchen sink as she smoked a cigarette out the window. Oisín had left his dishes in there. Hardened crumbs of porridge were sticking to the side of the bowl and the saucepan and it was so revolting that Sarah could hardly stand it. Why did Oisín insist on eating porridge anyway? It was 1st July – no one ate a cooked breakfast in July. Clearly, Oisín expected Sarah to clean up after him because she was on her school holidays. He would deny that, of course, saying he wanted to support her, why else would he always be encouraging her to paint, to get back into Oonagh's studio? But really, what was the point of her doing so? Sarah was never going to make any money from her art. She was never going to be good enough.

'But if you aren't painting,' Oisín asked her, 'then what do you do all day?'

'What do I *do* all day?' Sarah repeated. 'Do you want me to keep a diary? I didn't realise I had to report to you, Oisín,' she said, shouting after him as he left the room. 'But thanks for letting me know; I'll bear that in mind in future.'

He slammed the bedroom door.

'Asshole,' she said under her breath.

What do you do all day, Sarah?

She watched porn, the women waxed clean and dead-eyed, screaming their pleasure as if it were pain. She wondered if they were faking it, like she used to with Matthew. Had he known that she was pretending? Could he tell and just didn't care, as long as *he* was satisfied? (And she had smiled through it all and said, *Do it again, Matthew. Do it again, do it again.*)

Other days, she got stoned and lay on the couch, staring at the ceiling, thinking about him and the things she let him do to her. (*Touch yourself*, he had told her. *I want to see you touch yourself.*) Sarah's hands inched down her body, searching for relief, skin flushing red, and she couldn't tell if it was with shame or excitement. Maybe they were the same thing, she thought.

Her phone beeped. She stubbed out the cigarette on the outside windowsill and put it in the bin. It was probably her school friends' WhatsApp group, requesting photos from the wedding last weekend. *You promised us that you'd send them on the day,* Ciara had complained. *I wanted to see Aifric Conroy's outfit. She is such a ride.*

Ciara: Hi Auntie Aisling and Auntie Sarah! Mammy has put me in a new outfit for our day out shopping, do you like it?

There was a photo of Ciara's ugly baby, dressed in a pink sundress and matching hat. *Aww*, Aisling replied. *Holly has gotten so cute.* Sarah texted Aisling immediately.

Sarah: Cute? It's like Noel Gallagher and Matt Lucas had a love child.

Aisling: It's her daughter. What exactly do you expect me to say, Sarah?

It had been well over three years since Ciara had announced she was pregnant by texting Sarah and Aisling a screenshot of the ultrasound. Sarah and Matthew had still been together then and, as she stared at the formless blob, Sarah thought about what she would have done if this had been her ultrasound, her baby. Ciara was only twenty-four then, and it was an 'accident', she had said, as if she had simply tripped and fallen over, scraping her knee. 'But it's fine,' Ciara kept saying. She and Eoin were engaged anyway, they were building a house on a site that his parents had given them, saving every last penny they earned. 'This is just an acceleration of our plans,' Ciara had explained, and Sarah wasn't sure if she was trying to persuade her friends or herself.

When Holly was born, Eoin had sent photos from Ciara's phone. *Mammy and Baby both doing well*, the caption said,

Ciara red-faced and teary, the baby raw, wrinkled, its head warped from the forceps birth. Sarah couldn't stop looking at it, unable to believe that someone she had gone to school with had actually given birth. It had been Ciara whom Sarah had gotten drunk with for the first time, downing straight vodka they had stolen from Ciara's parents. It was Eoin who had given them their first pill at Electric Picnic when they were seventeen. Sarah had been scared, but Ciara had bitten it in two, handing half to Sarah and telling her not to be such a 'fucking wuss'. And now she was a mother. Holly was no longer a bump under increasingly unflattering maternity wear. She was a human being and Ciara and Eoin had created her. How had Ciara been ready for that responsibility when Sarah felt as if she had been treading water for the last ten years?

Oisín: I'm going for a few drinks after work. I'll be home late.
Sarah: Where are you going? I might come in to meet you.

She waited, checking her phone every few seconds, but there was no reply. She tried to call him, but it went straight to voicemail. 'Oisín,' she said. 'Oisín, give me a call when you get this, okay?'

She went into the living room, pushing aside the cream gauze curtain hanging from a stone archway so she could walk down the hallway. Up the stairs, in and out of all the rooms. When Oisín wasn't here, Sarah felt as if she was trespassing, as if Oonagh or William would arrive imminently and call the guards. She hesitated at the door to Oonagh's studio before pushing the door open. *Oh, don't call it my studio,* Oonagh kept insisting. *It's yours now.* But how could Sarah think of the studio as anything but Oonagh's? The splashes on the floor were from Oonagh's work. The walls were tacky with remnants of Blu Tack and tape where Oonagh had stuck postcards and *New Yorker* cartoons and photographs: whatever she was using for inspiration at any given time. This was the room in which the Howl at the Moon collection had been conceived, crushed flowers dripping blood from their buds, a 'stunning commentary on the patriarchy's fear of menstruation', the art critic in the *Observer* had called it. Oonagh was the 'best female artist to emerge from Ireland in the last fifty years' (*I don't know why they insist on calling me a 'female artist'*, Oonagh sighed. *I'm not sure what my gender has to do with anything*) and this room felt like hallowed ground to Sarah. Every time she picked up a paintbrush, she thought of Oonagh's success, of Oonagh's reputation. And fear would climb her limbs like ivy, stuffing its tendrils down her throat until she couldn't breathe.

Sarah sat by the window, scraping at a little clot of red (Cadmium Red, perhaps? Medium Hue?) on the wooden floor, holding a flake of it closer to her face so she could examine it, pushing all other thoughts away from her. She stared at that sliver of paint, waiting until the darkness came, waiting until it breathed into her eyes and turned everything black.

THEN

'Where the fuck have you been?'

'Fionn, I'm—'

'I said that we had to leave no later than six. I *told* you that.'

'I know,' I said, throwing my satchel on the ground, 'but Mrs Burke was being a—'

'I don't want to hear your bullshit excuses,' Fionn said. 'I'm leaving. You can make your own way into town.' He slammed the living-room door behind him.

Robbie and Aaron were watching me, Aaron sighing, '*Sarah*,' as if he was my father.

'It's not my fault.'

'It never seems to be your fault, does it, Fitz?' Aaron said, following Fionn. 'Rob, you coming?' he called over his shoulder.

'You can go,' I said to Robbie. 'Don't worry about me.'

'You have twenty minutes,' he said. 'Get ready as fast as you can. I'll phone Kevin and tell him to hold off until we get there.'

At the gallery, a waiter passed me and I took a glass of white wine from his tray. 'Keep them coming,' I said under my breath. The gallery was a small space, but Kevin had been clever with it – pale wood floors, cream walls, the front wall made entirely of glass to make the most of the natural light. Fionn's work could be imposing, overwhelming almost, but this was the perfect venue to show it off.

I could hear people whispering about him as they walked around the exhibition. 'Very important,' they said. 'Such an exciting new talent; he's going places, this one.' I wanted to tell them to stop talking about him like that. It was just Fionn. It was *my* Fionn.

'Oh my God, Sarah? Is that you?'

'Olivia,' I said, trying not to grimace. 'Wow. What a surprise to see you here.' She looked the same, an expensive scarf knotted in her curly red hair, dark lipstick and pale skin. Had Fionn invited her? Why would he do that? He knew how I felt about her and Matilda.

'It's so nice to see you,' she said, kissing me on both cheeks. Everyone did that at art college – some European affectation that they had picked up from their parents, I presumed. I tried to imagine how it would be received in Dunnfinnan and almost laughed out loud. 'You look great.'

'So do you,' I said. 'I love your head scarf. Hermès?'

'I got it for four euro in St Vincent de Paul, so I doubt it,' she said. 'But thank you. Isn't this deadly?' She waved at the room around us. 'I can't believe how many people are here! I always knew Fionn would do well; his stuff at DAC was fab, wasn't it?'

Fionn had been one of the only people in our year who had elected to work in a more 'traditional' medium. It wasn't fashionable at the time, not next to Olivia's collection of embalmed mice, painted to look like ladybirds, or Ruairí's exploration of lost masculinity in 'an increasingly matriarchal society' through performance art, but Fionn always did what Fionn wanted. I worked with oils too, not that anyone had cared. I couldn't compete with him. No one could.

'Are you two together now?'

'Me and Fionn?' I asked. 'God, no. We're just friends.'

'I always thought you would end up together,' she said. 'Didn't you have a thing at college?'

You don't have to pretend with me, Fionn had said that night as we lay down together on his bed, and it frightened me that he knew I was pretending in the first place. When he fell asleep, I thought of all the ways that I could fuck this up. I would hurt him. I would lose him.

Last night was a mistake, I told him the next morning. *We're better off as friends, don't you think?* And we agreed to forget that it had ever happened.

'I'm not really a commitment type of girl,' I said to Olivia.

'Fionn and I are like brother and sister at this stage. We live with two other lads that I met during my postgrad.'

'That's awesome,' she said, rubbing lipstick off the edge of her glass. 'I'm still living at home with my parents in Rathfarnham; I can't afford to move out while I'm working on my debut collection.'

'Still dealing with the mice?'

'Mice?' She looked puzzled. 'Oh, God – the *mice*. Stop; I'm mortified even thinking about them. The shit I did at college. I was so paranoid that people would figure out I wasn't a "real" artist, whatever the hell that is. The *rubbish* we all used to talk. No, I'm using acrylics now, actually.'

'Cool,' I said. 'Are you nearly done?'

'I hope so. I'm sick of being broke. My parents have been great, but I can't live off them forever, can I? I've had to sign on to the dole for the last few months.

'I know,' she continued when she saw my expression. 'I'm a disgrace, but Dublin is expensive. I'm thinking about moving to Lisbon; a few of the DAC gang are there. Rent is cheap, apparently, as is the drink. Jonathan Gilmartin has been on at me to head out there. Do you remember Jonathan?' I shook my head and she laughed. 'He would be devastated to hear that. He had such a crush on you in college. Not that you would have noticed. You were always so self-contained, just doing your own thing. I wish I had been like that at eighteen,' she said, her smile fading when I didn't respond. 'So, what did you say you're up to again?'

'I teach art at a private secondary school.'

'That's deadly,' she said. 'I wish I could do that, but I hate children, which seems like it might make the job a tad difficult. I probably shouldn't say that, should I?'

'Olivia . . .' I say. 'Olivia, you don't have anything on you, do you?'

'It's wonderful to see you, Sarah,' Fionn's mother, Fidelma, said to me. She was slight, the sort of thin that came from living on her nerves, her wiry frame drowned in a cerise suit jacket and fitted skirt.

'And you.' I took another sip of wine. Olivia wasn't carrying (*Sorry, Sarah,* she'd said, *I can't afford it. This is the first time I've been out in weeks*), so I had been forced to drink more.

'I can't believe how many people are here,' Fidelma said, looking around the gallery. She smiled at her husband. 'Can you believe it, Neil?'

'Here to drink the free wine, I bet,' Fionn's father said, leaning against one of the paintings a little too casually for my liking.

'So –' she turned to me – 'how are things with you, Sarah? Are you doing a line with anyone?'

'No, Fidelma,' I said. I didn't think the type of lines I was doing were something Fidelma and Neil would approve of. 'Still single.'

'Oh, don't worry; you'll meet someone yet,' she said. Fidelma was clearly still hopeful that Fionn and I would end up together, and I wished I could tell her that ship had sailed. 'A pretty girl like you will be snapped up in no time.'

'Thank you.'

'And how's work?' she asked.

'Fair play to you for getting that job,' Neil said, animated for the first time that evening. 'That was a piece of luck.'

'Yes,' I said. 'Very lucky.'

'Fidelma,' Neil said, 'isn't that Matthew Brennan over there?' He pushed himself up to standing, the painting quivering in his wake, and I rushed to steady it.

'Who, dear?'

'Jesus, Fidelma,' Neil said. 'The real-estate guy. He owns MBA.'

Kevin had also spotted Matthew, and was manoeuvring his way to the door so he could shake his hand and take his coat, calling a waiter over to offer Matthew a glass of wine. They talked for a few minutes, Kevin laughing at whatever Matthew was saying. Kevin handed him a brochure, then mouthed, 'Take care of him,' at a waiter behind Matthew's back.

'Do you think he will buy something?' Neil said loudly, people nearby turning to stare at him, and I tried not to wince.

Matthew also looked around to find the culprit, his face disdainful. Then he saw me and he smiled, as if I was the very person he had been hoping to see.

'Does he know you, Sarah?' Fidelma asked as Matthew waved me over.

I didn't answer her. I seemed to be moving even though I didn't want to, as if my legs were being controlled by the mere force of his will.

'Well, well, well,' he said when I was in front of him. 'If it isn't Sarah Fitzpatrick. It's been ages since we last met.'

'It was, like, a week ago.'

He tutted when he saw that my glass was empty. 'That won't do, will it?' He barely had to turn around before a waiter jumped to service, filling it with a 'Sorry, miss.'

'What are you doing here?' I asked him.

'Hi, Sarah; it's good to see you too. Isn't it nice that we're all here supporting the arts on such a wet and miserable February night?'

'Seriously,' I said, 'what are you doing here? Nothing better to do?'

His smile slipped, just for a second. 'No,' he said. 'Kevin invited me. I'm kind of a big deal.'

I had just taken a sip of wine and almost spat it out. 'Jesus Christ.'

'I wouldn't compare *myself* to Jesus Christ, but you're more than welcome to do so if you wish.'

'Who says that about themselves? Are you for real?'

'Always,' he said and I raised an eyebrow at him. 'Fine. The truth is that Kevin and I went to school together and he invites me to any exhibitions that he thinks I'll find interesting.'

'You went to Clongowes too?' I said.

'How do you know that Kevin went to Clongowes?'

'I think there's a rule that anyone who goes to Clongowes has to say that they went to Clongowes within five seconds of meeting you.'

'You're very funny,' he said, but he didn't laugh. 'But, yes, I did attend Clongowes.'

'You're not from Dublin though, are you?' I asked. 'I can't figure out your accent.'

'I'm from Limerick,' he told me. 'A mere blow-in.'

'No good schools in Limerick?'

'None,' he said. 'My father had notions. Only son and all that. Although I don't think my mother would have been too keen on the idea of boarding school, to be honest.'

'She spoilt you, didn't she? Mama's boy.'

'Well,' he said, 'I was until she died.'

'What about Harry?' I said quickly. 'He's an only son too, right?'

'My ex-wife also had notions, but they didn't include turning Harry into a mini-Matthew. Fate worse than death, according to Flo.' He pointed at the painting. 'You were right: your friend is incredibly talented.'

'Hey, Fitz.' Fionn snuck up on us, an arm around my stomach. He seemed to have forgiven me, the success of the evening and a couple of glasses of wine mellowing his anger.

'Ah, here is the man of the moment,' I said. 'Matthew, this is Fionn McCarthy, the incredibly talented artist. Fionn, this is Matthew Brennan. He's kind of a big deal, apparently.'

'I didn't know the two of you were an item,' Matthew said, looking from me to Fionn and then back at me.

'We're not.'

'Hey,' I said, elbowing Fionn in the ribs. 'No need to sound quite so relieved.'

'Your work is very impressive, Fionn,' Matthew said.

'Cheers.'

'I'm particularly taken with this one.' Matthew gestured at the painting in front of us. 'I'm going to buy it.'

'You can't have that one, I'm afraid.' Fionn said.

'Why not?'

'That one isn't for sale.'

Matthew looked at the pricing list, scanning down until he found the right one. 'I'll pay you three times as much as they're asking for it.'

'I told you, it's not for sale,' Fionn said again.

'Fine,' Matthew said, and for some reason I wanted to reach out and touch his face, tell him that it would all be okay. 'Congratulations on the exhibition.'

'What was that about?' I asked when Matthew had gone. We were still facing the painting, Fionn with his arms around me.

'I don't like him.'

'You don't even know him.'

'I know his type,' Fionn said. 'And why are you defending him? Do you fancy him or something?'

'Of course I don't fancy him, but there was no reason

to be rude. He could be an important contact for you; he's supposed to be minted.'

'He can't have this painting.'

'You don't need the money, all of a sudden?'

'No, it's because this one is for you. *Harbour Skies*,' he whispered into my ear. The canvas was enormous, it must have been seventy-six by thirty-eight inches at least, an ochre sky bleeding into a murky sea. 'Remember?'

We were in Fionn's house in Cobh last year. His parents had gone to Spain for a few days, so we had the place to ourselves. 'Don't worry about supplies, girl,' Fionn told me. 'I have everything in my room at home.' Packets of Haribo on the car dashboard, *Nevermind* on repeat, tapping cigarette ash out of rolled-down windows, bitching about Amelia, Aaron's new girlfriend. *She's awful*, we agreed, *what is he doing with her?* Fionn's place was tiny, one of many grey houses squeezed together in a terraced row, a scrappy patch of grass in the front. That night, we had taken pills, grinning as feathers unfurled in the back of our skulls, blooming large in our eyes. Hours later, we were coming down, our bodies wrecked but our brains too wired to sleep, when Fionn decided he wanted to go to the harbour to watch the sunrise. It was so quiet there, the light feeling like water on my skin. We found a bench to sit on and, for once, I felt as if everything might be okay.

'I do remember,' I said now. 'But, Fionn, I can't take this.'

'I want you to have it.'

'It's too much. You need the money.'

'This piece is you. It's *us*. I couldn't have made it without you.'

'Okay.' I told myself not to cry. 'Thank you.'

'You're welcome.'

'I'm sorry about earlier.'

'Ah, forget about it,' he said. 'Look at all these people. Kevin said all the paintings are sold. Already, Fitz.' He turned me around to face him. 'This is it,' he said. 'This is just the beginning.'

'I'm so proud of you, Fionn,' I said, and I was. Or I wanted to be. Maybe that would have to be enough for now. I kissed him on the cheek and walked away, pushing a path through thin women in black sheath dresses, men in patterned cravats, grabbing another two glasses of wine on my way.

I woke with shards of glass shattering in my skull. I was in my underwear, and there was blood scabbing on my knees and smeared on the sheets. Fionn was next to me, wearing only his boxers, the duvet half-thrown off him. I breathed through my nose, tasting the vomit as a promise. What had happened last night? How did I get home? And what time was it now? I fumbled around the bed until I found my phone.

'Fuck. Fuck, fuck, fuck, *fuck*.'

It was 10.45 a.m. There were five missed calls from the school, two from Mrs Burke's personal mobile, and three voicemails.

'Fionn.' I kicked him on the shin. 'Fionn, wake up right now.'

69

He groaned.

'I'm serious, Fionn.'

'Jesus Christ.' He sat up, squinting. 'What is it?'

'It's a quarter to eleven.'

'So?'

'So, I was supposed to be at work three hours ago.'

'Call in sick,' he said.

'I can't just call in sick. Burke is already pissed off with me.' I looked at my phone again, unsure if I was brave enough to listen to the voice messages. 'Why didn't you wake me?'

'Maybe because it's not my job to wake you, Sarah? You're an adult woman who should be able to set her own alarm.'

'Don't be mean to me.'

He didn't reply.

'Fionn? What happened last night? Did we . . . ?'

'Did we what?'

'You know what I'm trying to ask. Don't be a dick.'

He turned to me. 'Are you fucking serious?'

'I was only asking.'

'Sarah, you were a mess last night. You were so drunk you could barely stand. My father thought—'

'Did Matthew Brennan see?'

'*What?* No, actually, he had left before you went into complete meltdown. What a relief, since that rich cunt is the only one that matters.'

'I'm sorry, but it wasn't my fault. I didn't have time to get dinner because you were rushing us out the door.'

'So it's my fault you were paralytic?'

'No, of course not. I'm just trying to explain.'

'I can't believe you. You know how hard I've been working for this. I was killing myself trying to get ready for last night. I didn't want to leave my own private-view party early because I had to put you to bed. I would *never* have got that drunk if it had been your debut.'

'Oh, fuck off, Fionn; I said I was sorry.'

'Did you, Sarah? I don't actually think you did say you were sorry.'

'I—'

'And then to ask if we hooked up.' He pushed himself up to standing. 'I haven't been pretending to be your friend for all these years so I could fucking rape you some night when you were too pissed to know the difference.'

'I didn't mean it that way.'

'Yeah.' He opened the door. 'Yeah, I think you did mean it that way.'

I should have called Fionn back then, refused to allow him to leave until I explained to him that I was feeling jealous, that I had wanted it to be me last night. But I couldn't admit to that. I didn't want Fionn to know that I was insecure; I didn't want him to feel sorry for me or to see me differently. *Fionn. Fionn, please.* The clamouring thoughts were too heavy now, pressing down on me, anxiety swelling in my skeleton until it felt as if the bones might rupture through my skin. Breathe, I told myself. You're fine, nothing bad is going to happen to you if you keep breathing. My phone beeped and I reached out to grab it from my locker.

Dad: Hi Sarah. I hope last night went well for Fionn. Give me a call after school if you get a chance.

And there was another message.

Text: Hi Sarah, Matthew Brennan here. It was lovely to see you again last night.

I sat up in the bed. I hadn't been expecting this.

Sarah: How did you get my phone number?
Matthew Brennan: Well, that's not very friendly.
Matthew Brennan: You gave it to me at the gallery. Told me to contact you if I ever wanted to talk about Harry's artwork. Very kind of you, I thought. Did you have a good evening?
Sarah: Too much wine. 😖
Sarah: Do you mind not mentioning this to anyone else? Bit unprofessional of me.
Matthew Brennan: Don't worry, it'll be our little secret.

I focused on the screen: his name and his words and what this could mean. I didn't think about Fionn. I didn't think about Mrs Burke. All I could think about was this text message.

'Matthew Brennan,' I said out loud.

15TH FEBRUARY

Matthew Brennan: And how are you spending your Sunday, Miss Fitzpatrick?

Sarah: I've told you before, it's Ms.

Matthew: Oh, Christ – you're not one of those, are you?

Sarah: One of what, exactly?

Sarah: And I'm spending my Sunday trying to figure out how I'm going to explain why I didn't turn up for work on Friday. If I lose my job, will you hire me as your assistant? I poor. 😟

Matthew: I don't know about that. I think your talents may lie in other areas.

16TH FEBRUARY

Matthew: Watch this video.

Sarah: Ugh, I'm not in the mood. Had a terrible day at work.
My boss hates me.

Matthew: Just watch it. This woman is said to be the heir to
Martha Argerich's crown.

Sarah: Who dat is? I'm not old like you.

Matthew: Just watch the clip.

Sarah: Woah. Wishing I had kept up my music lessons now.

Matthew: She's beautiful, isn't she?

Matthew: Not as beautiful as you, though.

Matthew: Is it okay to say that?

Sarah: Yeah, it's okay.

Sarah: Thank you.

19TH FEBRUARY

Matthew: Doesn't this book look interesting?

Sarah: I think it's a little soon to be asking me for presents.

Matthew: But I already bought you something.

Sarah: What? Did you really buy me something?

Matthew: Of course.

Sarah: I can't believe that! Thank you so much! What is it?!

Matthew: It's a signed photo of me. It's in the post.

Sarah: How thoughtful.

Sarah: It'll be the perfect addition to the Matthew Brennan
shrine I've been building in my bedroom.

Matthew: Ah, yes, I know the shrine you speak of – thanks to
the technological triumph that is night-vision goggles.

Sarah: Just got weird.

Matthew: You liked it, didn't you?

Sarah: Kind of. Did you?

23RD FEBRUARY

Matthew: What do you think of this tux?

Sarah: 🔥🔥🔥🔥🔥🔥🔥🔥🔥🔥

Matthew: What is that supposed to mean?

Sarah: Ah here, Granddad. It means you look like a ride.

Matthew: I was going for handsome and debonair, Cary Grant style.

Sarah: Who?

Matthew: You don't know who Cary Grant is? What are they teaching you children in school these days?

Sarah: I don't know. Why don't you ask Harry?

Matthew: Touché.

Sarah: Where are you going? Your life seems so glamorous.

Matthew: Things are stupidly busy. Meetings, drinking, flirting, more meetings, charity balls where idiots like me get dressed up in order to raise money for charities we don't give a shit about.

Sarah: Imma ignore the flirting comment. We both know that I'm your favourite.

24TH FEBRUARY

Sarah: Are you hungover?

Matthew: I don't drink at these things. It's not professional.

Sarah: I think my boss might agree with you. Things are sliiiiightly tense at work right now.

Matthew: I had to fly to London at the crack of dawn this morning, so it wasn't worth it to me to be hungover.

Sarah: I love London.

Matthew: It's a wonderful city. You should come with me next time. I always stay in a suite at Claridge's and, really, everyone needs to experience a suite in Claridge's at least once in their life.

Sarah: Really?! That would be amazing! I'd love that! When are you going again?

27TH FEBRUARY

Matthew: I gave a lecture at Oxford today. All those nerds
love me.

Sarah: Cool! Hope you're having fun.

Matthew: Pots of fun, thank you.

Sarah: Were you a nerd in school?

Matthew: Absolutely not. How dare you imply such a thing.

Sarah: Pity. I ate nerds for breakfast in Dunfinnan.

Matthew: Still hungry?

Sarah: I might be.

Sarah: When are you back in Dublin?

28TH FEBRUARY

Matthew: Are you out in town tonight? I'm having drinks with friends at Residence if you want to meet me afterwards.

Sarah: I had to go home to Tipperary for the weekend. My dad's not well.

Matthew: The country, God help us. I try and avoid Limerick as much as I can these days.

Matthew: Doing anything fun tonight?

Sarah: Going out for drinks with the girls from school.

Matthew: What are you wearing?

Sarah: Are you serious?

Matthew: Yes.

Sarah: I'm wearing a skirt so tight I can barely walk. Happy?

Matthew: Please do not tell me about skirts of that nature on legs like yours when I'm about to go meet four middle-aged men. I will have concentration issues.

Sarah: Love the idea of giving you concentration issues.

Matthew: I'm distracted. And thinking . . . thoughts.

Sarah: What kind of thoughts?!

Matthew: Nothing I could commit to this medium but you probably have a rough idea given that you caused them.

Sarah: Not into sexting then? I'd better delete the nude pics I was about to text you.

Matthew: Enough. We need to sort this out.

Sarah: Sort what out?!!

Matthew: I just looked at my schedule. I'm free on Monday. I'll organise everything.

I reapplied my lipstick, my hand shaking a little. Matthew had sent a message forty minutes ago to say that he was here. *I'm in room 63*, the text said, *come straight up. Don't ask at reception. It's better if we keep this between ourselves for the time being.*

Where are you? he texted twenty minutes later.

I'm running late, I texted back. *I'll be there as soon as I can.*

I wasn't sure why I'd lied. I didn't know why I was standing in the hotel bathroom, staring at my reflection. Why was I there to meet Matthew Brennan, of all people? The strip lighting was harsh, the mirror speckled with black dots, a cheap, off-white laminate covering the sink countertop. I had suggested that I meet him at his house, but Matthew said no.

'I can't ask you to come all the way to Killiney,' he said.

'It's too far. I'll book somewhere near Heuston; that'll be easier for you.'

We arranged to meet at this hotel at 6 p.m. and I hadn't been able to think about anything else for the last two days.

'Are you listening to me at all, Sarah?' my father had said when he rang yesterday to tell me the results of his blood tests. 'You seem fierce distracted.'

'I'm fine, Dad,' I replied.

And then today, when I told Mrs Burke that I couldn't stay for the staff meeting, her eyes had narrowed. 'Are you all right?' she asked me. 'I hope you're not coming down with anything, *again*.'

'Of course not,' I replied. 'I have a dental appointment I can't reschedule.' And I walked out of school knowing that I should stay.

I couldn't afford to annoy her, not after the disciplinary meeting, the *You've let us down* and *The pupils deserve more*.

I'm sorry, I'd said. *I'll do better*, I'd said. *It won't happen again*.

Matthew: Are you still up for this?

I don't know.

I had been texting Matthew for a couple of weeks now, and every time my phone beeped, I felt a rush of excitement. Yesterday he had described in excruciating detail what he

83

wanted to do to me, what he was going to do to every inch of my body, and my breath fell short thinking about it. Matthew was older. Experienced. He would understand what I needed.

'I came twice last night,' Ciara used to tell us at school, after she'd lost her virginity to Eoin.

'Jamsie makes me come so hard that I feel like I'm going to pass out,' Aisling would reply, and I would nod, pretending that I felt the same about Tadgh Carey, who seemed to think my clitoris and belly button resided in the same area. I could only orgasm when I was alone, on my stomach and breathing into my pillow so that my father wouldn't hear me. But I couldn't tell Ciara and Aisling about that. Girls weren't supposed to do *that*.

Sarah: Nearly there.

The lift took me to the first floor. The corridor was long and narrow, the carpet fraying at the edges. It smelled musty with a faint hint of chlorine. Room 63. I knocked.

'Listen, Tony . . .' Matthew said as he opened the door, holding his finger up to his lips to silence me.

The room was small. There was a generic print of a Johannes Vermeer painting beside a black-framed window on the opposite wall, lace curtains turning the world outside opaque.

'I don't care what Geraghty says. This is a million-euro

84

development. Figure it out.' I could hear Tony speak, but Matthew cut him off, throwing his phone on the coffee table.

'A million-euro development?'

'It doesn't matter. Jesus. Look at you.' He held my face in his hands.

He could kill me, I thought, and easily – a snap of the neck and an abandoned body. No one knew that I was here with him, in this room, not even Fionn.

'It's nice to see you too, Brennan,' I said.

'Now that I have you here, I hardly know what to do with you.'

'We could—' I began, but he pushed me into the door, the handle pressing into my lower back. He pulled my polo-neck off and shoved my skirt down, scooping his hand under my legs and throwing me onto the bed. He unbuttoned his shirt and the flies of his trousers, lips moving down my stomach.

'Wait.'

'What?' He lifted his head.

'I don't like that,' I said. Legs spread open. Wondering what they're thinking, what they're going to tell their friends. Body tense. *Relax,* they always say, but I can't.

He smirked. 'That's because you've only been with boys until now.'

'No, I'm serious, I really don't—'

'Shush,' he said. 'You'll enjoy it this time.'

A few minutes later, I was pretending to come, writhing in

ecstasy. Anything to make it stop. He crawled back up my body and lifted my hips, shoving himself into me before I could tell him that he needed to put on a condom. He felt huge and this time I gasped for real. He dragged me into a kneeling position and thrust again from behind.

'You like that, don't you?' he said, pushing my body into the headboard.

I flipped my hair, looking at him over my shoulder, and I told him that I liked it. I told him to do it to me again.

'I'm close,' he said, and pulled out. Something hot across my skin. He collapsed on the bed next to me, groaning. *Jesus,* he kept saying. *Jesus.* 'Thank you for that,' he said to me after a few minutes. 'What a lovely way to spend an evening.'

'Yeah,' I said, but I didn't move. I stared at the velour fabric of the headboard, my fingers resting in one of its diamond-shaped indentations. I listened to my breathing, trying to find my way back into my body. It had all happened so quickly.

'Are you all right?' he asked me. 'You're very quiet.'

'I'm fine.' I hesitated. 'Okay, listen, I feel awkward even bringing this up and I don't want to be a pain, but . . . have you been tested recently?'

'Tested?'

'You know, for STIs.'

'STIs, how are you.' He snorted. 'Listen, the women I sleep with are all clean.'

The women. *The women.*

'Anyway, I hate condoms,' he said. 'You can't feel anything with them on.'

'Yeah,' I said. 'I guess.'

He stood up, stretching his arms overhead.

'Are you going already?'

'I have to go to Áras an Uachtaráin for an event to attract foreign investment in the property market,' he said as he pulled on his shirt. 'I know that sounds outrageously obnoxious, but this is my world, Sarah.' He tied his shoelaces. 'Feel free to tell me to get lost. I know I'm a nightmare.'

'It's fine,' I said, picking up my underwear. 'I have stuff to do this evening anyway.'

He was in the bathroom, the door open as he washed his hands. 'I'm sure you do; I've no doubt you're a busy girl as well.' I saw him notice me in the mirror, so I stayed still, allowing him to watch. 'You are incredible,' he said, turning around. 'I like that tattoo on your back. What's that for?'

'Édith Piaf,' I said, humming the tune for him. 'My mother used to listen to her all the time when I was little. It was her favourite song.'

'Very sexy,' he said, trailing his fingers down the words. He shook his head. 'What is someone like you doing with an old man like me?'

'You're not old.'

'Oh, but I am. Do yourself a favour and find a nice young man.' He kissed me, slowly this time. It felt like I thought it would with Matthew: more sure, somehow, more grown-up than the boys I had been with previously. 'And, with that, I must go.' He took his suit jacket from the back of the chair. 'I bought a present for you, by the way.' He pointed at the table with the plastic kettle and glass box full of teabags, sachets of sugar and UHT milk, and, sure enough, there was a green paper bag underneath it.

'Matthew! You shouldn't have. I can't believe you—'

'It's only small,' he cut me off. 'Don't get too excited.'

'Okay,' I said. 'But thank you anyway.'

In Stoneybatter, I sat at the kitchen table, the chair nudging back and forward on the uneven lino. Dust glistened in the light from the old reading-lamp that Fionn had stolen from his mother when we moved in. I stared at it, watching the particles in their twisting dance. There was a deep ache in my thighs already, my face raw from the scratch of his stubble. I stayed there for a long time.

When I remembered that I was at home and I was still holding Matthew's present, I peeled away the pinstriped paper carefully, like Nana Kathleen taught me to do. 'We can reuse that,' she'd say, putting it in the press for safekeeping. 'Sticks and stones,' Nana would say when I came home crying because the other girls sneered when they saw the birthday presents I gave them were wrapped in second-hand paper. 'They're only words, Sarah; they can't hurt you if you don't let them.' But words can hurt when no one wants to sit next to you on the bus or choose you for their red-rover team or invite you to their house to play. Words can hurt when nobody likes you. Things were better in secondary school; I had friends, Aisling and Ciara, to eat lunch with, boys approaching me at the disco, asking if I would shift their friends. I was calling myself an 'artist' then, ripped jeans and black nail varnish, listening to obscure bands that the boys from the Presentation College professed to like but my friends hadn't even heard of. 'You're not like the other girls,' my boyfriends told me, and I agreed. If I'd learned anything at the convent, it was how to pretend to be something I was not.

Matthew's present was an art book, one I'd told him I was waiting until payday to buy because it was too expensive. He had said that it sounded ridiculous: 'Anorexic models prancing around for gay photographers.'

'You're being such a dick,' I told him.

'It's been a while since anyone has called me a dick,' he replied, amused.

Sarah: I just opened the present. Thank you so much! I love it.

An hour passed. Waiting, Waiting. And finally:

Matthew: Not at all. Glad you like it.
Sarah: I'll thank you properly the next time I see you. We should go for dinner when you're back from Tokyo? Can't have you getting the wrong idea 😌

89

I sat there, waiting for a reply. My arms were bare and I could see speckled skin where his fingers had prodded and dug in, marking their territory. I knew I would be bruised tomorrow. It was exciting, I told myself.

'Oh,' Fionn said, 'I didn't hear you come in.' He opened the fridge and grabbed a packet of cooked ham. He had that dazed look on his face that he got when he was in the middle of a painting, when he could only stop to go to the bathroom or to eat something as fast as he could, as if talking to someone might break the spell, cut the brush out of his hands before he could finish.

'Fionn,' I said, and his shoulders tensed. 'I need to talk to you.'

'Is it important, Fitz? I'm kind of in the middle of some-thing.'

'No.' I looked at my phone again. 'No, it's not important.'

NOW

Sarah woke early, unable to sleep in the sticky heat.

'I don't know how they expect farmers to make a living in this kind of weather. Hottest July on record,' her father told her when she phoned home.

'Really, Dad?' she said every time. 'That's interesting.'

Oisín turned to her, his hand under her pyjama bottoms. She wanted to say no, but when she tried to think of the last time they had done this, she couldn't remember. So Sarah let Oisín have sex with her, felt him moving inside her, and she closed her eyes and thought of Matthew. She thought of Matthew wanting her, taking his pleasure from her in whatever way he desired, and she came with a sharp cry.

She got out of bed, closing the bathroom door as Oisín asked, 'Are you okay?'

Behind the free-standing bathtub was a mirrored wall.

'Kinky,' she had said to Oisín when they moved in, and he had stood her in front of the mirror and taken her clothes off, making her watch what he was doing to her.

Oisín was the only man who had ever made her come. 'What do you like, Sarah?' he said. 'What do you want me to do?' And she told him, whispered her needs to him in the dark of night. Why hadn't Matthew done the same? Didn't he care? There were so many things Sarah wanted to ask Matthew these days, but knew that she could not. Sometimes she felt as if she would go mad with the not asking.

Her body was softer now than when she had been with Matthew. She had been thin then, sharp collarbones and jutting ribs. 'You're in such good shape,' he would tell her which somehow made Sarah want to eat everything in sight while simultaneously vowing never to consume solid food again. 'Your body is incredible.' Sarah had long been aware of the power she could exert over men, of the effect her body had on them; she had learned that lesson when she was twelve years old and a man had screamed crude obscenities at her from the safety of his passing car. But, even then, she knew that it shouldn't be used for her own pleasure. Her body was there to be looked at, to be admired by others, and, as such, it would never entirely belong to her.

'Sexy bitch,' Matthew would say, and then ejaculate on her back or on her stomach.

'I'm on the pill,' Sarah told him. 'You can come inside me.'

'I'm ridiculously fertile,' he said. 'We don't want any

accidents now, do we?' And Sarah tried to guess how many other accidents there had been, how many girls had been sent over to England to 'take care of things'. Matthew would pay for it, of course. He was good like that.

'Sarah?' It was Oisín, calling her from the bedroom. 'Babe, are you okay?'

'I'm fine.'

She could hear him sigh. 'If you say so. I'm going downstairs to make breakfast. Do you want scrambled or poached eggs?'

They sat at the kitchen table, Sarah's hair frizzing out of its ponytail, Oisín badly in need of a shave. *Why would anyone even* want *to be in a relationship?* Matthew used to say to her. *People give up, and they start wearing tracksuits around the house* – he'd almost recoiled – *until a Chinese takeaway on a Saturday night is the highlight of their week. You're far too young and cool for that,* he'd said to her. *It's one of the things I like most about you.*

Sarah had wanted Matthew to like her, so she'd agreed with him. She remained quiet and he rewarded her by staying. For a while, anyway.

'Your mother texted again,' Sarah said, picking up her phone to read the message.

'Oh yeah?'

'Yet another exhibition she wants me to go see with her. That's the fourth one this month. I wish she would just take the hint.'

93

Oisín didn't reply. The scrape of his knife against the plate, the clang of teeth against the metal, the slurping of tea. Sarah slammed her cutlery down with a clatter and he looked up in surprise.

'Are you not enjoying it?' he asked her. 'I made them the way you like.'

'I've lost my appetite, for *some* reason.'

'Oh,' he said, continuing to shovel eggs into his mouth.

'Did you wash out the saucepan?'

'What?'

'The saucepan? You know, that metal thing you used to cook the eggs in, Oisín?'

He sneaked a look at the sink. 'I didn't get a chance to do it yet.'

'Jesus fucking Christ, Oisín; you know what scrambled eggs are like; it'll be impossible to clean now.'

'I told you, I didn't get a chance to do it yet.'

'Because it's so hard to put some Fairy liquid and hot water in a saucepan, is it?'

'Sarah,' Oisín said. 'Sarah, why are you so angry with me all the time?'

'What? What are you talking about? I'm not angry with you all the time.'

'It feels like you are. Like when we had sex earlier. I just . . .'

'You just what? If you've got something to say to me, Oisín, then just say it.'

'Oh, come on, Sarah. I'm sick of feeling like everything I do is wrong. It's not fair to me. This isn't what I signed up for.'

Break up with me then, Sarah thought. Get it over and done with. Then we can both move on with our lives. But she just asked, 'What do you mean?'

'Are you still going to Dunfinnan for the weekend?' he replied, ignoring her question.

It had been months since Sarah had gone home. 'But you're on your summer holidays,' her father said during their phone call yesterday. 'Surely you can spare the time now?' She had felt guilty then so she promised Eddie that she would visit this weekend and that she would bring Oisín.

Sarah had been anxious about bringing Oisín to Dunfinnan in the beginning, unsure of what Eddie would make of her new boyfriend, with his sharp suits and his fancy job in finance, but Oisín had insisted. 'I want to spend the rest of my life with you,' he'd said, 'and that means meeting your father.'

Eddie had been waiting at the front door, his hand outstretched to shake Oisín's. They hit it off immediately, much to Sarah's disbelief, discussing GAA and the horses, Oisín talking about summers spent on his aunt's farm in West Cork. 'That would be on your mother's side, I presume. She's the Irish one, isn't she?' Eddie had asked him, and Oisín nodded, eating the overcooked carrots without complaint.

It was late before they went to bed, Eddie showing Oisín to the spare bedroom where Nana Kathleen used to sleep.

95

'He's a nice lad,' Eddie said to Sarah. 'You deserve someone nice, after everything.'

Later, Sarah crawled into the bed next to Oisín.

'Sarah,' he said, 'we shouldn't, not here. Not in your father's house.'

But they did.

'You're amazing,' he said. 'I've never met anyone like you. I'm so lucky.' And Sarah had felt lucky too.

'Of course I'm still going home. Dad wants to see me before my birthday next week,' she said now. 'You're coming with me, aren't you?'

Oisín didn't reply.

'Oisín, I've told Dad you're coming. And we went for dinner with your parents on Tuesday, it's only fair that—'

'It might be better if I don't go down.'

'Why?'

'I don't know,' he said. 'Maybe we could do with a weekend apart.'

'What are you trying to say, Oisín?'

'Nothing. It's just a weekend apart,' he said. 'It'll give us both some time to breathe.'

THEN

'Why are you calling me?' I asked Matthew the first time he phoned. 'Is someone dead?'

'Why would anyone be dead?' he said.

'Because that's the only legit reason anyone would have for *phoning* me rather than texting.'

'Christ Almighty.'

'Seriously, it's rude. You're presuming that I'll have time to talk to you.'

'Well, do you have time to talk to me?'

'I might.'

'You are very annoying,' he said, but he kept talking.

He kept phoning too, telling me about his trips to Hong Kong and New York and Berlin, mentioning new artists that he had come across on his travels that he wanted me to look up. He was funny, charming, successful. He could have whomever he wanted and, for some reason, he'd decided that he wanted me. And Matthew Brennan wanting me made me forget about the *You have insufficient funds for this transaction*, and the Koka noodles for dinner the week before pay day, and the *Are you coming home to Dunfinnan this weekend, love? I miss you.* Before I knew it, I was looking forward to his calls. Waiting for them. A simple text from him could lift my entire day, and I became uneasy when they didn't arrive as frequently as I wanted, bordering on euphoric when they did.

'You're positively giddy,' Stephen said as I shimmied around the staffroom when Matthew had texted me after two days of silence. 'What's going on?'

'I . . .'

I imagined telling Stephen, his reaction, Florence finding out, Mrs Burke jumping at any opportunity to reprimand me for my 'lack of professionalism', losing my job, moving back to Dunfinnan and that single bed, and my father mentioning a 'great position going in the convent'. I was putting so much in jeopardy, being with this man. What was he risking to be with me, in return? I told myself that it was not worth it, that Matthew was not worth it. I told myself I had to be careful.

'I'm going to break it off,' I said to Fionn when Matthew hadn't texted me back, again.

I had confessed to Fionn about Matthew after that first time in room 63, showing him the text messages so I could get his opinion. *You're a man, Fionn; what do you think of this? Look at this one, Fionn. He put an x in this one. He never puts an x after his text messages. What do you think this means? And what do you think this one means? And this one? And this one?*

'It's too much hassle and he's not even my type,' I said. 'He's obsessed with CrossFit, of all things. I mean, it's pathetic, at his age. He never laughs at my jokes, he just says, "Very funny," but I'm expected to find him *hilarious*, of course, and—'

'Cool,' Fionn said, leaving the kitchen or the living room or wherever we were hanging out to go into the tiny studio upstairs, closing the door firmly behind him.

'You never listen to me anymore, dude,' I said, and Fionn sighed and asked why I couldn't talk about Matthew to my other friends. Why did it always have to be him?

'Because . . .'

'Because you're not allowed to, I guess?' Fionn said.

'It's not that I'm not *allowed* to tell anyone,' I said. 'It's for my own protection. Matthew doesn't want me to have to deal with the drama I would get if it hit the papers.'

'Why would anyone give a fuck about who some CEO is dating?'

'It's not about him,' I said. 'It's because of her – Florence Kavanagh. The papers are obsessed with her.'

'Matthew Brennan must have loved that,' Fionn muttered under his breath.

Later that evening, I was still talking about Matthew as I watched Fionn finish a painting. I was sitting on the landing, never able to go all the way into his studio these days, as if an invisible line had been drawn across the entrance. He was using the thin edge of a blade to scrape at the canvas and I itched to do the same. Then I thought of my work at DAC, trying and trying, only to be told that it was a 'good effort, Sarah', and I curled my fingers into my palms. I would rather have cut them off, one by one, than fail again.

'The reality is,' Fionn said to me, 'the situation with Matthew is bothering you the way it is. So why don't you say it to him?'

'Say what to him?'

'That you don't want to meet him at that shitty hotel anymore.'

'It's not shitty.'

'You just said it was shitty.'

'It's not the best,' I admitted.

'It's not like he can't afford better.'

'Yeah, but we might meet someone we know in a nice hotel in town.'

'Someone *we* know?'

'Fine. We might meet someone that Matthew knows.'

'And that would be so terrible because . . . ?'

'Because we're not ready to tell anyone yet.'

'But you're not happy with the way things are, right?' Fionn asked.

I paused, glad that Fionn was looking at the painting rather than at me. 'I could be happier, I guess.'

'Grand. Tell him that.'

'I can't just *tell* him that, Fionn.'

'Why not?'

'Because . . .'

'Because what?'

'Because it's not that simple.'

He groaned. 'I can't keep having this conversation with you, Fitz.' And he threw the paintbrush into the tin of water, wiped his hands on the ragged cloth and left without saying another word.

'I am going to break it off,' I said aloud, when he was gone. 'I am.'

But then Matthew texted. (I'll give it another week, I told myself. It's too soon.) He texted again. And again. And, before I knew it, I was back where I'd started, knocking on the door of room 63, waiting for Matthew.

'Your legs are fantastic,' he told me. He had lifted them over his shoulders earlier, thrusting in deep. It hurt when we had sex like that, gritted teeth and chafing skin, but Matthew liked it.

'I grew them myself,' I joked, and he curled his body around mine.

'Very funny, for a girl.'

'What's that supposed to mean?'

'Women aren't funny, are they?'

'Oh, *God*,' I said, trying to pull away, but he tightened his grip until I stopped fighting. I closed my eyes, breathing in sweat and his expensive cologne, and I felt dizzy with wanting. Wanting him, wanting money, wanting to feel happy, wanting my life to finally begin. I didn't know what I wanted. All I knew was that I *wanted*. I wanted so much.

'Okay,' he said, letting go of me. Matthew was always the first one to step back, to get dressed, to leave. And every time, I felt as if I had failed a test I didn't even realise I was taking. 'I have to go; there's a conference call with LA in an hour.'

'You are so busy and important,' I said. 'Are we talking millions?'

'Of course.'

'So,' I said, as he thoroughly soaped his hands in the bathroom, always so eager to wash the smell of us off his skin, 'when will I see you again?'

'I'm not sure,' he replied. 'I have to go to Paris next week. Business, mostly, but I'm hoping to extend it by a few days.'

'By yourself?' I asked.

(A French girl, roughly dried hair, a cigarette hanging between wet lips. She told Matthew that she didn't care what he did or who else he saw, but, unlike me, she meant it.)

'Yes,' he said, coming back to the bed. 'I prefer travelling alone.'

'I lived in Paris for a summer when I was at college,' I told him. 'It was incredible. You *have* to go to Père Lachaise. I know it's a cliché, but I used to hang out by Édith Piaf's grave there, all the time. That's when I got my tattoo.'

'Ah, yes,' he said, bending down to kiss the tattoo. 'My own little bullseye.'

I flinched.

'What?' he said.

'Nothing,' I said.

He got dressed with the precise efficiency he seemed to do everything with – socks, underwear, shirt, trousers, shoes, belt – the routine never varied. I picked his coat up from the back of the chair.

'Alexander Wang?' I said as I handed it to him. 'Very "trendy", as you old folks like to say.'

He shrugged it on, then pulled me closer to him, wrapping the sides of the coat around me, and I leaned my head against his chest, listening to his heart beat.

'I have to go,' he said again. 'I'll call you, okay?'

'Yeah, cool,' I said. 'Be good.'

I stayed there after he left, sitting on the bed, trying to summon up the energy to move. The crumpled sheets, the thin windowpanes letting through a whistling wind. It felt cheap and I shivered, as if the dampness of the room was seeping into my bones. I looked down at my naked body, the promise of bruises dusting my inner thighs, and I grabbed the duvet to cover it up. I didn't want to see what I had done to myself.

★

My phone was the first thing I looked at when I woke up in the morning. I stared at the screen on the DART to work. I kept it half hidden under my desk so I would be able to see if it lit up, my heart pressing into my spine when I had a message (please, please), but then it wasn't from him. I felt a flash of irrational hatred for the person that had bothered to text me and then I started waiting again. Another text would arrive but it wasn't from him, and it wasn't from him, and then it wasn't from him again.

Two weeks passed and he hadn't texted me.

'Are you okay?' the lads in the house asked when I said I was going to bed early again.

'Sarah, is something the matter?' they asked me in work, when I sat silently in the staffroom, cramming chocolate biscuits into my mouth. I didn't even like them – Matthew preferred it when my body was made up of edges – but they were filling the hole in my stomach, the hole of *not good enough* and *not pretty enough*, and him pulling my hair back, tight, and a sharp palm to flesh, tender flesh but willing, always willing, and *You like that, don't you, Sarah?* And I said yes and I looked at him with wanting eyes, because that's what he liked. He liked it so much that it must have been good for me too.

Dad: What time will you be home this weekend?

Dad: I presume you are coming home.

Dad: I hope you haven't forgotten, Sarah.

Dad: The Mass is organised and everything.

Dad: Are you getting my texts?

I was at Heuston Station. Tomorrow was 25th May and I always went home at this time of year. It was important. Train ticket in one hand, overnight bag in the other. The robotic voice saying, 'The train now standing at platform three is the five o'clock service to Cork.' I checked my phone to see what time it was, and there it was. A message from Matthew. He was sorry that he hadn't texted, he said, work had been crazy, he had been travelling.

Come meet me now, he said. And so I did.

Ducking past the receptionist in the hotel. The lift, the worn-out carpet. Room 63.

'Sarah,' he said, and without warning he was inside me, fucking me against the wall, his face contorting. I wondered why men never felt embarrassed about their facial expression as they came, when I almost felt compelled to practise mine, to make sure that it looked attractive enough. 'Fuck,' he said. 'Fuck, you feel so good.'

In the bathroom afterwards, I stared at my reflection. My face was flushed, a rash bleeding its way down my neck and onto my chest. I licked my fingers and rubbed at the smudged eyeliner, wishing I could get into the shower and scrub my entire body clean, make it forget what just happened to it. I should have been on the train, going to Dunfinnan. I had never been away from home on her anniversary before. I could see Matthew in the reflection, stretched out on the bed, his phone in his hand.

'I can't keep doing this.'

His eyes on mine in the mirror. 'What do you mean?' he asked.

'This. Us. Whatever this is,' I said. 'I need—'

'More,' he said, as if he had been expecting this. 'You need more.'

I turned to face him. 'I'm sick of meeting in this hotel. It would be nice to actually go for dinner sometime and not be treated like I'm a fucking whore that you hired for the evening.'

He winced. 'Please don't swear, Sarah. I don't like it when girls swear.'

'You sound like Eddie.'

'Who's Eddie?'

'My father,' I said, my voice rising.

'How am I supposed to remember his name?' he asked. 'You always call him "Dad".'

Because I remember. I remember everything about you.

'Look, I'm sorry if you're feeling as if I'm taking advantage of you, Sarah. That was never my intention. I thought we were having fun.'

'We are,' I said.

'I completely understand if you don't want to see me anymore.'

'What? That's not what I said.'

'No, you're right. You deserve better. And I wish I could be the one to give it to you, but I can't,' he said. 'So, if you want to end things,' he continued, 'I get it.'

'I don't want to end things. I never said that.'

'You want to keep seeing me?'

'I want to keep seeing you, but—'

'Well, if you want to keep seeing me, what's the problem?' He pushed himself off the bed and, with each step that he took towards me, I forgot what I'd been going to say, because he was here with me now and that was all I had wanted anyway. 'We're still having fun, aren't we?'

'Yes,' I said. 'Yes.'

'It's not just sex for me, Sarah. I hope you know that.'

He kissed me, silencing me before I could ask him for more. His words sliced through my skin, humming in my throat with what they could mean, the promise of them.

I can wait, I told myself. I've always been good at waiting.

'Why didn't you come home?'

'Dad, I can't really talk right now.'

'I don't care, Sarah. Why didn't you come home? I bought your ticket and everything, all you had to do was get on the train.'

'There was an emergency in work, Dad. I was stuck in a meeting until five thirty and I missed the train, it wasn't my fault—'

'Why didn't you phone me? I was standing at Clonmel for over an hour.'

'I'm sorry, but it wasn't my fault.'

'I kept trying to call you.'

'I couldn't look at my phone during work, could I?'

'You said you would come home, this weekend of all weekends. You *promised* me, Sarah.'

'Dad, I can come home tomorrow morning. I'll get an early train.'

'No. Don't bother. I just . . .' His voice faltered. 'I never wanted you to forget about her.'

'Dad.' I couldn't breathe. 'Dad, of course I'm not going to forget her; that's not possible.'

The phone went dead. I put it back in my bag, waiting at the traffic lights to cross in front of the Courts of Justice. I made my mind go blank, like I used to do when I was a child and my mother had just died. Nana Kathleen wasn't living with us then; it was only the two of us left behind, trying to survive. My father sitting at the kitchen table when the last of the cousins had gone home, rocking back and forth, one hand over his mouth to muffle the high-pitched noise, like an animal with its leg caught in a trap. Men weren't supposed to cry. Men were supposed to be brave.

'Daddy,' I had said, and I tried to hug him. 'Daddy, don't be sad.'

My father stared at me, his eyes unseeing, as if he wasn't sure who I was or what I was doing in his house. I wasn't enough for him either.

NOW

As a child, it had baffled Sarah how Nana Kathleen and her friends would express surprise when it was Christmas or their birthday or a wedding anniversary. 'How in God's name is it that time again?' they would say, shaking their heads in disbelief that another year had passed and they had found themselves at the exact same date once more, as if they hadn't been expecting it. It was stupid, Sarah would think, stupid how ill-prepared they were for the way the future carved through their lives, claiming their youth for its own.

But when she woke that morning, rubbing the damp off the back of her neck, she understood. It was 29th July and it was her birthday. She was twenty-seven. And, somehow, she could not believe it. Her mother had been married at her age, and pregnant. Sarah tried to imagine herself married to Oisín, a baby clawing in her stomach, needing sustenance, love, demanding sacrifices, because that's what mothers did for their children – they sacrificed. First their wombs, then their hearts. Children were greedy that way.

Sarah unplugged her phone. There were the usual *Happy Birthday!* messages on Facebook from people she hadn't seen in years, messages in the WhatsApp group from Ciara and Aisling. A text from Oisín saying that he had gone to work early, but he would see her at dinner tonight. *I love you,* he said, and Sarah wondered if that was still true.

Dad: Happy birthday, love. Have put €100 into your AIB account. Phone you later for a chat.

Her mother had always sent her a card. 'It's nice to get post, isn't it, pet?' she would say on the morning of Sarah's birthday. 'It makes it special.' Helen had believed in making birthdays special.

Sarah brushed her teeth, wincing at how worn her skin looked in the bathroom mirror, nascent lines forming around her eyes. In the kitchen, there was a package on the table, in cream and black paper, and an envelope beside it. She unwrapped the box to find a Louis Vuitton handbag from Oisín. It was expensive, she knew, something she would never be able to afford on her salary. She should be grateful to have such a generous boyfriend. The envelope was from William and Oonagh, a voucher for an all-inclusive weekend stay at

111

Ballyfin hotel. *It'll be good for you and Oisín to get a break!* The card said, in Oonagh's handwriting.

Fionn: Happy Birthday. I owe you a drink.

Fionn didn't buy her presents anymore. Not after what she had done to him.

The doorbell rang, startling Sarah. No one ever came to the Booterstown house without texting first. Unannounced visitors tended to be Jehovah's Witnesses (*No*, Sarah felt like telling them, *I do not want to accept Jesus Christ as my Lord and Saviour. Yes, I'm fine with the fiery pits of hell for all eternity, thanks for asking*) or local kids raising money for charity, their mams standing behind them, as if daring Sarah to refuse to support orphans in Syria or jerseys for the local under-twelves' rugby team. The doorbell rang again, a finger on the buzzer for longer than was strictly necessary. Her phone lit up, Oonagh's name on the screen.

'Yes?' Sarah said.

'Hi, Sarah. It's Oonagh.'

I know, Sarah thought. Caller ID is amazing.

'I'm outside the front door,' Oonagh continued. 'Is the doorbell broken?'

'No,' Sarah said. 'It's not broken. Give me two minutes.'

Oonagh was standing on the front porch, immaculately dressed in a sleeveless linen top and cropped trousers, blonde hair freshly blow-dried. 'Well, there's the birthday girl,' she said, kissing Sarah on the cheek. 'It's good to see you.'

'Yes,' Sarah said, breathing in. No matter how much expensive perfume Oonagh wore, she always smelled of paint and turpentine, her art stitched to her as tightly as a shadow. If Sarah closed her eyes, she could pretend she was back in the garden shed in Dunfinnan, the shed Eddie had told Sarah was hers when she turned fifteen.

You'll need somewhere to work, sure, he'd said. *You'll be asphyxiated from paint fumes in that room of yours, if things carry on the way they are.* Sarah could see herself in that tiny space, the Killers on her iPod dock while she finished her Leaving Cert coursework. It was an imaginative composition based on an old photo hanging in their living room, of Sarah and her mother and Eddie in Tramore: Sarah's first trip to the beach as a child. Sarah remembered feeling as if she was trying to draw blood, drag her memory of that day up from her bones and scratch it into life on the canvas – salt tangling hair, skin tightening with sunburn. But Sarah knew that what she really wanted to capture was how it felt to have a mother again. Helen's hand in hers. The weight of it. Both of them ignoring Eddie's fussing about the price of ice creams and how the sand was too hot and how the shells were too sharp and how there was sand in his ham sandwich. Eddie had been fourteen years older than Helen, and it was at moments like that when the age gap became most apparent. He looked wrong when he was away from the farm, somehow, as if he was posing for an artistic study in his shorts and sandals (Sarah Fitzpatrick. B.1990. *Father at the Beach*, 1994. Oil on canvas). *Beautiful, Sarah*, Ms Ryan, the art teacher, had said when she saw the painting of Sarah's family. That was when Sarah had been the best art student at the convent. That was before she went to college and discovered thirty other people who had been the best students in their schools too.

'I've been texting you,' Oonagh said. 'I was hoping you might come to the Annual Exhibition in the RHA with me. I was supposed to attend the opening shindig, but I had to go to the States with William; he's on tour with the new book and you know how he gets.'

Sarah didn't respond.

'Anyway,' Oonagh said, 'I thought we could go together, maybe get lunch in the gallery afterwards; the food is good there. My treat.'

'I didn't get any texts from you,' Sarah replied. 'My phone must be broken.' She gestured at her dressing gown and slippers. 'You'll have to excuse what I'm wearing. I would have changed if I knew you were coming.'

'Oh, it doesn't matter. We can go another time. Whenever suits you,' she said. There was an awkward pause. 'Can I come in, then?'

'Oh,' Sarah said. 'Sorry. Of course. Come in, come in.'

They walked through the hall into the kitchen, Sarah apologising for the mess. 'Magda was sick this week and Oisín said he would tidy up last night, but then he had to have dinner with a client, *again*, and he wasn't home until late, so I told him I'd just do it myself, but I haven't had a chance to get around to it yet and—'

'It's fine,' Oonagh said. 'Don't worry about it. This is your house now; you can do what suits you.'

Can I? Sarah thought, but she smiled at Oonagh anyway, turning on the Nespresso machine and searching the cupboards for biscuits. 'How's William?' she asked. 'That was an incredible review in the *New Yorker*; he must have been thrilled.'

'It was super, wasn't it? Unfortunately, they got the initial sales figures the day after.' Oonagh lowered her voice as if to ensure no one would overhear her. 'And let's just say that they're not quite what we had hoped for.' She picked up the Louis Vuitton bag and stroked the leather. 'This is beautiful. A birthday present?'

'Yes,' Sarah said. 'From Oisín.'

'Isn't he so good? I love Louis Vuitton, but I have to smuggle the Brown Thomas bags into the house when William's at Trinity; he thinks it's a criminal waste of money.'

'Well,' Sarah said as she placed a cup of coffee in front of Oonagh. She picked up the sugar canister and grabbed milk from the fridge. 'It is your money, after all. You can do what you want with it.'

'It doesn't quite work like that in a marriage. William and I share everything equally. That's the deal.'

That wasn't the deal in Sarah's relationship. There was

Sarah's money and there was Oisín's money, and although Oisín was generous, although Sarah knew that he would give her anything she wanted or asked for, that money still wasn't hers. And, ultimately, it wasn't Oisín's either. He was paid well as a private-client adviser at Bryant, but they both knew that it was Oonagh's money that funded their lifestyle. Oonagh had always supported her men and their artistic ambitions, paying for yet another new guitar for Domhnall, covering the initial touring costs so the Principles could play every small venue in Ireland and build up their rabid fan-base, shelling out for acting classes and headshots for Oisín before he decided that he wasn't cut out for the constant rejection of the thespian life. Oonagh's money seemed to mean a lifetime pretending that, no, William didn't mind that his critical success wasn't matched by the sales figures, and, no, William didn't care that his wife made more money from selling one painting than he did in a year from his award-winning novels. And, Oisín had told Sarah in confidence, in exchange for William 'not caring', Oonagh's job was to reassure her husband that he was brilliant, that his work was important, *necessary*, bolstering an ego that was punctured every time he looked at their joint bank account. Was that part of the marriage deal too?

'Yes,' Sarah said. They sat in silence, the *ting* of metal against china as Oonagh stirred milk into her cup, the roar of a lawnmower from next door.

'Martina Morrison still working poor Johnny to the bone?'

116

'Nonsense, Oonagh,' Sarah said. 'Mrs Morrison does all the work herself. It's the green fingers, you see, and God Almighty himself has blessed her with them.'

Oonagh snorted. 'That woman is lethal. I hope she hasn't been driving you mad.'

'Ah, she's harmless.'

'So,' Oonagh said, taking a sip of her coffee, 'what are you doing for your birthday? Anything special?'

'Not much; just going to chill out, I think. Oisín is taking me to Blowfish later.'

'That'll be lovely. JJ and Alannah are doing an incredible job with the place, aren't they? You should have the monkfish for your main – it's incredible.'

'I know.'

'Or the blackened salmon is amazing as well. I would go with either of those two dishes, if I were you.'

'I have been there before, Oonagh.'

'Of course,' Oonagh said, breaking a biscuit in half, but not eating any of it. 'I'm sorry if I'm annoying you. I only came over today because I wanted to give you your present.'

'You already gave me a present.'

Oonagh frowned, so Sarah forced herself to keep talking.

'And thank you. It was very generous.'

'I'm glad you liked it,' Oonagh said dryly. She reached into her handbag, pulling out an envelope. 'Maybe you'll be more excited about this.'

Sarah didn't move.

'Well,' Oonagh said, 'aren't you going to open it?'

Sarah took the envelope from her. Inside was a one-thousand-euro voucher for an art-supply store, the best in Dublin. The one that Fionn and she used to go to when they were students. The same one her father—

'Buy yourself some frivolous colours,' Oonagh said, her hands gesticulating wildly as she imagined the paints Sarah might choose. 'Just experiment, don't worry about the end result. Allow yourself to create for the sake of creating again, rather than thinking about whether it's "good" or not. I think that's the key to true creativity, don't you? If you look at how children make art, they're so *present*, they never worry about—'

'I can't accept this, Oonagh.'

'What?' She stared at Sarah in confusion. 'Why not?'

'It's too much money.'

'Oh, money,' Oonagh said, as if the concept was nonsensical. 'Money isn't important, Sarah. If you're an artist, then you make art. It's as simple as that.'

'Maybe money isn't important for *you*, Oonagh, but for the rest of us it tends to come in handy.'

'Please don't talk to me like that, Sarah.'

'Like what?'

'Like I'm some class of simpleton. Do you honestly think I became an artist to make money? This was the seventies, Sarah, in *Ireland*. There was no money in the country and the only option for a woman was to become a teacher or a nurse, or to go into the civil service.' Oonagh shuddered at the thought. 'Do you think my parents jumped up and down with joy when I said I wanted to go to art school? And then I brought William, of all people, back from London and told them that this was the man I was going to marry . . . Well. You can imagine how that went down.' She almost laughed. 'Black and a Protestant. I'm not sure which they thought was worse. My father told me I would die penniless and alone, and that I wasn't to come crying to him for help when that happened.' Her smile faded. 'As if I would have asked him for anything.'

Sarah rolled her eyes. 'Your father was a doctor, Oonagh; I don't think you were exactly facing the mean streets of Dublin, now, were you?'

'My father was a lot of things.'

'You still had a mother, didn't you? You had your sisters.' Sarah's voice spiked. She was being rude, Nana Kathleen would have told her, but she couldn't stop. 'What did I have?'

'What did you have?' Oonagh banged the cup down on the table. 'What did *you* have? Oh, I don't know, Sarah, maybe you had a *normal* father, who loved you, and supported you and encouraged you to go to art school because all he wanted was for you to be happy?'

'My father left me in that house when my mother died so he could go on yet another binge with his drinking friends.'

'Oh my God, would you stop? For once? I'll admit that your father didn't cope well after your mother died. Can you blame him?'

'Well, Oonagh, maybe he should have paid more attention to her when she was alive. He never seemed to think of that, did he?'

'That doesn't negate the fact that he had just lost his wife to cancer, Sarah. Grief manifests in strange ways.'

'I'd just lost my mother. And I was only a child.'

'I know. And I'm sorry,' she said. 'But your father did his best. Didn't he go get professional help to stop drinking? Didn't your grandmother move in to take care of you while he was in the hospital?' She waited for Sarah to nod in acquiescence before continuing. 'And didn't your grandmother love you and mind you until your father was well again?'

'Yes. But . . . but . . .' Sarah was stuttering now, trying to remember her point. 'But he left me *alone*, Oonagh.'

'Sarah –' Oonagh took Sarah's hands in hers – 'I'm sorry that happened to you. Truly, I am. But don't you think you should do something about it? Go to therapy. Read some self-help books. Break up with Oisín, if he's making you so bloody miserable.'

'*What?* Oonagh, you can't just say that to me. What's wrong with you?'

'I think the real question, here, Sarah, is what's wrong with *you*? Do you think that we don't notice, William and Domhnall and I, how you treat Oisín? How you snap at him and order him around and pick at every little fault? Do you think that's easy for us to be around?'

Sarah flushed. She thought she had been clever, that she

had managed to fool the Wilsons into thinking she was the perfect girlfriend and prospective daughter-in-law. And, if they had noticed, who else had? Aifric? Oisín's friends? His colleagues?

'I've tried not to get involved—'

'Is this what you call not getting involved, Oonagh? Staging some kind of intervention?' Sarah pulled her hands away. 'I bet you wouldn't do this to Aifric, if Oisín was still dating her.'

'Aifric?'

'I know you prefer her to me. You've made that painfully obvious.'

'Aifric is like a daughter to me, Sarah; I've known her since she was a child and—'

'Oh, please. Just because Aifric is rich and her family are the fucking Conroys, you think that she's better than me. "Poor little Sarah" – am I right? "Up from the country, with her dead mother and her farmer father" – is that it?'

'Sarah,' Oonagh said through gritted teeth, 'I don't know what is wrong with you. Your father is a lovely person. *Lovely.* I would far rather have him in my house than Charlie Conroy, on any day of the week; all that man does is sleep around and blithely ignore the fact that his wife has had a chronic eating disorder for the last twenty-five years.'

'But Oisín—'

'"But Oisín" what? He and Aifric dated in secondary school – they were kids. He doesn't want to be with Aifric. He wants to be with you. But, I have to ask you, Sarah, do you want to be with him?' Oonagh moved her chair closer to Sarah's. 'I know it's impossible to tell what a relationship is like from the outside, sometimes it only makes sense to the two people involved. God knows there have been times when people have questioned why I stayed with William. If you and Oisín are blissfully happy, then feel free to tell me to get lost. But it doesn't appear that way, and I have to admit that I want my son to be with someone who really loves him. And I think you deserve the same.' She took Sarah's hands in hers again, and this time, Sarah didn't pull away. 'Are you happy, Sarah?'

Sarah dropped her head, willing herself to be strong.

'I didn't think so,' Oonagh said. 'Do you want to talk about it?'

'It's not Oisín,' Sarah said. 'It's not him. He hasn't done anything wrong. It's . . .'

'It's what?' Oonagh's voice was gentle. She sat very still, waiting for Sarah to confide in her. And Sarah wanted to. She wanted to explain to Oonagh about Matthew Brennan and how he had treated her and how she couldn't understand why she had allowed it to happen, but the truth was that she had. Sarah was haunted by that, by her own complicity in the whole affair. Every time she looked in the mirror, she saw a body that could be used for someone else's gratification; she saw a woman who could be easily discarded and forgotten about, as if she was nothing.

'I was with this man.'

'And?'

'And he . . . And he . . .'

'What did he do to you?' Oonagh's hand tightened on Sarah's. 'Oh, Sarah, I'm so sorry. Did he *hurt* you?'

'He didn't love me,' Sarah said. 'If you love someone, you'll do anything to be with them, right? But Matthew just used me for sex; he thought he could treat me whatever way he wanted to, and I let him.' She was talking so fast; she wasn't sure if she was making any sense, but she needed to say this, to get it out of her. 'I let him treat me like I was a worthless piece of shit that he could fuck whenever he wanted.'

'Matthew? Matthew who?'

'You have to swear you won't tell anyone,' Sarah said. Even after all this time, she continued to keep Matthew's secrets. 'Do you promise?'

'Of course.'

'Matthew Brennan.'

'Matthew *Brennan*? The real-estate guy who was married to Florence Kavanagh?'

Sarah nodded.

'I know him; he sold us the house in Killiney and I felt like taking a shower after he left. He's an absolute sleaze.' Oonagh lifted Sarah's chin so she looked her in the eye. 'You are worth ten of Matthew Brennan.'

'No, I'm not.'

'You are. You're young and talented, you have the world at your feet.'

'Not talented enough, am I?'

'Sarah, give me a break.'

'What? It's true. I'm not like you or Fionn; it was never going to happen for me.'

'You haven't even *tried*,' Oonagh said. 'From what I can gather, you just gave up at the first hurdle. No one said this job was going to be easy, Sarah; it takes determination.'

'Don't lecture me, Oonagh. I can't afford to paint full-time; I wouldn't make enough money to survive on. I don't have a rich daddy to support me, do I?'

'Do not bring my father into this again,' Oonagh said.

'So, you're going to ignore my point?'

'What point, exactly? You're a teacher, aren't you? Paint in the evenings, after school. Paint during the Easter holidays and every summer. It's the end of July now; you still have a month left to get some work done. Make *art*, Sarah, not excuses. That's what real artists do,' Oonagh said. 'Are you a real artist?' She stood up, pulling the strap of her handbag over her shoulder. 'I hate to be blunt, Sarah, but surely you don't think you're the first person to have your heart broken by some idiot who didn't deserve you in the first place? Or the first woman to have a difficult childhood?'

Sarah flinched.

'I'm sorry,' Oonagh said, and she did look sorry. 'I don't mean to be harsh. I'm sure it was devastating to lose your mother at such a young age.' She took an unsteady breath.

'But there are worse things that can happen to a child than the death of a parent. Believe me.'

★

Blowfish used to be an infamous nightclub on Leeson Street, the sort of place you would only go at 3 a.m., when everywhere decent was closed, the walls slimy with sweat and someone else's credit card behind the bar. Sarah had never gone there; it wasn't considered cool at DAC, but all of Oisín's stories from college seemed to revolve around the club. It had come up for sale around the same time that JJ was looking for premises for his first restaurant, and he had bought the place on a dare, all of them in hysterics that JJ owned the club they used to be thrown out of on a regular basis for snorting coke in the toilets. When the sale had been confirmed, Sarah asked Oisín about the price of the place.

'JJ's parents are giving him the deposit, obvs,' he'd told her, and the banks were eager to give him the rest because, 'they know a good thing when they see it. The boom is back, baby.' Sarah had thought of Aisling, still waiting on mortgage approval, desperate to move into her own house. It didn't seem as if the boom was back in Dunfinnan.

'Sarah!' JJ said when he saw her. 'Happy birthday.' He came out from behind the maître d' stand to hug her. 'I haven't seen you since the wedding, I don't think.'

I don't know how much longer I can do this.

It's obvious to all of us that—

'Yes,' she said. 'Such a great day.'

He led her through the crowded restaurant. There was a bleach-blonde DJ in the corner, sneering when someone asked for a song she didn't approve of. Men in suits were throwing back shots at the horseshoe-shaped bar in the centre of the room, and leather-seated booths for customers to eat at lined the walls. The table JJ had given them was tucked into a corner, far enough away from the DJ's sound system to allow them to hear one another speak. There was a bottle of champagne in an ice bucket, two glasses poured. She handed her coat to JJ and sat next to Oisín rather than opposite him, resting her head on his shoulder.

'Hey baby,' she said. 'I missed you.'

'Someone's in a good mood,' Oisín said. 'I missed you too. Happy birthday.'

'Thank you,' she said.

'And happy anniversary.'

Two years ago. She had still been waiting for Matthew to call her then and say he had made a mistake, scanning through photos of him on the MBA social-media accounts to see if he looked like he was struggling to sleep or to eat, like she was. But he looked better than ever. Of course he did, Sarah reminded herself. They had never been in a real relationship; they had just been having some fun. Matthew was reacting to their break-up (no, not a break-up. They had never been in a real relationship in the first place, Sarah had to accept that) in a completely normal way. It was she, Sarah, who needed to get over it.

'Two years,' Sarah said to Oisín. 'Hard to believe.' She moved to the other side of the table. 'It was weird us sitting next to each other like that, wasn't it? We were right on top of each other.'

'I thought it was nice,' he said.

'It was weird,' she said, picking up her menu, hiding Oisín from view.

'Hey,' he said, tapping the back of the menu until she lowered it. He seemed to be waiting for her to say something else. Her stomach tightened. Did Oisín know that his mother had come to the house today? Did he know that Oonagh thought they should break up?

'"Hey" what?' Sarah said, buying herself time.

'Did you like your present?'

'Oh, my present. Yes. Of course.'

'I was just asking because you didn't text about it.'

'I was busy today.'

'Too busy to send me a text?'

'Jesus, Oisín, I thought this was supposed to be my birthday dinner. Can we not do this?'

'Sure,' he said, forcing a smile. 'You look really pretty, Sarah.'

'Thanks,' she said. Oisín's eyes lowered to the deep cut of her neckline and she knew he would want to have sex with her tonight. 'What are you having?'

'The monkfish,' Oisín said. 'I'm not hungry enough for a starter.'

'You always get the monkfish.'

'Because I love it.'

'But it's so boring; would you not even think of trying something else?'

'Sarah. Let me have what I want, okay? I don't think that's too much to ask.'

The waiter came to take their order. Oisín asked for the monkfish, swallowing a smirk when he was told that was an excellent choice: 'One of the finest dishes on the menu, sir.' Sarah would have the ling, she told the waiter, even though she wanted the blackened salmon. That was what she always ordered, but she couldn't get it now, not after needling Oisín over his predictability. *It's not a competition,* he would sigh, if he knew what Sarah was thinking. But it was. Oisín didn't realise that, because he was always the one who was winning.

'Did you open my parents' card?' Oisín asked her.

'Yes,' she said. She wasn't going to tell him about his mother's visit, she decided. Let Oonagh talk to Oisín if she was so desperate for him to break up with her.

'I'm excited,' he said, buttering a bread roll. 'I've been dying to get down to Ballyfin.'

'I don't know if I'll be able to go; I'll be back at school in less than a month.'

'We could go before then.'

'I have plans for next month.'

'What plans?'

'I can't have plans, now?'

'Ling for the lady,' the waiter said, before Oisín could reply, placing the plate in front of her. 'And the monkfish for the gentleman.'

Sarah looked around the room, taking note of the couples stroking hands, knees touching under the table, high on the promise of what was to come later. She remembered when she and Oisín had been like that. They used to point out people making stilted conversation or checking their phones and vow they would never end up like that. They would be in love forever, Oisín said.

'All done here?' The waiter was back. 'Was it not to your satisfaction?' he asked Sarah, as she pushed her full plate away from her.

'It was lovely,' she said. 'I lost my appetite, is all.'

Oisín took out his card to pay the bill, leaving a generous cash tip on the table. Sarah didn't thank him. He could afford it.

'Are you okay?' Oisín asked her, once they were inside the house.

No. 'I'm fine.' I'm not fine. 'You?'

'I'm going to bed,' he said.

Sarah's eyes followed him as he walked upstairs. There was so much she needed to say to Oisín and so much she knew she could never tell him. It was too late.

In the kitchen, Sarah put the kettle on. She stood there, waiting for the water to boil, and she began to think about last year's birthday. Twenty-six. She and Oisín had only been living in Booterstown for three weeks then. They were in love, the house was free, Oonagh MacManus was insisting that Sarah claim the studio as her own. It seems like fate, Sarah had thought as she unpacked her suitcases. After an early birthday dinner in Jay's Tavern, she had gone to the shop to pick up another bottle of wine and, when she returned, Oisín was waiting for her, holding a cake with twenty-six candles. The hall had been transformed with balloons and a home-made *Happy Birthday, Sarah!* banner hanging on the wall.

'Did you do all of this?' Sarah had asked him. 'Did you do all of this for me?'

'Of course I did,' Oisín replied. 'I love you, Sarah. I love you so much.'

THEN

'Happy twenty-fourth birthday, babes,' Robbie said as I shuffled into the kitchen in my slippers. 'I can't see any new wrinkles. Yet.'

'How kind of you to say so.' I grabbed a mug from the draining board. 'And terribly kind of you to remember what an important occasion today is.'

'It would be hard to forget,' Aaron said. He was sitting at the table, already scanning through work emails on his phone. He nodded at the calendar hanging on the kitchen door, a *Farmers Journal* one that I had put up as a joke. I had circled 29th July with pink highlighter, writing '*SARAH'S BIRTHDAY!*' in capital letters.

'Yes, well,' I said, 'I didn't want you to get caught out. So embarrassing.' I sat down next to Aaron, Robbie standing behind me and rubbing my shoulders. 'Now. Where are my presents?'

'I'm giving it to you right now,' Robbie said. 'It was a voucher for a massage.'

'Very generous. And what did you get me, Aaron?'

'Why do you need us to get you anything? Fionn's present will be impressive enough for the three of us, no doubt,' he said, then added, under his breath, 'I don't know why he bothers.'

'I'm sorry,' I said, choosing to ignore him, 'I expect individual presents from each of you.'

'Fine.' Aaron rolled his eyes. 'I'll raid the samples closet at work today. You're a ten, right?'

'No,' I said. 'I'm an eight.'

His eyes scanned down my body. 'Amelia was right, you *have* lost a lot of weight.' He stood up, wrestling with his coat. 'I'll see what I can do. Talk to you later.'

'I'd better go too,' Robbie said. 'My boss is so strict on time. There's no telling *what* he might make me do if I get in late.'

'Gross,' I said. 'Give Kevin my love.'

'Will do.' He squeezed my shoulders. 'Any nice plans for the day, birthday girl?'

'I'm not sure yet,' I said. 'I'm waiting on a few offers. You know how it is.'

When I was alone, I checked to see if Matthew had texted me. He hadn't, but it was early yet; it was only 8.30 a.m.

It was early yet; it was only nine thirty a.m.

It was early yet; it was only ten a.m.

Aisling and Ciara texted into the WhatsApp group, *Happy*

132

birthday, babe! 24 – you're ancient! May as well give up now
xxxx.

Aisling: On a side note, niiiiice new profile photo. 🔥
    You seem to change it every week. I can't keep up with
    your hotness.
Sarah: What can I say? I have commitment issues.

I changed it so that he would notice and text to tell me
that I was pretty. I changed it so he would remember that
I existed.

He hadn't texted but it was early yet; it was only 11.30 a.m.

I picked up my phone and reread our messages from yesterday.

Matthew: I have to do the unspeakable and cancel our plans
    for this afternoon. There are some issues with Harry I
    need to sort out. I totally understand if you never want to
    talk to me again.
Sarah: Don't apologise!!! Harry comes first. What about
    tomorrow?
Matthew: No luck, it's insanely busy. I have a meeting with
    SexBomb – they're hoping to roll out in Ireland next year
    and I am determined to get that contract. I'll see if I can
    get any freebies for you.
Sarah: What perfect timing! It can be my birthday present.
Matthew: Your birthday?

Sarah: Yes. On 29th July, twenty-four years ago, a miracle happened.

Sarah: I mean, some might call it the Second Coming, but I'd hate to put words into your mouth.

Matthew: You know me – I've always been a fan of coming.

I was sure he had something special planned. Flowers, probably; Matthew seemed like the sort of man who would send a girl flowers for her birthday. We had been getting closer, these last two months – since that day in room 63 when he promised me it wasn't just sex. Since that day that I had decided to wait. I had more free time when the school year finished, so I could afford to be flexible. *I'll fit in with your schedule,* I told him. I shaved my legs and bikini line every day, and I ran packs of the pill together to ensure I didn't get my period. The blood made him squeamish, he said. Waking up every day, waiting for his text. *Come meet me now.* An afternoon quickie or a stolen hour between morning meetings; once, twice, sometimes three times a week. 'I don't have much time,' he would say to me, unzipping his trousers as I knelt down. 'We have to be quick.' He kissed me on the cheek afterwards. 'Thank you, Sarah,' he always said. 'I needed that.' And I told myself that he needed me.

'Hey, Dad,' I said as I answered the phone.

'Sarah,' he said. 'Happy birthday.'

'Thanks.'

'Did you get the money?'

'I haven't had a chance to check my online banking, but I'm sure I did.'

'Check it, will you?'

'I'm on the phone to you now; can you not wait until we're finished?' I read *SARAH'S BIRTHDAY! SARAH'S BIRTHDAY! SARAH'S BIRTHDAY!* on the calendar, over and over again. This year was supposed to be different.

'Sarah . . .'

'Fine, Dad.' I gave in. 'I'll check my internet banking once we've hung up.' I had been giving in a lot since my mother's anniversary. Apologising, trying to explain why I had missed that train. *I'm not angry, Sarah,* my father said to me. *I'm just disappointed.* 'And I'll text you straight away and let you know that the money's there. Okay?'

'Grand,' he said, and he cleared his throat. 'I met Ciara Grogan after Mass yesterday.'

Ciara still went to Mass? 'That's nice.'

'She's going to have a baby, you know.'

'Yes, Dad, I'm aware.' It would have been hard not to be, with the photos of Ciara's bump that were flooding the WhatsApp group.

'Her parents were with her. Eoin English too. The whole lot of them went to Mass together.'

'That's –' weird as fuck – 'nice.'

'They were all chat about the wedding plans. August, Ciara was saying. In Clonmel.'

'Yes, Dad. I know.'

'It's nice to see her settled down.'

'I mean, she's only twenty-four, so some might say it's a bit early for her to be settling.'

'I said "settled down", Sarah, not "settling". That's not a very nice thing to say about your friend.'

I pinched the bridge of my nose. 'No, Dad. I'm sorry.'

'That's okay.' He paused. 'While I have you, did you apply for any of those jobs that I sent you?'

'I have a job.'

'But these jobs are in Tipperary.'

'I don't want to live in Tipperary, Dad. I want to live in Dublin.'

'Ah, sure; what's so great about Dublin? I know you like living with Fionn and the lads, but that house is fierce damp, Sarah; I'm convinced that's why you get a chest infection every winter. And, if you were in Tipperary, you might have more time to yourself; you could get back to the painting. I always thought—'

'My boyfriend lives in Dublin,' I said, before I could stop myself.

'You have a boyfriend?' he asked. 'Since when do you have a boyfriend? How come this is the first I've heard of it?'

'It never came up before.' I had always refused to talk about my relationships with my father, for fear that he might want to discuss his own (hopefully non-existent) love life in return.

'What does he do? Is he an artist too?'

'He works in real estate.'

'There's no money in that anymore, is there? Not since the recession. I hope the poor lad has a decent backup plan.'

'Yeah, well, it's Matthew Brennan, so I don't think he needs a backup plan just yet.' As soon as the words left my mouth, I knew that I shouldn't have said that.

'Matthew Brennan?' my father said slowly. 'The man who was married to Harold Kavanagh's daughter?'

'They've been divorced for ages, Dad.'

'And didn't you tell me that his son went to your school?'

'Yes. Harry.'

There was silence on the other end of the phone.

'Well?' I asked. 'Aren't you going to say something?'

'Could you lose your job over this?'

'Two minutes ago, you wanted me to quit my job and move home. Some consistency would be nice.'

'Don't get smart with me, Sarah.'

'I'm not trying to be smart,' I said. 'And I doubt they could fire me over this.'

'You doubt it? Well, that's very reassuring, isn't it? And how long has this been going on, then?'

'Only about five months.'

He didn't say anything.

'I thought you'd be happy about this. He's so successful, Dad; he has the most amazing house. You should see the photos of it; it's—'

'You think I care about how much *money* this man has? Are you for real?'

'I didn't say that.'

'Good. Because I don't care. And I hope I raised you better than for you to care either.'

'Dad.'

'I have to go, Sarah.'

'Dad,' I said again. 'You can't say anything about this to anyone. It's –' *a secret* – 'private.'

'What do you mean, "It's private"?'

'We're keeping it between ourselves for now,' I said.

'So he's your boyfriend in private. How many other "private" girlfriends does he have? Is there an entire harem of you?'

'Jesus – of course not,' I said. But the truth was that I didn't know, and, worse, I couldn't ask. Not yet. 'Look, Dad, I don't expect you to understand.'

'I'm glad,' my father said. 'Because I don't.'

'Fitz?' Fionn's voice shouting up the stairs. 'Fitz, where are you? I have your present.'

The door to my room was thrown open.

'You're still in your pyjamas? It's 7 p.m.' He was standing at the door frame, a large box covered with Care Bear wrapping paper in his hands. 'I'm so excited about this one,' he said. 'I think I might have outdone myself this year.'

I didn't move.

'Fitz?' He sat next to me on the bed. 'Fitz, are you okay?'

'I'm fine,' I said. 'It's just my dad.' I pushed myself up onto my elbows. 'It's so typical of him; he can never be happy for me. He has to ruin *everything*.'

'Fitz, come on,' Fionn said. 'He's not that bad.'

'He is,' I said. 'He's ruined my birthday; he's put me in a bad mood; he didn't even send me a card, for fuck's sake. How hard would it be to send your only child a birthday card?'

'Sarah – you're twenty-four, not fourteen. Let's have a little bit of perspective, shall we?'

'Why are you sticking up for him?'

'Eddie's a good guy. Do you know he texts every time he sees an article about me in the papers? Just to make sure that I've read it. He's sound out, like.'

'Pity he couldn't support me in the same way.'

'What?' Fionn was staring at me. 'He paid for you to go to art college.'

'Using Nana Kathleen's money.'

'So what? I had to work two jobs for three years before I could go to DAC,' he said. 'My father still thinks I must be gay because I decided to become an artist. You're being . . .' He stopped himself. 'Look, aren't you going to open your present?' He held the box out to me, but I couldn't find the energy to take it from him.

'Can I do it later?' I said, curling into his side.

'He didn't text, did he?' Fionn said.

'He had a million meetings today.'

'It would have taken him two seconds to send a text.'

'I know, but there was some stuff going on with Harry too. I don't have kids, I don't have a demanding job like he does. Maybe that's half the problem.'

'How do you mean?'

'It's because I'm on my holidays, I have too much time to be thinking. If I had more going on right now, I wouldn't . . .' I wouldn't waste my days, thinking, *thinking*. Thinking of Matthew, about what he was doing and who he might be doing it with. 'And Matthew is so busy, his job is incredibly demanding.'

'You already said that.'

'Look, it makes more sense that I—'

'That you what? That you be the one to make all the sacrifices?'

'He's busy,' I said again.

'This isn't like you. I've never seen you act like this over a guy before.'

That's because the other boys were easy, I thought. The other boys lay down before me and I walked over them without a second thought.

Fionn pushed my hair off my forehead, the gesture so gentle that I felt as if I might cry. 'You deserve more than this, Fitz,' he said. 'I hope you know that.'

NOW

The morning after her twenty-seventh birthday, Sarah met Fionn at the Irish Museum of Modern Art. He had protested when she first suggested it, saying that she would be hungover and inevitably cancel last minute. 'I don't do that anymore,' Sarah had said. 'I'm like an old married woman, these days.'

Fionn was different these days, too. He woke at 5 a.m. to chant mantras, a new devotee of transcendental meditation. He ate vegetarian food; he practised hot yoga; he had finally given up the hash. He dated girls who were too thin and too cool, girls who dabbled in graffiti art or expressionist dancing in their spare time, but who never seemed to have proper jobs, as far as Sarah could see. When Sarah asked Fionn if she could meet them, he said that they wouldn't have anything in common. He was getting good at compartmentalising, putting her in one box, the people he met through his art in another, never allowing the two to mix. He had become similar to Matthew in ways Sarah could never have anticipated.

Fionn and Sarah walked around IMMA the same way they always did: separately, but with an acute awareness of where the other one was in the room at all times.

'Why?' Sarah would ask Fionn when he stood for too long in front of a painting. 'Why this one?'

'Because it makes me feel something,' he said, and Sarah understood. They stayed there, side by side, in front of the painting. Sarah wanted to feel something too.

'Do you want to go in?' Fionn asked as they passed the narrow entrance into the room containing a retrospective of Oonagh's work, explaining her historical importance in both Irish art and feminism.

She shook her head. 'I've seen it already.'

Sarah had gone to the opening of the exhibition with Oisín, listening intently as he explained each piece in great detail to her. 'This is my favourite,' Oisín had said of a painting from the They Shoot Daughters, Don't They? collection. 'Mom was really coming into her own in the eighties.' And Sarah smiled, loving how proud he sounded of his mother. They went for dinner afterwards, Oonagh and William, Oisín and Sarah, Domhnall and his girlfriend, Eimear.

'To Mom,' Domhnall had said, raising a glass of champagne in her honour, the rest of the table following suit.

Oonagh was flushed with happiness; she couldn't have

done any of this without them, she said. 'Especially you, my darling,' she said to William.

He grunted in reply. He was feeling sick, he said, and the food wasn't as good as it normally was, and the waiter was taking too long, and did they really need to get sparkling water? What was wrong with tap water?

Afterwards, when Sarah thanked them both for a lovely evening, William shrugged. 'Nothing to do with me,' he said. 'It's Oonagh's money, after all.'

'I saw it a couple of weeks ago,' Fionn said now. 'I really liked it; they've curated the collection brilliantly. She's a clever woman, your mother-in-law to be.'

At brunch, a little later on, Fionn ordered the veggie scramble, Sarah the pancakes, and they talked about Robbie and Kevin's new dog ('Why don't they just adopt a baby?' Fionn said. 'It's obvious that's what they want to do.') and Aaron and Amelia's upcoming wedding plans.

'Another wedding,' Fionn said. 'That's four, next year, plus the stags. I'll be broke.'

'What are you talking about?' Sarah said. 'You're doing so well, it's amazing.'

'Fitz, I made twenty-one grand last year, and that was a good year.'

'*What?* But every time I open a newspaper there's an article declaring you the "future of Irish art". I spend my life boasting about my famous friend Fionn. I don't get it.'

'Sure look it, I didn't get into this to become a millionaire.

It is what it is.' He bit off a piece of toast. 'How are things with you?' he said, mid-chew.

Sarah wanted to tell him about Oonagh's visit to the house, about her advising Sarah to break up with Oisín. *Do you think I should do it?* she wanted to ask Fionn. *Do you think I should leave Oisín?*

Sarah wanted to tell Fionn that she was afraid. Afraid of making a decision and regretting it afterwards, perhaps for the rest of her life. Afraid of being by herself again, alone. Alone forever.

'Sarah?'

'Sorry,' she said. 'I'm fine. Everything is fine with me.'

'Good,' Fionn said. 'Glad to hear it.'

When the waitress came with the bill, Fionn handed over his debit card. Sarah always seemed to be surrounded by men who handled the bill. She had gone from her father paying for food and clothes and school trips, to Matthew, who paid for hotel rooms, to Oisín, who paid for, well, everything. A lifetime of pretending to reach into her bag at restaurants and bars, knowing that the man beside her would insist that she put her wallet away. The only woman Sarah knew that earned more money than the man in her life was Oonagh. Oonagh didn't need William to pay for her lunch. Oonagh didn't need William to do anything but love her. Sarah couldn't imagine what that felt like, to see a man as a source of love rather than needing him to take care of her.

'Thanks, Fionn,' Sarah said. 'You didn't have to do that.'

'Not a bother, girl,' he said. 'It can be your birthday present.'

Sarah remembered another birthday. 'What did you get?' Fionn had asked her over a breakfast of Honey Loops and tea.

'Money,' she'd replied. 'That's what my dad always gets me.'

'Ah, here, girl,' he'd said. 'We've got to sort this shit out.'

Coming home that afternoon, she found a sheet of A4 paper on the front door, with an arrow pointing down, saying, *Look under the mat*. A piece of paper waiting there. *Riddle me this, Sarah*. The treasure hunt took her all over the house and back out the front door, until she discovered Fionn by the Wellington Monument in Phoenix Park. A red and white checked picnic blanket, a bottle of cheap wine, green olives, a couple of spliffs and a packet of Percy Pigs. He had thought of all of Sarah's favourite things.

'Thanks,' Sarah had said to Fionn as the sky turned black, and for some reason she couldn't help thinking of her mother. Helen would have loved this, would have loved Fionn too. 'This is the best birthday I've had in a long time.'

After that, there had been Christmas presents and elaborate Easter-egg hunts, sweets handed over by bemused neighbours when Fionn insisted they dress up as Gomez and Morticia Addams for Halloween and go trick-or-treating. Sarah had never known anyone like Fionn before, someone who could turn a trip to the supermarket into an adventure that she would never forget.

'Ah, you're too good to me,' she said to him now, as he smiled at the waitress, throwing a few euro coins into the tip jar on the counter.

'Anything for you, Ms Fitzpatrick.' He opened the cafe door and gestured at her to go first.

'My turn next time,' she said as they walked through Stoneybatter, past Mulligan's.

'Good stuff,' Fionn replied, reaching into his pocket for a packet of cigarettes, offering one to Sarah.

It didn't even have to be for a special occasion. Fionn had given her sketches, doodles of her stretched out on their couch in Stoneybatter, dying of a hangover; little cartoons he had drawn, imagining what Sarah was like at school, rows of adoring students hanging on her every word. But the painting from his debut was the first proper piece he had ever given her. When the exhibition was finished, Fionn had collected it from the gallery, hanging it carefully on Sarah's wall. She told him she loved it, but surely he must have seen that it was too big for her room. It took up so much space, and it was, like all of Fionn's work, so commanding that you couldn't look at anything else when you were in its presence. Sarah felt as if she was drowning in it.

And she hadn't asked for it. She had been shocked at the exhibition when Fionn had told her that he wanted her to have it. He had insisted. It had been Fionn's decision. And, if it was hers, then surely she should have been allowed to do whatever she wanted with it?

Fionn and Sarah stopped outside a tattoo shop on the quays, looking at the photos of the artists' handiwork. 'Would you get any more?' Sarah asked him, and Fionn pulled a face.

'Mam will kill me if I get any more tats,' he said, and Sarah laughed at the thought of Ireland's hottest young artist still having to answer to his mam, down in Cork.

Matthew had turned forty-four the year they were together – 5th August, a week after her own birthday. (Twenty years between them, Sarah had told herself; it was a huge gap; what was she doing?) There had been photos of his party in *Sunday Life* magazine: a big crowd, every 'important' person in Dublin invited. Everyone except for Sarah. Florence was there, standing next to Matthew as he blew out the candles, her arm around Harry's shoulders. They looked happy. *I'm so lucky to celebrate my birthday with all my friends and family,* Matthew told the journalist from the magazine. *But I'm especially fortunate to have my son and my extraordinary ex-wife here tonight.* When Sarah read that, she thought she was losing him. She panicked.

'How is your mam?' Sarah asked Fionn as they crossed the street to walk beside the river. 'I haven't seen Fidelma in ages.'

'Close your eyes, Matthew,' Sarah had told him when she knocked at room 63 that day in August, the weekend after his forty-fourth birthday. 'I have a surprise for you.' He was sitting on the bed, his face upturned like a child's, and his trust in her caught her breath. She was doing the right thing, she reassured herself.

Matthew's face when he opened the present, his fingers gripping the frame. 'Sarah,' he kept saying. Sarah. Sarah. Sarah. Sarah. 'It's too much,' he said.

'No, it's not,' she said. 'I want you to have it for your birthday. I know how much you loved it at the exhibition.'

And Matthew looked at Sarah and it was as if he was seeing her for the first time.

'She's grand,' Fionn said, slowing down to let a man in a wheelchair pass him on the narrow footpath. 'I phoned her yesterday and she was giving out about those photos of Charlotte and me at the premiere of . . . Oh, fuck, I've forgotten the name of it. Some stupid rom-com that Charlotte insisted I bring her to.'

'*Same Difference?*'

'Yeah, that's the one. It was a piece of shit. I'm on some PR's mailing list and I can't seem to get off it.'

Sarah would have loved to go to the premiere, get all dressed up and meet Iris Bailey, Hollywood's latest teen phenomenon. But Fionn didn't ask Sarah to that type of thing now.

'Why is your mam cross?' she asked.

'She says Charlotte's too thin.'

'No child-bearing hips there, right?'

'I'm not sure how she thinks I can even afford to pay for

a kid.' Fionn rolled his eyes. 'And Charlotte is twenty-three, for fuck's sake.'

'Twenty-three,' Sarah said. 'Jesus. Were we ever that young?'

'You're twenty-seven.'

'That's not twenty-three.'

'I'm thirty-three,' Fionn said. 'Let's not play this game.'

'Where is it?' Fionn had asked that night when Sarah came home from room 63.

'Where is what?' she replied, although she knew what he was talking about.

'Sarah, stop it,' he said.

'What were you even doing in my room, Fionn? That's not on; that's a total invasion of my privacy,' Sarah said.

'Where is it?' he asked again. And she looked away. 'No,' he said. 'Sarah, you didn't.'

'It was Matthew's birthday,' Sarah tried to explain, 'and I had to, Fionn, Florence was—'

And Fionn's face broke.

They reached O'Connell Bridge. 'I have to go to Grafton Street,' Sarah said, pointing to the right.

'I'm heading this way,' he said. 'I'm meeting Charlotte at the Ambassador. There's an exhibition on the history of bloodletting that she wants to see.'

'That'll be fun,' Sarah said.

How could you? Fionn kept saying, while she begged him to understand. *How could you do this, Sarah?*

They hugged now, Fionn letting go before Sarah did. 'Happy birthday again,' he said. Sarah watched as he walked away from her. She wanted to tell him she was sorry. But she had said sorry to Fionn too many times.

THEN

I blinked in the sunlight as I got off the bus, temporarily blinded. I heard his voice before I saw him.

'Sarah.'

There was a large shape in front of me, solid. 'You're looking fierce thin,' it said.

'Thanks, Dad.'

'It wasn't a compliment.'

The bus driver opened the luggage hold, and I reached in to grab my bag.

'Let's go,' I said.

'Thank you very much, Cormac,' my father said to the driver. 'Sarah wanted me to tell you that on her behalf.'

'I was just about to thank him, Dad.' Was it possible to get on the bus again and head straight back to Dublin? 'Thanks, Cormac,' I said.

'How was the journey?' my father asked.

'It was fine,' I said.

Two and a half hours, the sun beating through the glass. The woman next to me peeling tinfoil away from her sandwich, the smell of tuna curdling the air. She was so close to me, her body clammy against mine. *Excuse me,* I kept saying, every time her arm touched me. *Excuse me.* A guy in his late teens, behind me, having a loud conversation on his phone: *Yeah, man, we were fucked. I drank, like, ten pints; puked my ring when I got home.* A mother and her teenage daughter, sitting in front, surrounded by shopping bags. *I should never have allowed you to buy that top,* the mother said. *Your father will have a conniption when he sees it.* The daughter sullenly kicking the seat in front of her, as if having a mother was a burden, something to be endured.

Fionn: Don't text me again.

Fionn: I don't care if you're sorry. It's done now.

'Nice weather we're having,' my father said, pointing me in the direction of the jeep. 'August can be a funny month, though; I hope it lasts for them, for tomorrow.'

'I'm sure it will,' I said. Never mind the Child of Prague, Ciara had probably sacrificed an entire village of virgins to pacify the sun gods on her wedding day.

'No boyfriend with you?' Dad asked as he put my suitcase into the boot.

'What?' I said, climbing into the front seat. 'Ugh, it's such a mess in here. When was the last time you got it cleaned?'

'Not that long ago.'

'Just get it valeted. Seriously.'

'I'll get it valeted when I want to get it valeted, Sarah. And I'll thank you not to talk to me like I'm one of your students.'

A twist of a key in the ignition. Clonmel in the rear-view mirror, disappearing slowly. Driving through Dunfinnan. The road narrowing into a tiny boreen, tufts of grass sprouting in the middle, the jeep dipping into potholes that our local TD promised to fill before every election. (*It's a priority, Mr Fitzpatrick*, he always said. *I can assure you of that.*) Driving down to our house, the lane lined on both sides with electric fences to keep the cattle out.

'This is it,' I'd told Fionn when I brought him to Dunfinnan for the first time. It was our second year of DAC, and he'd said he wanted to get out of the city for the weekend.

'Come on,' he had said. 'Let's go to your home place. It'll be fun.'

I said yes. Everything was fun with Fionn.

'See this?' I'd said when we arrived at the farm, waving a hand at the surrounding fields. 'Everywhere the light touches belongs to the Fitzpatricks.'

'Okay, Mufasa,' Fionn replied, and we had both laughed.

'So,' my father said now, when we were sitting at the kitchen table, two cups of tea in front of us and a packet of Viscount biscuits open. 'The boyfriend?'

I looked behind me. 'He's not here, is he?'

'You're not as funny as you think you are, you know.'

'Oh, I think I'm pretty hilarious.'

'So, tell me, why didn't Mr Brennan come with you for the wedding?'

'Dad, can you give me a break?'

'It was a simple question, Sarah; there's no need to bite my head off.'

'Nothing is just a "simple question" with you.'

'I can't ask about my daughter's boyfriend?'

'He's not my . . .'

'He's not your what?'

'Jesus Christ, Dad, just let it go. He had to go to Paris this weekend, okay?' I said, taking one of the biscuits. I imagined myself putting it in my mouth, chewing, swallowing. I put it back in the packet. 'Some work thing.'

'Busy man.'

'That he is.'

I had asked Matthew to come to Ciara and Eoin's wedding with me. I wanted him there, handsome and tall by my side.

'A wedding?' he'd asked.

'It'll be fun,' I said, already planning to buy a new dress, to get my hair and make-up professionally done. I would be beautiful. I wanted Matthew to see me looking beautiful.

'I hate weddings, Sarah,' he said. 'Cheap Prosecco and small talk, watching two people make the biggest mistake of their lives. It's not for me, I'm afraid.'

154

'Okay,' I replied.

'You're the easiest girl I've ever met, do you know that?' he said, and I smiled, as if it was a compliment.

'I'm going to throw my bag upstairs,' I said to my father. 'I might take a shower as well.'

'Grand,' he said. 'The *Late Late* starts in half an hour. Will we watch that?'

'Sarah?' my father asked again when I didn't respond. 'The *Late Late*? That comedian you like is going to be on.'

'Fine,' I said. I turned at the door. 'Dad? You didn't say anything, did you?'

'Didn't say anything about what?'

'About Matthew Brennan. You didn't tell anyone about him, did you?'

'No, Sarah,' he said, crumpling the biscuit foil. 'I didn't say anything.'

It was always strange waking up in my old bedroom. My father hadn't moved anything since I had left for Dublin, keeping it as a shrine to my eighteen-year-old self, movie posters and scraps of paintings still tacked on the walls. The only concession Dad had made to admitting that I didn't live in Dunfinnan anymore was to swap the ironic Barbie bed sheets for a plain yellow cotton. Other than that, it was as if nothing had changed.

'Sarah,' Dad called up the stairs. 'Aisling is here already. Hurry on.'

I heard them chatting while I checked my handbag – debit card, house key, phone, lipstick, powder, eyeliner.

'Still in Clonmel,' Aisling was telling Dad. 'I have sixth class again . . . Yes, I really like that age; they're great. Very bright group, this year . . . No, Jamsie can't make the Mass – he has to work. Hopefully, he'll get to the afters . . . I know, they're so lucky with the weather. August can be tricky, can't it? Ciara will be thrilled.'

'What's that you're wearing?' my father asked when I walked into the living room.

'A dress,' I said.

'Why has it got that, that *thingy* on it?'

'Okay, Dad,' I said, shepherding Aisling out the front door. 'I'll see you tomorrow.'

'Sorry about that,' I told her, as we got into her pristine Mini Cooper. I flicked the air freshener hanging from the rear-view mirror. Why would anyone want their car to smell of 'forest fresh'?

'Don't apologise.' She twisted around to look out the window as she backed down the drive. 'Eddie is a dote.'

'So,' I said, 'Jamsie has to work, does he?'

'Yes.'

'He seems to be working a lot, these days.'

'I don't want to talk about it.'

'Fair enough,' I said. 'In other news, you look cute.'

'So do you. Very . . . Dublin.'

I looked down at my outfit, the black mini-dress with a

cape attached, two thick gold cuffs on my wrists. 'I'm going to take that as a compliment.'

The Mass was in Dunfinnan, the same church where I was baptised, received my communion and my confirmation, where I stumbled inside a pitch-black box to admit my eight-year-old sins to the parish priest. *Bless me, Father, for I have sinned; this is my first confession.* Kneeling down, hands clasped, praying for redemption.

There were air kisses as we told the mother of the bride she looked great.

'Oh, thank you, girls,' she said. 'We went to this fantastic boutique in Athlone; I've been dieting for six months to get into it, but it was all worth it; sure, I'm nearly thinner than Ciara now. Can you believe that she got pregnant? I mean, we're delighted, of course, but it did make dress-shopping difficult, and they're both so young and . . . Oh, sorry, girls, I have to go get a photograph taken. Eoin's brother will show you where to sit.'

'She's never liked me,' I said to Aisling as we took our seats. 'Not since I had to go into the pharmacy to get the morning-after pill from her.'

'Didn't you get Canesten cream as well?'

'And Solpadeine. It was a good night.'

'Clearly.'

The couple sitting in front of us turned around to say hello to Aisling. Gemma Daly and her boyfriend, Padraig, still together after all these years.

'Oh my God, Sarah Fitzpatrick,' she said. 'We haven't seen you in ages; do you ever come home? Too good for us, now that you're up in Dublin, I suppose.'

The organ music started and Ciara's sister appeared in a pastel dress, clutching daisies in her hands. Then it was Ciara in a strapless meringue, her father, pale-faced, by her side. A string quartet playing Adele songs; the priest giving advice on maintaining a healthy relationship; Aisling walking up to the altar for a reading. 'Love is kind,' she said, with such certainty, as if she believed it, but I didn't think that was true. Love was holding your breath until they texted you. Love was waiting for them to decide that you're good enough. Candles were lit, vows said. *I now pronounce you husband and wife.* We lined up outside the church to shake hands and hug the bride.

'What are you wearing?' Ciara asked me. 'You look like a superhero.' She elbowed her new husband. 'Eoin, doesn't Sarah look like a superhero?'

'Hey, Eoin.' I gave him a kiss on the cheek. 'Congratulations.'

'A fucking superhero,' I said, when Aisling and I were driving to the River View Hotel. 'And she's one to be giving fashion advice, is she? The state of her wedding dress. My outfit is amazing, but I don't know why I would expect anyone in fucking Dunfinnan to understand that; everyone here is so backward. Did you see what Gemma Daly was wearing?

Someone needs to tell her that Kate Middleton isn't an appropriate style icon for someone in their early twenties.'

Aisling was silent until we reached the car park. 'Okay.' She pulled up the handbrake, her voice brittle. 'Firstly, I live in Dunfinnan, so I would appreciate it if you stopped calling us backward.'

'Ais, I—'

'And secondly, I think mocking the bride's dress – the *pregnant* bride, I might add – is sort of beyond the pale. What's going on with you?'

'Nothing.'

'This is Ciara's wedding day. Today isn't about you.'

'I know that, Ais. I've just got some stuff on my mind right now.'

'What kind of stuff? Is it a boy?'

I looked out the window and she gave a cackle of laughter.

'Of course it is. Sarah Fitzpatrick, up to her old ice-queen tricks again. What poor craythur have you got eating out of your hands this time?'

I knew I shouldn't say anything to her, but I wanted to. I wanted to say his name, to hold it in my mouth, feel its weight on my tongue. I needed to own him in a way that I knew I wasn't allowed to.

'It's Matthew Brennan.'

'Who?'

'You know,' I said, 'the real-estate guy. He owns MBA.'

Aisling still looked uncertain.

'Florence Kavanagh's ex-husband.'

'Oh, *that* guy.' She screwed up her face. 'But he's old, Sarah.'

'He only turned forty-four last week.'

'Exactly. He's practically the same age as my dad,' she said. 'How long has this been going on?'

'A few months.'

'A few *months*? Why didn't you tell me?'

'We're keeping it a secret, for the time being.'

'A secret?' she repeated. 'That's a bit weird. Why?'

'Well, I teach his son, for one thing, and—'

'But I don't see why that means you have to keep it a secret. If it's serious between the two of you, surely you could just get his son transferred to another class?'

'I'm the only art teacher at St Finbarr's.'

'And? I know it's not exactly professional, but it's hardly a fireable offence, is it? Have you checked? I'm sure it would be grand.'

'It's not just that.'

'What do you mean?'

'Well . . .'

I hesitated, tempted to tell her about work, Mrs Burke's eyes following me around the staffroom, the official warning after Fionn's exhibition and the promises I made to try harder. But somehow it felt as if saying it out loud would make it real.

'Everything is fine,' I said. 'This is just the way it is, for the moment. And you can't say anything to anyone, okay?'

'Okay.' She smirked at me. 'Now, give me the dirt. What's the sex like? Is it amazing? I bet it is, especially if he was married to Florence Kavanagh. I doubt she would put up with less than two orgasms per ride.' She laughed, and I tried to laugh too.

Her eyes narrowed. 'It is good, isn't it?'

'Yes,' I said. 'It's good.'

She stared at me.

'It's fine,' I amended.

'Fine? That doesn't sound very promising. Have you told him what you need him to do to get you off?' she asked. 'It's not like Jamsie magically knew how to make me come. I had to teach him. And then teach him again. And again. And then – oh, God – he bought this book, *The Multi-Orgasmic Couple*. I hope he bought it from Amazon and didn't go to the Easons in Clonmel; can you even imagine?'

'I am not giving Matthew Brennan a book called *The Multi-Orgasmic Couple*, Aisling.'

'I'm just saying that good sex is about communication. How is this guy supposed to know what's good for you, if you don't tell him?'

'I don't need a lecture, okay?' I said. 'Should we go in? We're going to miss the free drinks.'

We walked into the hotel, a large, squat building painted in the palest pink. 'Famous for weddings,' Ciara's mother told us. 'One of the best in Tipperary, if not *the* best.' Glasses of

Prosecco were waiting in the foyer. One down, then another. We found our table and I introduced myself.

'Hi, how are you? I'm Sarah, and this is Aisling. Aren't they blessed with the weather?'

It was Gemma Daly and her boyfriend, me and Aisling, an American cousin of Eoin's called Maura Cliff, who looked to be seventeen or eighteen, and Tadgh Carey who were all at the same table.

'Tadgh, are you by yourself?' Aisling asked, and he looked at me and said yes.

Whispering *toilet* to Aisling, we went to the bathroom, where I raided the basket with deodorant and mints and tampons to see if there was anything worth stealing.

'Why would Ciara put us with Tadgh, of all people?' I said. 'What's that about? It's been years.'

'I don't know. Oh my God, can you stop checking your phone?'

'What?' I said. I hadn't even noticed I was doing it.

'Red or white wine?'

'Beef or salmon?'

'Would you like more mash with that? We have potato gratin too, if you'd prefer.'

'Was there something wrong with it?' the waiter asked when he saw how little I had eaten, and I told him I wasn't hungry.

'Shhh. The speeches.'

Each of us put a ten-euro note into a pint glass. Ciara's

father talking, people stifling yawns, Tadgh watching the time. It was twenty-five minutes – oh, the humanity – Maura, the American cousin, had guessed correctly; she won the money. Shots for the table?

'Tequila? Sambuca?'

'No, let's have Jägerbombs.'

'Ah here, I'll feel like I'm having a fucking heart attack tomorrow if I drink any more Red Bull.'

The band was setting up. It was traditional Irish music to begin, older aunts and uncles and grandparents waltzing on the dance floor.

'Why doesn't anyone know how to dance properly any-more?' someone asked.

At the bar later, I smiled at Tadgh Carey.

'What are you having, Fitz?' he asked, and I could see him hoping, but I allowed him to buy me a vodka and Diet Coke, anyway. And another one. And another. 'Thanks, Tadgh,' I said. 'You're always so good to me, do you know that?'

The DJ playing AC/DC, Eoin's friends sliding on their knees across the dance floor, their ties wrapped around their heads. 'A vodka and Diet Coke,' I told the barman. 'And another one,' I said. 'And another.'

Good sex is about—

I doubt Florence Kavanagh would put up—

'Are you okay, Sarah?' It was Ciara, coming out of the toilet cubicle.

I was at the sinks, staring at myself in the mirror. I must

163

mean something to him, I told myself. And he must mean something to me, if I allow him to treat me this way. He just needs time.

'Fine,' I said. My voice was slurring, curling over the corners of the words. 'I'm fine.' I tried again. I drank some more of my vodka. 'Are you having a good day?'

'Yeah,' she said. 'It's been good. I just wish . . .' She paused in front of the floor-length mirror, tugging at the wedding dress. 'It would have been nice not to look like a heifer in the photos.'

I stood beside her. I was so much thinner than she was now.

'Do you regret it?' I asked.

'What?'

'Getting pregnant.'

'What? No, Sarah.' She frowned at me. 'Of course not. It's a bit sooner than expected, and I would have preferred to wait until after the wedding but—'

'You don't look *that* bad,' I told her. 'Honest. White is a hard colour to pull off, at any size.' I stumbled, almost spilling my drink on her. 'Oops. Sorry, babe.'

And then she was gone. I checked my phone (no text) and it was 1.30 a.m. (no text) and I was tired; it had been a long day. I needed another drink.

'Sarah.' It was Aisling and she looked annoyed. 'What did you say to Ciara? She just told me to take you home.'

'What? I don't want to go home. I want another drink.'

'You've had enough.'

Coats and bags were retrieved, a taxi ordered: 'Can you pick us up immediately? At the River View.'

The man greeted Aisling by name when he arrived, asked her how the wedding went.

'It was lovely,' she told him.

'Sarah,' she whispered to me as we got into the car, 'what you did tonight was not on. You really upset Ciara.'

Did I? 'Sorry.'

'I'm serious, Sarah. You can't say things like that to people, especially not on their bloody wedding day. What's *wrong* with you?'

'I didn't mean anything by it.'

'You never mean anything by it, do you?'

'Why are you so mad at me? I said I was sorry, didn't I?'

'Look,' she said, 'I know you haven't always had it easy, Fitz. God knows what I would be like if, well, you know. And I've tried to make allowances for you, I really have, but sometimes . . .'

'Sometimes what?'

'Sometimes I wish I didn't always have to be your minder.'

When we reached Dunfinnan, she leaned forward and pointed the driver in the right direction.

'I don't have any cash on me.'

'I'll take care of it,' Aisling said.

I unclipped the seatbelt, pausing before I got out of the car. 'Are you mad at me?' I said.

'Just get some sleep. I'll talk to you tomorrow.'

I waited until the taxi disappeared before I turned towards the house. I crept upstairs, trying to be as quiet as I could, because I was afraid of waking my father. If I woke him, maybe I would ask him why he had married my mother if he was going to spend most of his time nursing a pint in Donie's pub. I would ask him why we weren't enough for him, even when my mother was alive. *Why did it take Mam's death for you to change, Dad?*

I would ask him if he had ever loved her at all.

19TH AUGUST

Matthew: Greetings from Paris.

Sarah: Oh my God – you went to Père Lachaise!

Sarah: I can't believe you remembered, I'm so touched!

Sarah: You should go to Derrière for lunch if you're near the 3rd & 4th arrondissements. Get the floating island for dessert – it's insane.

Sarah: And go to the Musée d'Art Moderne. Everyone goes to the Louvre, it's passé.

20TH AUGUST

Matthew: At the Louvre. This place is amazing.

Sarah: Oh, cool. Hope you're having fun.

Sarah: What have you planned for the rest of the day? Do you think you'll have a chance to go to Musée d'Art Moderne?

Matthew: I'm heading home this evening.

Sarah: Are you busy this week? I'd love to see you if you have time. x

Sarah: No worries if it doesn't suit.

30TH AUGUST

Matthew: Apologies for the lack of contact.

Sarah: No need to apologise! I've been crazy busy too. Have so much stuff to organise for going back to school.

Sarah: Can you believe we're back tomorrow? It doesn't seem fair when it's still August.

Sarah: Is Harry looking forward to going back?

Matthew: Good news. I am off child duty on Sunday and have the afternoon free if you would like to catch up.

Sarah: I'd love that! What do you want to do? I read a review of this new restaurant in Killiney called Pecan – it sounds amazing. It might be easier for you than having to schlep all the way across town.

Matthew: I don't know if it's safe for me to meet you in public when I haven't seen you in a while.

Matthew: Room 63 at 2 p.m.?

1ST SEPTEMBER

Matthew: Well, that was spectacular, wasn't it? You do
   continue to amaze me.
Sarah: Why, thank you, Right back at you, Brennan. xx
Sarah: Let's do it again soon!
Sarah: When are you free?

18TH SEPTEMBER

Sarah: Hey, are you free for a chat?

Sarah: It won't take long – sorry.

Sarah: Sure look it, just text me when you're free.

24TH SEPTEMBER

Matthew: Sorry re: the lack of contact, I've been up to my
teeth with work.
Sarah: No worries! I know how busy you are.
Matthew: I'll need to see you soon, Sarah. I'm free tomorrow
evening. I'll book the room.

NOW

The weak September light was seeping through the blinds when Sarah woke, tilting the room into a watery grey. She showered, tiptoeing into the spare bedroom, where she had left her work outfit: the pencil skirt and floral blouse, the low-heeled court shoes. She stood in front of the mirror when she was ready. She looked neat, she thought. Professional.

'Very nice,' Oisín said as he walked into the room, still in his boxer shorts.

'Did I wake you?'

'Nah, it's grand.' Oisín put his hands around her waist. He looked unsure, as if asking Sarah for permission to touch her. Sarah wanted to enjoy it. She imagined herself leaning into him and feeing warmth spreading through her, the way it did before.

'You're all sweaty, Oisín.' She pushed him off her. 'I don't want you to stain my new blouse.'

'Okay,' he said, stepping back. 'I only came in here to ask if you wanted a lift to work, not to get the head taken off me.'

'I didn't mean—'

'I knew I shouldn't have bothered.'

'I'm sorry,' she said. 'Really. I didn't mean to snap at you. First-day-back nerves. I'd love a lift.'

Sarah kissed Oisín when he pulled up outside the convent, wiping lipgloss off his cheek afterwards. That's what good girlfriends did, she thought. They were affectionate. Maybe if she pretended to be a good girlfriend, it might come true. A few of the pupils were standing outside, one making a comment that Sarah couldn't hear through the car window, but which caused the others to dissolve into fits of giggles.

'Move along, girls,' she said, getting out of the car. 'I'm sure you have classrooms to go to. Let's start this school year as we mean to go on.'

'Yes, Ms Fitzpatrick,' they chorused.

One of the braver girls, a tall redhead who played with the senior basketball team, asked slyly, 'Is that your boyfriend, miss?'

'That's none of your business, Ella. Please go to class immediately.'

They swarmed before her, and she could hear, 'The Principles,' and, 'Domhnall Wilson,' and, 'Oh my God, I love him,' floating out of their chatter. Teaching teenage girls was different from what Sarah had expected. The girls could be mercurial, prone to dramatic fights and fallings-out, oscillating rapidly between vulnerability and defensiveness, but Sarah was surprised by how much she liked them. She enjoyed their sincerity, how earnest they were in their affection for boy bands and their favourite authors and the latest child star attempting to throw off the shackles of an early Nickelodeon career. When teenage girls loved something, they loved it fiercely and without shame, unburdened by the same desire to be 'cool' that she had seen in her old school. At St Finbarr's, the boys had wielded their burgeoning masculinity as if it were a weapon.

Sarah had started working in this new school last year. She'd wanted a fresh start, somewhere where no one knew her, so she could reinvent herself. Ms Fitzpatrick, who was always on time for work. Ms Fitzpatrick, who was quiet and kept to herself. She taught her classes efficiently, refusing to feel annoyed by the abject lack of talent, as she had at St Finbarr's. Sarah had lost the urge to take the paintbrush off the students and show them what they were doing wrong. She never picked up a brush anymore.

'Very good, girls,' she said at least fifty times a day. 'That's a very good effort.'

After work, Sarah walked home alone. The school was only twenty minutes from the house in Booterstown and it was a typically warm September day. 'So predictable,' Nana

Kathleen used to say when Sarah arrived home after her first day back, as a teenager, the wool jumper tied around her waist and the shirt sticking to her armpits with sweat. 'The sun always comes out blazing once the children go back to school. You can set your watch by it.'

Sarah took her shoes off as soon as she was through the front door, the marble cool beneath her bare feet. In the kitchen, she poured herself a glass of juice and sat at the table, running her fingers across the worn oak with its water rings and grooves, a tapestry of a life well lived.

'Hi, Dad,' she said, answering her phone.

'Hi, love. Just wanted to check in about your first day back.'

'It was grand. Some lively girls in second year; I'll have my work cut out for me as their year head.'

'You're well able for them,' he said. 'You know, I always thought teaching was a good job for an artist.'

Sarah was tired of hearing people say that, the unspoken insinuation that Sarah was lazy for not utilising her spare time more effectively.

'Like William,' her dad went on. 'Sure, isn't he the same as yourself?'

'William is a professor of literature at Trinity College, Dad,' Sarah said. 'It's not quite the same thing, is it?'

When they hung up, Sarah sat there, reading the comment sections on the *Mail Online* as she waited for Oisín to come home.

★

176

'Sarah?' Oisín called out, almost three hours later.

'I'm in the kitchen.'

'Hey,' he said, flinging his briefcase on the floor.

'Do you have to do that?'

'Do what?'

'Just throw your stuff all over the place. I'm not sure who you think is going to pick them up, but I'm not your servant, Oisín.'

'I am very much aware of that,' he said, tucking the briefcase into a corner beside the bookcase. The book that Matthew gave her was still there, on the second shelf – Sarah looked through it occasionally as if trying to convince herself that her memories were real, that she hadn't simply imagined everything that had happened between them – but the rest belonged to Oonagh: texts by Judith Butler and Naomi Wolf and Germaine Greer and Susan Faludi, and a history of feminism in Ireland which featured an essay on Oonagh and the countrywide protest she had organised after an abortion case involving a teenage rape victim in the nineties. 'You should read them,' Oonagh had told Sarah. 'You might find them illuminating.' Sarah had tried, eager to ingratiate herself with the great Oonagh MacManus in those days, but she gave up midway through an angry polemic about how 'heterosexual relationships are an archaic form of slavery' and 'women who accept traditional gender roles in their marriage are complicit in upholding the patriarchal status quo and set a damaging example for their daughters'. Was this what rich white women were worried about? Sarah thought of her own mother, washing the kitchen floor and scrubbing the toilets and making the beds and helping Sarah with her homework and dropping her off at the school gates and cooking pots of potatoes and lamb chops for the farmhands who came in at lunchtime, ravenous, smelling of sweat and manure, their hands raw from over-soaping, and Sarah supposed she could see the validity of the author's argument. In a way, marriage did seem like a form of slavery. Helen's sense of fun, her sense of adventure, had appeared to bleed out with each passing year. She had been trapped in her relationship with Eddie, taking care of Sarah while he was in the pub playing Mr Popular and buying rounds for his friends. But to call her complicit seemed grossly unfair. What could a woman like Helen do? Or Helen's mother before her? 'I didn't know your mother's people that well,' Nana Kathleen had told Sarah when she was a teenager and begging for stories about her mother, desperate for any scrap of information she could find. 'But the Hayeses were considered notoriously old-fashioned in Dunfinnan, even for the eighties.' Sarah's grandfather had declared university a waste of time, especially for girls, and forbade Helen from applying for a grant. 'It's a pity,' Nana Kathleen said. 'Your mother was an intelligent woman; she would have done well, I think.' But Helen hadn't been given the choice. Maybe she hadn't even been aware she had one.

'How was your first day back?' Oisín asked her.

'Fine.' Sarah's tone was sharp. *You think we don't see, Sarah, how you treat Oisín?* She tried again. 'Sorry. I'm hungry and cranky. Will we order takeaway?'

'I'm grand. I took a client out for lunch today. Four-course meal, the works. I'm stuffed.'

'Well, what am I supposed to eat?'

'Order takeaway. I'm not stopping you,' Oisín said. 'You can use my card if you want.'

'I have my own money, thank you very much.'

'Sarah.'

She looked up in surprise. His voice sounded so thin, as if it might crack in half. He was leaning against the kitchen table, his hands by his sides.

'What did I do wrong this time?' he said.

'Nothing,' she said. 'You did nothing wrong, Oisín. I'm sorry.'

Oisín shuffled into the nook attached to the kitchen, like his feet were too heavy for him to lift. Sarah was left there, searching for the words that would make things better.

Remember, Oisín? Remember when we moved in here? Their relationship had been relatively new then, only a year old, and people said it was too soon for them to move in together; what was the rush? Sarah didn't know how to explain that she needed Oisín by her side at all times, that she felt as if she couldn't breathe without him. There were so many movies that she didn't know the ending to, books left discarded, TV shows unwatched because she was unable to concentrate with Oisín so close to her; she needed to climb onto his lap, to feel him inside her. After she came, Oisín would tell her he loved her. And when he said that to her, Sarah forgot about Matthew, something she had previously assumed was impossible, and the relief of letting Matthew go was almost unbearably intense. She hadn't realised how heavy the weight of her shame had been, and how tired she had become of carrying it.

'Tell me your secrets,' Oisín would say as they made a duvet fort and pretended that it wasn't a Wednesday afternoon when they should be out meeting friends or buying groceries or doing normal things, like normal people. Maybe they weren't normal, though, Oisín and Sarah. Maybe they were special. Maybe all they needed was each other.

'I'll tell you my secrets if you tell me yours,' Sarah had whispered into Oisín's ear, licking it with the very tip of her tongue, feeling him shiver against her. And he did tell her.

Oisín told her how much he wanted to please his father, and how he feared that he would never be able to do so. He told her he loved his brother, but he was jealous of Domhnall, that he wished he had had the bravery to follow his passion and become an actor, instead of fleeing at the first bad audition. He knew it hadn't gone well, Oisín told Sarah. He had forgotten his lines, had asked once, and then twice, if he could start again. He had left the room, but the director's voice was loud and Oisín had heard what the man said about him: 'Handsome, but stiff as a wooden plank.' Oisín hadn't told anyone else that, he said to Sarah, and she felt oddly triumphant. She wanted to own Oisín in a way no other girlfriend had, particularly Aifric Conroy.

One night, Sarah had noticed a group of lads staring at them in Stephen's Green, one of the men sneering and saying something to his friends that made the rest of them bray with laughter. 'Don't bother,' Oisín had said when Sarah wanted to confront them. 'It's not worth the hassle. It never is.' Sarah asked Oisín then what it was like to grow up in Ireland as a mixed-race kid. ('Biracial,' he corrected her, and she apologised, embarrassed.) Oisín said that he had never experienced 'proper racism' as a child – the odd slur muttered on the rugby pitch, perhaps, but JJ had always sorted that out for him, tackling the culprit to the ground with a devastating blow. It was harder as an adult, Oisín admitted, and he began to understand the degree to which he had been insulated at school, protected by his parents' wealth and his tight-knit circle of friends. He experienced more of it now, he said – old women clutching at their handbags when he passed them on the street, or the sudden realisation that he was always the one person of colour at parties. People confused him with Cooper at work because they were the only two black men in the office even though Cooper was ten years older than Oisín and five inches shorter. When Kanye and Jay-Z songs were played in clubs, colleagues would sing the N-word, looking at Oisín afterwards, expecting him to laugh and to reassure them that he didn't mind, that he wasn't 'too sensitive'. He was often told by drunken strangers on nights out that he

181

looked like a certain celebrity, and he knew he didn't, Oisín told Sarah. He didn't look like Obama or Chris Brown or Jesse Williams; there were no similarities between them at all except for the colour of their skin. Then there was the time he accidentally knocked against someone on Mary Street and heard, 'Fuck off home, will ya? Black cunt.'

'But that doesn't happen very often,' Oisín rushed to reassure a furious Sarah. 'It was much harder when Dad moved here in the seventies; he and Mom were practically ostracised in the beginning.' Oisín was lucky, in comparison, he told Sarah.

'Why didn't your parents stay in London? Wouldn't it have been better there?' she asked him, and Oisín shrugged.

'They wanted to take advantage of the artist exemption, I think,' he said, 'and, anyway, Dad said the Irish weren't the worst; they got used to him after a while.'

Did they get used to William or used to his growing fame? After he won the Booker, everyone wanted to claim William Wilson as a Paddy, no matter the colour of his skin or what nationality his passport said he was. *More Irish than the Irish themselves,* people said about Oisín and Domhnall now, with their fluent Irish and traditional names, thanks to their Gaeilgeoir mother. A credit to their parents, all told.

'So,' Oisín had said to Sarah, 'now it's your turn.' He asked her what happened when her mother got sick.

'I was only nine when she was diagnosed,' she told Oisín, 'ten when she died.'

'Too young,' he murmured into her ear. 'I'm sorry, babe.'

Sarah told him about the morning she'd woken to find Helen had shaved her hair off, her skull bumpy and misshapen. 'It was falling out anyway; thought I may as well do it myself,' she had said. Sarah asked if she was going to wear a wig and Helen told her she wasn't sure yet, and Sarah had been mortified at the idea of anyone seeing her mother like that.

'I wish I had asked her how she felt,' Sarah said. 'I wish I wasn't always so selfish.'

She told Oisín how, initially, Eddie had seemed happy to pretend like the entire thing wasn't happening. 'Sure, you'll be grand,' he'd said to Helen. 'You've always been such a fighter.' But her mother became weaker and weaker, until the doctors were talking about making Helen 'comfortable'. Sarah told Oisín how she had wished her mother was dead by the end, just so she could escape that hospital. The antiseptic smell, the wretched people clutching at their family's hands, begging to be allowed go home, one last time. The flat beep of the life-support machine, then Helen taking that final, desperate gasp. And it was done. Her mother was dead.

Sarah had found it almost exciting: time off school and so many people in the house; her mother's corpse in the parlour, people shivering as they touched Helen's yellow hands. There were sandwiches and cake; Sarah was consumed by the insatiable kindness of strangers wanting to be seen giving her a hug as they told her she was 'a brave girl'. But then it went quiet. The neighbours and the relatives continued with their own lives; the girls in school got bored with her numbing sadness.

And she told Oisín about the months when her father didn't speak to her, didn't utter one word from morning until night. Eddie was grieving, she explained, and drinking too much because he didn't know how to deal with it. Her father had always been a social drinker, his nightly habit of going to the pub in Dunfinnan for 'the one' had been the primary cause of the many arguments that Sarah had witnessed as a child. But it had never been like this before.

She didn't tell Oisín about the cold house, or how the cupboards were bare for days, no food in the fridge and nothing for her lunchbox in the morning. She didn't mention how her eyes had begun to look huge as her body shrank. Meetings in the school, and Sarah repeating, 'I'm fine.' (She had lost one parent; she couldn't lose the other.) And then Nana Kathleen moved in while Eddie went into hospital, saying prayers with Sarah before bed, that 'the good Lord will help your father find his way again'.

Her father came back after two months. 'I'm sorry, Sarah,' he said, hugging her awkwardly. He was more patient with her after that, more present, encouraging her with her artwork, asking her how her day went when she came home from school. He never drank again, but Sarah knew now. She knew how easy it was for things to fall apart. And she couldn't unknow that.

Sarah didn't tell Oisín about Matthew either. Some secrets are meant to be kept, in case people use them against you, she thought. Oisín believed she was funny and interesting and confident and Sarah liked that. She liked how Oisín saw her, and she liked how she felt when she was with him. He made her so happy. He made her forget.

Until, one day, he didn't anymore. They moved in together and he left his dishes in the sink and he cracked his knuckles while she was trying to watch TV and he threw his towel on the bed after his shower, so the sheets were cold with damp by bedtime. Sarah didn't feel like she had enough space, the space she needed to hide the parts of herself that she was most ashamed of: her impatience, her tendency to be critical, how quick she was to snap if something annoyed her. Oisín saw all of it, all of her flaws, everything she had tried to suppress for so long, and Sarah hated him for being a witness to that, for realising that she wasn't perfect after all.

As the months passed, Sarah began to remember how flat the world could seem, how boring it was when the realities of everyday life crept in and hiding away underneath a duvet for hours no longer seemed like a viable option.

'Oisín, can you just grow up?'

'Oisín, is it so hard to put your dirty clothes in the laundry basket?'

'Oisín, did you have to get so drunk last night? I was mortified by you.'

It was like a vicious fever rising in her, urging her to lash out at him, to draw blood. Sarah couldn't seem to control it.

'Why are you being so horrible to me?' Oisín had asked when she said he was so thin that it felt like being fucked by a twelve-year-old boy. He left then, coming home that night with whiskey scorched onto his breath.

'I don't know what I did wrong, Sarah,' he said, before passing out on the bed beside her.

'I'm sorry,' Sarah whispered. 'But you were supposed to make me happy forever. And I'm not. I'm not happy any-more.'

Sarah could never quite forgive Oisín for that.

THEN

'Fionn.' I banged my fist on the door again. 'Fionn, come on.'

He turned the radio up, Mariah Carey's warbling 'All I Want for Christmas Is You'.

'Fine,' I said, raising my voice so he could hear me. 'Be like that.'

Downstairs, Robbie was stirring a pot of porridge on the hob, Aaron reading a fashion magazine with a pen in hand, circling items he wanted to show to his buyer.

'Fionn's door is locked,' I said, slumping in a chair. 'When have any of us ever locked our doors? This is getting ridiculous.'

'Maybe he's afraid you'll nick one of his paintings,' Aaron said.

'Excuse me?'

'I can't believe how selfish you are sometimes, Sarah.' He

shook his head. 'It was a big deal for Fionn to give you that piece, and you just hand it over to some random dude?'

'Who told you about that?' I said.

'I finally got it out of Fionn last night. I couldn't figure out why he hadn't said a word to you for four months,' Aaron said. 'Can't say I blame him. That was cold as fuck, Sarah.'

'Oh, shut up, Aaron,' I said. 'And it's not just some random guy. He . . .'

He hadn't texted in ten days. I thought giving Matthew the painting would bring us closer together, and it did, for a while. 'We should go on a holiday,' he had said to me. 'Somewhere where no one will know us.' But then he was busy when I'd tried to set a date, and there were business trips to London and to Washington and Sydney that had to be prioritised, obviously, and, 'I couldn't bring you with me, Sarah; you would be far too distracting.' And then Harry needed him this weekend and that weekend, and messages were left unanswered, and dates for room 63 were cancelled.

'It's fine,' I said, every time. 'Don't worry about it.' And I was left waiting and waiting and waiting, morning turning into afternoon, turning into evening, my world shrinking, folding itself around the phone, willing Matthew's name to flash onto the screen. The less he texted, the more I seemed to want him.

'Whatever,' Aaron said, washing his mug out and turning it upside down on the draining board. 'You know what you did wasn't cool.'

I waited until he left. 'Are you fighting with me too?' I asked Robbie, as he placed a bowl of porridge on the table, shaking flaxseed into it.

'Of course not,' he said. 'Although, I'm not sure Matthew Brennan is worth all this hassle.'

I had told Robbie a few weeks ago, after a bottle of red wine and half a valium. I knew I wasn't supposed to tell anyone, but I kept letting it slip. Had Matthew told his friends about me? Did he find that my name was at the tip of his tongue every second of every day as well?

'What are you talking about, Rob? Kevin told you that Matthew was a good guy, that he was the only one in Clongowes who was nice to him, even though he was gay.'

I had been so proud when I heard that story. I knew Matthew was kind, deep down.

'Oh, Sarah,' Robbie said. 'That was a long time ago, my love.'

19TH DECEMBER

Sarah: Brennan! So, listen, Dunfinnan calls on Monday . . .

Matthew: Okay. What's Dunfinnan?

Sarah: It's in Tipperary. It's my home town.

Sarah: I want to give you your Christmas present. You free this
weekend?

Matthew: I can't this weekend, I have Harry.

Sarah: Ah, I was looking forward to seeing you.

Sarah: Is there any half-hour you can spare me? I'm going
home on Monday and I'd love to see you before I go
back.

Matthew: No can do, I'm afraid.

Sarah: I don't think I'm asking for too much. All I want is
to see you before going home for Christmas. Come on,
dude.

Matthew: Sarah, I don't want to be causing you upset. Just

190

tell me to leave you the hell alone if this is getting to be too much for you.

Sarah: No, of course not.

Sarah: I really am sorry, okay? Just forget I said anything. I'll see you in the New Year.

I was on Dawson Street, battling through crowds of panicked people doing last-minute Christmas shopping, when I saw him. He was sitting on a long stool by the front window of a cafe, his iPhone pressed to his ear. I pushed the door open and walked in. I should not have been doing this. I was breaking all the rules (his rules) by doing this.

'Please,' he said to whomever he was talking to, 'I'm begging you, please just give me—' He looked at the screen, then put it back to his ear. 'Hello? Hello?' He placed the phone on the table in front of him, rubbing a hand across his jaw.

'Matthew,' I said.

He looked up, seemingly unsurprised to see me. 'Sarah,' he said. 'How nice. You look fantastic.'

'Thank you,' I said. 'It's been a while since we've hung out.'

'Yes,' he said. 'I'm sorry; I meant to get back to you.'

'Oh, don't worry. I know the way it goes.'

He pointed at my shopping bags. 'Anything interesting?'

'I had to pick up something for Fionn's present.' I'd bought a book on Wes Anderson and another about feminist artists of the new millennium, neither of which I could afford, but I was hoping it would make him forgive me. I would give him the books and I would tell him I was sorry, yet again. Maybe this time he would believe me.

'Very good.'

'That's Fionn McCarthy.'

'I thought as much.' He cut up a section of his crêpe, but he didn't eat it.

'Speaking of Fionn, how's *Harbour Skies* doing?' I asked.

'I haven't been telling it bedtime stories or anything, but I think it's coping okay.'

'Ha.' What did I expect from him? Eternal gratitude? (Yes.) Did I expect the present would make him realise how much I understood him? (Yes.) Make him realise we should be together properly? (Yes.)

'Okay,' I said. 'I'd better ...' I gestured towards the counter.

'Sit with me.'

'Oh, I don't want to intrude,' I lied.

'You won't be.'

'Are you sure?'

'Sarah, I'm sure. I'd like the company. Honestly.'

'I thought you had Harry this weekend,' I said, as I took a seat opposite him, tucking my bags beneath the table.

'Yes,' he said. 'So did I.'

'Jesus.' I looked at my phone for the first time since I had met Matthew. 'It's eleven o clock.'

Lunch had turned into coffee which turned into cocktails.

'I should go,' I said after our second drink, pleasantly light-headed.

'No,' he said. 'Please stay out. 'Tis the season, and all that.' He said he was starving, and we should go for dinner. 'Come on, Sarah; it'll be lovely. My treat. Please say yes?'

'It's the Saturday before Christmas,' I argued. 'There's no way we'll get a table anywhere.'

Within ten minutes, we were being seated at Fade Street Social.

'It's nice to see you again, Mr Brennan,' the hostess said. Was this what life would be like with Matthew? No more queues or waiting, the implicit understanding that I would be welcomed everywhere once I was on his arm?

'We'll have a bottle of your finest champagne,' he told the sommelier, and, when that was finished, there was wine and more wine again.

At the end of the meal, Matthew paid the bill and walked me outside.

'I can't believe it's that late,' I said.

'Time flies when you're having fun,' he said. We were in

the doorway of the restaurant, waiting for the rain to stop so we could decide where to go to next.

'It *was* fun,' I agreed.

'Although, I can't remember the last time I was out with someone who got asked for ID. You're such a baby.'

'I don't know,' I said. 'I'm old enough for lots of stuff.'

'Oh, really?' He touched his fingers to my stomach, and the promise of what was to come ripped through me.

'Taxi,' he said, hailing down a passing car.

His hand on my knee in the back seat, inching up my thigh. He was watching me closely, too closely, as if he was trying to learn my face off by heart. It felt so intimate that I had to turn away from him.

'Just here,' Matthew said to the driver, leaning out the window to key in the code to the iron gates. The taxi made its way up the tree-lined drive, gravel crunching, until the house came into view. It was enormous, the biggest house I had ever seen in real life, and seemed to have been carved out of glass and stone, clinging onto the cliff edge, over the sea.

'Jaysus. This your place?' the driver asked with a whistle.

Matthew didn't reply, handing him a fifty-euro note and telling him to keep the change. 'Happy Christmas,' he said.

'Your house is beautiful,' I said as he turned the alarm off, trying to sound nonchalant, as if I had been in dozens of houses like this and was accustomed to such wealth.

'It keeps the rain off,' he replied, leading me into the

kitchen, metal and glass gleaming, light bouncing off hard surfaces.

'Big house for one person,' I said, the wine making me brave. 'Do you ever get lonely, all by yourself?'

'I'm never here,' he said, opening the fridge to grab a bottle of water. 'And I have Harry every second weekend, so . . .'

There was a photo stuck to the fridge door with a tacky Eiffel Tower magnet. In it, Matthew looked happy, his head thrown back with laughter, one hand on Harry's shoulder, the other around Florence's waist. The perfect family.

'Whoa,' he said, as I backed him against the countertop, kissing him. I dropped to my knees, unbuckling his belt. He grabbed my wrist and I looked up in surprise.

'What's wrong?'

'Nothing,' he said. 'But I don't want to do that right now.'

'What? Why not?'

'I just . . .' He broke off. 'I've had a little too much to drink. I don't think I'm going to be able to . . .'

'Oh,' I said. 'Is there anything I can do to, eh, help things along?'

He pulled me to standing. 'Happens with men my age, I'm afraid.' I tried to look as if I understood. 'I just want you to sit with me for a while, Sarah,' he said. 'Please?'

The living room had a plush velvet sofa, an antique grandfather clock and a ten-foot Christmas tree, stacks of beautifully wrapped presents beneath it. After lighting the already-set fire, Matthew claimed the couch, while I knelt by the fireplace, smiling nervously. Matthew wanted me to play a new role tonight, but he hadn't given me the script; he just expected me to know what to say and how I should behave.

'Here,' he said. 'Have some of this Merlot; it's an excellent vintage,' and I drank it carefully, trying not to stain my lips or my teeth in front of him.

The clock chimed midnight, and we talked about art mainly, but about books too, and music. He asked me what I was currently working on, frowning when I told him I was taking a break.

'You're an artist,' he said. 'You can't "take a break" from that. It's part of who you are.'

I closed my eyes, breathing the words in. Maybe I would be an artist, if I was with him.

'Fuck,' I said, as I spilled wine on the carpet. 'Fuck, I'm so sorry.'

'Taxi for one, please.'

'Oh, shut up, Brennan; you're as drunk as I am.'

'You know, I think I might be.' He took the glass from me and placed it on the coffee table.

'I'll get a cloth from the kitchen.'

'Don't bother,' he said. 'The housekeeper is here every morning.'

'Even on a Sunday?'

'Every morning. She'll take care of it tomorrow.'

'But it's red wine – that'll stain.'

'I said, don't worry about it.' He pulled me closer to him,

until I was sitting between his legs, my back against the couch. He leaned down, resting his chin on top of my head, and I felt as if he was putting us into position, readying our pose for a portrait painting. A replication of *The Lovers* by Magritte, perhaps. We would turn to kiss, grey hoods covering our faces and our mouths, the fabric coarse against our searching tongues. Never quite able to find our way to connect with one another, no matter how hard we tried.

'You know when you asked me earlier if I was lonely?' he said.

'Yes?'

He stayed silent, the grandfather clock chiming 1 a.m.

'I was supposed to have Harry this weekend,' he said eventually. 'Did I tell you that?'

'You mentioned something in your text the other day.'

'I was supposed to have him this weekend, but Flo . . .' He stopped. 'Well, Flo had other ideas, didn't she? She always has ideas for Harry that don't include me.'

I didn't know what he wanted me to say.

'It's hard, this time of year,' he continued. 'This big house and that stupid goddamn tree. I keep buying him more presents, you know? As if that will make things better. This isn't what I wanted for Harry. I wanted things to be different. I wanted . . .' He leaned back against the sofa. 'I didn't want to end up like *him*.'

'Christmas can be a tough time for everyone,' I said. 'No point in letting it get to you.' I reached for the bottle. 'This will help.' I poured some more into his glass. 'Come on, Brennan. Don't let the side down.'

'No,' he said. 'I've had enough. I'm going to bed.'

'Bed?'

'Yes. Do you want to go to sleep?'

The two of us lying in his bed, my head tucked under his armpit. He wouldn't want to have sex with me; he would want to talk. Harry and Florence, his dead mother, and fathers that are so easy to disagree with. Matthew's arm tightening around my neck until I couldn't breathe. He would expect me to listen to him, to soothe him, and to tell him everything would be okay. Maybe he would expect me to share my secrets in return.

'You go,' I said. 'I'll be up in a minute.'

His footsteps on the stairs – slow, tired. I watched the logs burn, blue flames licking at their corners. The clock chimed two. I'm safe, I thought. He must be asleep by now. I examined the presents under the tree, turning the tags over to read the messages. There was a gift from Harry, a small box from Florence. *Love, Flo X*, the tag said, and I wished I could see what it contained. His bookshelves were sparse. 'I'm not much of a reader, can't see the point in it to be honest,' he had told me earlier, and there were only a handful of books, hefty tomes on art and culture, the odd memoir of a successful businessman. A few novels: Hemingway, Thomas Pynchon, Philip Roth. There was no television, no DVDs or box sets; he found 'all that nonsense' to be 'a waste of time'.

There were framed photos on the walls, a few faded pictures of a woman I guessed was Matthew's mother, the rest mostly of Harry. Harry on his first day of school. Harry smiling gap-toothed at the camera. Harry and Matthew sitting side by side on a sofa in a different house to this one, both asleep, heads drooping to the side.

I moved through the rooms as if I was scavenging for clues, something that finally would reveal the truth of Matthew to me. Something I could use to make him mine at last. The downstairs bathroom – L'Occitane hand wash; Egyptian-cotton towels; quilted toilet paper with folded tips, like you saw in hotels; a spare deodorant and toothbrush in the cabinet. The kitchen – coffee capsules and wine glasses in the cupboards; the fridge full of stacked containers with days of the week written on them. Caveman Cuisine was the company that provided them, the labels listing the number of calories, macros and the amount of protein in each meal.

In the hall, an intricate chandelier was dripping diamond light onto a mosaic-tiled floor. Another room. A study. A framed photo of a baby Harry in a Santa hat on the desk, a Mac computer, filing cabinets. I sat in the desk-chair, twirling around until I was dizzy. Then I opened the drawers, one by one. Nothing out of place; everything was so tidy and well organised. A fountain pen, a leather-bound notebook, an iPad, a stress ball. Then I opened the last one. Bottom left. Photographs. Matthew and Florence, on their wedding day. Florence wearing a cream slip dress, her beauty having no need for embellishment. Florence pregnant, swollen belly huge in a bikini, lying on the deck of a yacht. Matthew and Florence kissing, the camera close on their faces. Matthew holding a newly born Harry, his eyes bright with unshed tears.

There was a cigar box hidden underneath the photographs. It was beautiful, ornately carved out of dark wood, with a mother-of-pearl fastening. An antique, I thought. I flipped it open. Sheets of thin paper, spider handwriting scrawled across the page. A crinkling noise as I unfolded it and I looked at the door in panic, as if Matthew might have heard me from upstairs.

Please, Florence, the letter began. It was dated a few days previously, and was only half finished. *I know that I've made mistakes. I know that I shut you out when we were together and I never really talked to you about my feelings. But it can't be too late for us, there has to still be a chance for us to be a real family with Harry again. I love you, Flo. I love you more than I have ever loved anyone, more than I ever thought was possible. You have to understand, with my history, with my father the way he was, that it's not –*

'No,' I said. I folded the letter back up and placed it back in the box, shutting the drawer. I walked out of the study, closing the door behind me.

I left before Matthew could wake up.

'Sarah.'

'Sarah.'

'*Sarah.*'

'*What*, Dad?' I turned off the shower and shouted downstairs. 'I'm trying to wash my hair.'

'Mass is at twelve. Will you be ready in time?'

'I'd be ready a lot quicker if you let me finish washing my hair.' I turned the water back on, his voice muffled in the background.

'That was a fierce long shower you had,' he said when I walked into the kitchen.

'Happy Christmas to you too.'

'It was lucky I had my shower before you, or there would be no hot water left. Did you turn the immersion off, like a good girl?'

'Yes, Dad.' I filled a pint glass with water, dropping Berocca, Dioralyte and Solpadeine into it. 'And it took me ages to wash the conditioner out of my hair, the pressure is so bad. Why do you still refuse to get a new shower?'

'I'm so sorry,' he said. 'Here's the number for the ISPCC; I'm sure they'll have something to say about my shocking negligence.'

'I'm not in the mood, Dad,' I said.

'Ah, Sarah, will you have a sense of humour?' he said. 'Come on. Let's go.'

It was cold outside, my breath smoking before me, the car seat like ice beneath my legs. The radio came on: Sinéad O'Connor singing 'Silent Night', my mother's favourite carol.

'Maybe we'll just . . .' my father said, as he switched off the music. We didn't talk for the rest of the journey.

It felt as if everyone in Dunfinnan was at the church, dressed in smart winter coats and suede gloves. There were kisses on cheeks, 'Happy Christmas to you too.' Bending down to ask small children what Santy brought them, 'Oh, you must have been very good to get all of that.'

I followed Dad up the aisle, genuflecting half-heartedly. The altar was dripping in candles and ivy, a nativity scene assembled to the left-hand side. I felt faint, grabbing at the pew in front of me. I shouldn't have gone out last night, but after two hours sitting in the parlour with my father, watching *Die Hard* and eating Quality Street, I had texted Aisling and pleaded with her to come meet me for a drink.

Matthew: Hey, where are you? I woke up and there was no sign of you.

Matthew: Presume you got home safely.

Matthew: I hope you're okay.

Matthew: Sarah, I would appreciate it if you let me know you got home all right.

I walked up Main Street of Dunfinnan, the wind cutting through me. Aisling was in front of Donie's, waiting for me.

'Ciara couldn't come,' she said. 'Holly is too small, and you know she's breastfeeding.'

I didn't know that. I hadn't seen or spoken to Ciara since the wedding.

'Will we go on rounds?' I asked Aisling, when we were inside, and she pulled a face.

'I don't want to be hungover on Christmas Day,' she said. 'I have to help Mam with the dinner and—'

I blew a kiss at her, ordering two vodka and Diet Cokes at the bar. 'Just the one,' I said.

'Your turn,' I said.

'My turn,' I said.

'Your turn,' I said.

'My turn,' I said.

'Your turn,' I said.

'My tur—'

'I can't, Sarah,' Aisling protested. 'I'll be dying tomorrow.'

I called her a lightweight and ordered a double vodka.

Moving through the bar, waves and hugs and, *Hi! Hi; how are you? What are you doing now? I haven't seen you since last year. Are you still in Dublin? Are you still in London? Are you still in Boston? Are you still in Brisbane?*

'How are things with Matthew Brennan?' Aisling asked me, when we'd found a corner to hide in.

'I don't want to talk about it.'

'Why not?'

'I don't know,' I said. 'I think I'm over it.'

'Okay; what went wrong this time?'

'Nothing went wrong,' I said. 'It's just that I went back to his house a few days ago and he was a bit . . .'

'A bit what?'

'A bit needy, maybe?' I said. 'He's forty-four; isn't he supposed to be over all that by now?'

'Typical Sarah Fitzpatrick.' Aisling laughed. 'Bail at the first sign of reality. Another man's heart shattered.'

'Oh, whatever,' I said. 'It'll be grand. Enough about that, I'm being a real *mé féiner* tonight. How's life with you?'

'Fine,' she answered, but she said she was tired then and she called a cab to go home.

I had another drink and found Tadgh Carey in the smoking area, wearing a battered leather jacket and too much hair gel.

'Are you going out in town for Stephen's?' he asked, and where would I be going? Did I want to meet up for a drink?

'Sarah,' he said. 'Sarah, you look so beautiful.'

I didn't want to remember what happened after that.

Sarah: Brennan! Sorry for the lack of contact, I've been having some issues with my phone and I only saw your texts now. HAPPY CHRISTMAS EVE! Or Happy Christmas!!! It's past midnight, isn't it? I am drunk AF. Ring me tomorrow, okay? Xxxx

'Sarah,' my father muttered. 'Put that phone away this minute, do you hear me?'

'Calm down; no one cares.'

No one was going to notice my phone when it was the Children's Mass, toddlers and preschool kids scrambling across the altar while the Monsignor pretended he didn't mind.

'So important that they understand the *true* meaning of Christmas,' he said. 'It's not just about Santa and presents, you know.' He looked relieved when it was over. 'You may go in peace to love and serve the Lord.'

Outside, my father found his friends, slapping them on the back, asking if they'd make the point-to-point tomorrow.

'I hear Above and Beyond is tipped to win,' he said. 'Could be a handy little number there, I'm telling you.'

'Ais!' I called when I saw her, blonde hair scraped into a high ponytail, her face grey beneath her make-up. I hugged her parents and her older brother, Barry.

'Happy Christmas, Sarah,' her mother said to me. 'That's a beautiful coat you have on you.'

'Thanks, Liz.'

'Liz. Sean.' My father shook hands with them. 'Happy

206

Christmas to you both.' He nodded at Barry, then turned to Aisling. 'You're looking a bit delicate today, young lady,' he said.

'She should do, by the sounds of how much vodka you two put away last night,' Barry said. 'You're a bad influence, Fitzpatrick.'

'Oh, yeah, I was pouring the shots down her throat,' I said. 'Totally my fault.'

'We had better get going,' my father said. 'Have a good day, folks.'

I gave Aisling another hug. 'Text me later, yeah?' I said to her, as Dad and I left the church car park.

'You couldn't have taken it easy – on Christmas Eve, of all nights?' he said, rattling his car keys. 'How much did you have to drink last night?'

'The normal amount.'

'What's the "normal amount"?'

'The normal amount that normal people my age drink, okay, Dad?'

'Drinking to excess is no joking matter,' he said.

You should know, I felt like replying.

'That poor girl has been going through enough; I doubt she needed to drink herself into a stupor, on top of everything else.'

'What do you mean? Aisling is grand.'

'Well, maybe *you* think breaking up with your boyfriend of seven years is grand, but—'

'What? What about Aisling and Jamsie?'

'They broke up last month. She moved out of the apartment they were renting in Clonmel and she's back at home with her parents.'

I waited until he'd unlocked the jeep door. 'And how exactly do you know all of this?'

'Sean told me when I bumped into him at the post office last week. Himself and Liz are devastated. They considered Jamsie to be a part of the family.' He put the jeep into reverse. 'Did you not know?'

'Of course I knew,' I said. 'Don't be stupid.'

I wondered what my father would say if I told him that I dreamt about the journey home sometimes. Floating in that pause between consciousness and oblivion, trying to push myself up through the sticky film of sleep. The narrow street of Dunfinnan, faded houses, dirt gathering where the paint was peeling from the walls. The sharp turn away from the town, into the country: patchwork fields and open spaces. The fields were always empty in my dreams, brimming with stillness. It was always so quiet, so very quiet. The tyres squealing over the cattle grid. The outhouse, thrown up with grey concrete and a corrugated roof; the abandoned washing machine, the ghost of laundry past. My father had said he would get rid of it – 'I'll do it next weekend, I promise.' But he never did. The house key under a filthy flower pot; a cat with matted fur slipping through my legs, a swish of a ginger tail against my shins. I always woke up before I could open the door – sweating, aching for something that I could not name.

Back at home, I sat in Nana's old rocking chair while my father set the fire, the same way he always did it: the foundation of firelighters and briquettes, three lumps of coal and six small sticks on top. In the kitchen, he washed his hands in the sink, like he used to do every Sunday before Mass when I was a child, dunking his face in a plastic basin full of hot water, scrubbing himself dry in front of the broken piece of mirror propped up against the kitchen window.

'Should we open our presents?' he asked me. 'I wanted to wait until you woke up this morning, but then you—'

'I get it. I woke up late. I've ruined Christmas morning. I am the worst daughter ever.'

'I was going to say that we didn't have time to do it before we went to Mass. There's no need to be so dramatic.'

The Christmas tree was in the hall, tucked under the staircase. It was small, the green branches sprayed with white in an approximation of snow – a cheap thing that Nana Kathleen picked up after she moved in with us. My mother used to say it wasn't Christmas without the smell of a fir in the house; we would drive to Clonmel on 8th December to pick one out together. 'Just us girls,' she would say, and I knew that it was us against my father. The December after she died, there was no tree, real or otherwise. I woke up that Christmas morning and ran downstairs to the living room. My stocking was draped over the rocking chair, where I had left it the previous night, but it was empty. It had never been empty on Christmas morning before. My father was still in bed. I went in to wake him, the room tight with stale breath, and I put a hand on his bare back, slick with sweat.

'Dad,' I said, but he didn't move. 'Dad, there are no presents.'

'Go away, Sarah,' he said.

'But, Dad,' I insisted, 'it's Christmas and—'

'Would you just stop?' he said. 'What do you want from me? You're too old for Santa. Just cop on and leave me in peace.'

I sat in front of the television for the rest of the day, eating the selection box that our neighbour had given me. ('Poor child,' she'd said to her friends, over my head, as if I was deaf. 'Sure, there'll be no Christmas in that house this year, will there?')

'What did you get?' the girls had asked on our first day back in school after the holidays.

'What? Do you still believe in Santa, or something?' I said, laughing at their hasty denials. 'Cop on, will you?'

'From Aisling,' Dad said now, as he crouched down next to the tree, peering at the gift tags. He handed me a book wrapped in red paper.

'Thanks.'

One present from Aisling, a joke gift from my work Kris Kindle. Presents for both me and Dad from my uncles and aunts on his side: hampers and candles and soap sets.

Nothing from my mother's family. I hadn't seen any of them since the funeral.

'Nothing for you from the Brennan man?'

'Of course there was,' I lied. 'It was too big to bring home.'

'And what did Fionn get you?' My father's face lit up. Fionn's presents had become the highlight of our Christmas morning, over the last few years, and he always remembered to include something that my father would enjoy as well. A ridiculous board game that was suitable for two players, a DVD of a TV show from the seventies, some old-fashioned sweets that my father had confessed to loving as a child. 'It's not Christmas without Fionn's gift.'

'We decided not to give each other presents this year,' I said.

It had been four months of silence. Day after day, I'd knocked on the door of the studio. 'Fionn,' I'd said. 'Fionn, I know you're in there.' I could smell the paint and the weed, could hear the creaking of the floorboards as he shifted from one foot to the other. Our house was too small for anyone to disappear within its walls, and yet I was never able to catch him. I left the art books outside his bedroom door on 22nd December, with a card begging him to forgive me. I needed Fionn to forgive me so I could tell him about what had happened at Matthew's house, about the photos that I had found. And the letter, the words seared into my brain (*I love you, Flo*). It was the first thing I thought about when I woke up, the last thing at night, my fingers worrying the words like Nana Kathleen did with her rosary beads. *What should I do, Fionn?* But Fionn went home, leaving the books and the card behind. I crept into his room and I sat on the bed. 'I miss you, Fionn,' I said to myself.

'Ah,' my father said now, gathering the paper for recycling. 'That's a pity.'

'It was my decision,' I said, avoiding his gaze. 'It was getting weird, the amount of effort he put into my presents. It's not like we're dating or anything.'

'Hmm,' he said, picking up the last present under the tree: an envelope. 'This is from me. It's probably not as exciting as whatever Fionn would have dreamt up for you, but I hope you like it.'

I opened it, presuming it would be money, as always. But it wasn't.

'Where did you get this?'

'I asked Fionn for help,' he said.

It was a one-hundred-euro voucher for an art-supply shop in Dublin, the same one that Fionn and I used to go to when we were at college. We would spend hours in there, making lists of all the things we would buy if money was no object.

'I don't make art anymore.'

'I know,' my father said. 'And that's a real shame. When I think of you, out in the garden shed, happy out, splashing away . . .'

'I was a kid.'

'And you have to be a kid to paint, do you?'

'What's the point, Dad? There's no money in it. Fionn is up to his eyes in loans, and he's about ten times more talented than I am. Dublin is expensive, you know.'

'You could move home. I saw a four-bed house for sale on Bridge Street for eighty-five grand. You wouldn't get anything like that in Dublin.'

'But I don't *want* to live in a four-bed house on Bridge Street.'

'And why not? What would be wrong with it?'

My father's face was weathered from the sun and the wind, lines scored across his forehead, his lips chapped. He was wearing his best suit, bobbling on the lapels, for Christmas Day, his tie a swirling relic from the eighties. He wanted me to move home and meet a man like him and live a life like his, a life that would make more sense to him. My father seemed destined to be surrounded by women he was unable to understand.

'There's nothing wrong with it.' I looked at the voucher again. 'Thanks, Dad.'

'Not a bother, pet,' he said. 'I'd better go check on the dinner.'

I put the voucher back in its envelope and I placed it back under the tree. I didn't think about it or that letter (*love you more than I have ever loved anyone*). I refused to allow myself to do so. Instead, I set the dinner table. The white linen tablecloth that was used for special occasions, the faded mistletoe placemats my mother had bought in Clonmel for their first Christmas as a married couple, the crystal glasses they received as wedding presents.

'I got us a turkey breast,' Dad told me. He'd been something of a tentative cook since Nana Kathleen died. 'Didn't see the sense in getting a whole bird when it's only ourselves.'

We pulled crackers and put the paper hats on our heads; mine was red and my father's was purple. 'Like royalty, I am,' he said.

I laughed because I could tell that he thought he had made a joke. I gathered up the dishes, stacking them in the dishwasher.

'Will we play Monopoly? Or Trivial Pursuit?' I asked.

'Not with you, thank you very much.'

'What's that supposed to mean?'

'It means you're a terrible sore loser, Sarah. You have been ever since you were a child. Let's spare ourselves a repeat of 2006, shall we?'

He turned the TV on instead, for *Mrs Brown*. We watched the *Fair City* special, the *Coronation Street* special and a horrifyingly violent movie, which seemed an odd choice for Christmas Day.

'Are you not having anything yourself?' he asked, as I made him a toasted cheese sandwich and a hot chocolate that evening.

'I'm not hungry.'

'But you barely touched your dinner.'

'I told you,' I said, sitting back down. 'I'm not hungry.'

'You've gotten very thin. I'm worried about you.' He took a bite of the sandwich, barely chewing before he swallowed.

'And you've been checking that phone all day.' He sipped the cocoa, inhaling through his teeth at the heat. 'Did himself not call?'

'Who?' I asked.

We both knew that Matthew hadn't called. He hadn't texted back either, but he must have read my message by now. Maybe he was angry with me for sneaking out of his house without saying goodbye? Or annoyed that I hadn't texted him back for four days?

'The Brennan fella.'

'He's with his son,' I said. 'He probably hasn't had a chance to look at his phone yet.'

'It would've only taken two minutes for him to call you.'

'Yeah,' I said. 'I guess that's true.'

I returned to my phone, scrolling down, down, down. Twitter. Facebook. Instagram. Snapchat. New shoes and new phones and new handbags. *#LuckyGirl #SantaCame #BoyDoneGood #Spoilt*

The official MBA Instagram was silent, the most recent post a generic *Happy Christmas to friends near and far* on Christmas Eve. I tried Florence's Instagram account – private. Harry – private. I went onto Facebook and dug deeper. Florence's mother – private. I was surprised at that; usually the mothers provided the best stalking opportunities, with their apparent inability to fix their security settings. I could only access one photo on Florence's page: her profile picture. Three hundred likes, and a woman called Evelyn Kavanagh

215

had commented on how beautiful she looked. *Thanks, Auntie Evie!* Florence had written underneath. Evelyn Kavanagh was a woman in her sixties, I guessed, with a silver bob and a jaunty scarf tied around her neck, and her photo albums were public. *Hitting the mulled wine hard!!!!!* she'd posted, two hours ago. I skipped past photos of Florence and her parents and Harry and their golden retriever and their beautiful Christmas tree – real, of course, and tastefully decorated in creams and golds – until I found it: a photo of Harry and Matthew and Florence in matching Rudolph sweaters, rosy-cheeked and beaming at the camera. The perfect, happy family. Mother, father, child. Everything as it should be.

'I'm going to bed,' I said.

'But we haven't watched *Meet Me in St Louis*,' my father said. 'We always watch that on Christmas Day.'

'I'm tired.' I got up, resting my hand on his shoulder.

'Okay then, love.' He placed his hand over mine, but he didn't look at me. 'Sarah? Can I ask you something?'

'What?'

'Are . . .' His voice was hesitant. 'Are you happy?'

My father had never asked me that question before.

'Sure, Dad,' I said. 'Of course I am. Night.'

Am I happy? I asked myself as I brushed my teeth. Am I happy?

I didn't know how to answer that question. I'm not sure if I ever did.

On 4th January, I kissed my father on the cheek and promised that I would visit more often, both of us aware that I was lying.

Boarding the bus to Dublin, I recognised someone from school getting on before me. We avoided eye contact, afraid of having to sit next to each other and make small talk. *What have you been up to? Teaching? Wow. I didn't think you'd end up a teacher. Haha.*

The two women behind me were talking about how much they'd eaten over the holidays. *I can barely zip up my jeans; I'm a disgrace. I'll have to be so good for January now.*

Sarah: Hey! Happy New Year! Hope you had a good
Christmas! Did Harry like that book I recommended?

217

Outside, the land had been stripped bare by winter, the trees whittled thin. As we drove through a series of towns and villages, I watched the men and women and children – people I would never know and who would never know me. I wondered if they were happy. I wondered if they knew what 'being happy' meant. I had a sudden urge to wave at them so they would look at me, so they'd remember my face. I wanted them to know that I existed.

The bus pulled into the station at Dublin and I bumped into the girl from school as we grabbed our bags from the hold.

'Julie,' I said. 'I didn't see you there at all. Good Christmas?'

Sarah: I'm heading back to Dublin today. Would be good to
see you.
Sarah: If you have time, obvs. xx

'Hey,' I called out as I pushed the door open. 'Anyone home?'

I found Fionn in the living room, a woman sitting next to him. They were holding hands, her legs intertwined with his.

'Hi,' she said, smiling at me. 'I'm Natalia.' She glanced at Fionn, waiting for him to say something. 'I'm Fionn's girlfriend.'

'Girlfriend?'

'Yes.' She squeezed his knee. 'I thought you'd told all your friends about me, Finny?'

Finny?

'Well,' I said, 'I didn't hear anything about—'

'Come on, babe,' Fionn said, standing up. 'Let's go to my room.'

'She seems nice,' I heard Natalia say as they climbed the stairs. 'Nice' was what girls like Natalia called you when they decided you didn't pose a threat because you weren't as pretty as they were. I waited to hear if Fionn replied, but there was only the slam of his bedroom door.

> **Sarah:** I'm sorry that I left that night without saying goodbye.
>
> I was feeling a bit sick and I didn't want to disturb you.
>
> You seemed like you needed your sleep!!

In the staffroom, the fridge was packed high with Tupperware boxes of salad and soup, everyone discussing their New Year's resolutions.

'I'm going to go to the gym three times a week. Maybe four.'

'I've signed up for a boot camp.'

'I'm on a juicing cleanse.'

'Apparently, it's sugar is the problem now, not fat. And, in the eighties, they were telling us to avoid fat like the plague. You wouldn't know what to believe, would you?'

'Yes,' Mrs Burke said, pouring milk into her coffee, watching me. 'A new year, a new start. No harm at all, I think.'

Sarah: Could you text me? I'm worried that you're not getting my messages.

Sarah: If you're mad with me, then just say it. This is getting ridiculous.

Sarah: Matthew?

There was a phone ringing.

'Stop it,' I said, as I opened my eyes. '*Stop*.' But it rang and it rang and it rang.

It was too bright in this room. This room that was not my bedroom. (Not Dunfinnan, not Stoneybatter either. Where was I?) I was in a double bed, soft cotton sheets, flamingo-patterned wallpaper. I remembered. I was in Kevin's house on Mountpleasant Square. He and Robbie had thrown a party last night.

'Dry January be damned!' Kevin had toasted the room, raising a glass to the men in shirts unbuttoned too low and women in jewel-coloured dresses that didn't wrinkle when they stood up to go to the bathroom. They talked about school fees and villa rentals and how much their houses were worth since the crash, and I pretended to be interested. (What is he doing right now? And where is he? And who is he with? And why hasn't he texted me back? And maybe his phone is broken? And maybe he hates me? And maybe I should text him again to check? No, Sarah. No. Wait.)

'Didn't seem to affect Matthew Brennan much, did it?' one man had said, and I'd started at the mention of his name. Robbie met my gaze, an almost imperceptible shake of the head warning me to stay quiet. 'Every year, he seems to have crawled up the Rich List by another few places. He's such a wheeler-dealer, a real Del Boy in a fancy suit.'

'Don't be mean about that poor man,' a woman said. 'I take Pilates with Florence Kavanagh, and I'm telling you now, Matthew Brennan is not over her.'

'Really?' someone else asked. 'How so?'

'Pining after her, especially since she started dating Daniel McGuinness. Apparently, Matthew literally *begged* to spend Christmas with her family this year because he had nowhere else to go. Florence feels sorry for him, she's so soft, and he *is* the father of her child, so I suppose—'

'Any more wine?' I interrupted her, waving my empty glass at Kevin.

The phone rang again now and I could hear the mattress springs creak in the room next door. I threw the duvet cover onto the floor, the mascara-smeared pillows following, and I found my phone hidden down the back of the bed.

'Hello?'

'Sarah?' my father said. 'What's wrong with your voice?'

'Why are you phoning me this early?'

'It's 11.30 a.m. That's a perfectly acceptable time to phone someone.'

'Not on a Sunday morning, it's not.'

'Out again last night, I take it.'

'I went to a dinner party at Kevin's house,' I said. 'It was all very civilised.'

There was a pause. 'Kevin? Is he . . . ?'

'Yes. Kevin is Robbie's boyfriend.' Pressure was building at the base of my spine. 'Listen, Dad, is there something you wanted to talk to me about?'

'There is.' I could hear a rustle of newspaper. 'I was reading the *Sunday Independent* today—'

'I'm delighted for you. I'm really sorry, Dad, but I don't have the energy for this right now. I'll phone you tomorrow, okay?'

'It's about Matthew Brennan.'

'What?' I said. 'What about Matthew?'

'There's a photo of him in *Life* magazine, at some shindig, and he's with a woman.'

'Dad, he's allowed to talk to other women, you know. This is a ridiculous conversation.'

'I was only trying to help,' he said. 'I don't want to see you getting hurt.'

'Oh, spare me. You've never liked him, have you? You have these preconceived notions about who Matthew is, just because he's rich and he's Harold Kavanagh's son-in-law. You refuse to give him a chance.'

'Give him a chance? Sarah, I've never even met the man. If you had bothered to bring him to Dunfinnan, I might be better equipped to form an educated opinion on his character.'

As if I would have brought him to the farmhouse. 'I'm not doing this with you, Dad,' I said. 'Bye.'

Matthew Brennan gave the opening speech at a gala in aid of Barnardo's on Friday night, the *Sunday Independent* online told me, *a charity close to the property tycoon's heart.* The accompanying photo was of Matthew with a woman who had elbow-length blonde hair, his hand was perilously high on her ribcage. *Millie Shaw,* the caption said.

'You have such a type,' I'd said to him one day. We were lying in the hotel bed, the LUAS roaring past outside, talking about our sexual fantasies.

'A threesome,' he'd said. 'That's what I want, but it would have to be with someone we trusted, someone we knew wouldn't blab afterwards. Do you know anyone suitable?'

I had smiled, pretending I wasn't picturing another woman, thinner than me, prettier, *better*.

'What about that friend of yours, the one in your new profile photo on WhatsApp?' he asked.

'Aisling?' I asked, and I felt sick. 'Aisling is far too square to have a threesome,' I said. 'She's boring as fuck. Anyway, what is this obsession with blondes about?' Matthew had previously mentioned other women he found attractive, all ghost versions of Florence. 'Was your mother blonde, Matthew?' I teased him. 'Is this an Oedipus type of thing?'

He had stiffened at the mention of his mother and I knew that I'd made a mistake.

'Wouldn't it be hilarious if I dyed my hair?' I rushed on before he could get up and leave me. 'If I just turned up, one of these days, with blonde hair?'

He wound some of my thick, dark hair around his fingers, the hair that reminded me of my own mother every time I looked in the mirror. 'I wouldn't object to that,' he said.

'Hello?' Aisling said now, as she answered her phone.

'Hey.'

'Sarah? Why is your number on private?'

(Because I phoned Matthew last night and hung up when he answered, like a teenager with a pathetic crush.)

'You sound fucked,' she went on, without waiting for an answer. 'Good night, I take it?'

'I went to Kevin's house with Robbie. They were throwing a dinner party.'

'Girl, you *fancy*. That's some grown-up shit, right there.'

I tried to agree, but I couldn't get the words out, each attempt cracking into a heaving sob.

'Sarah?' she said. 'Sarah, what's wrong?'

'It's Matthew.'

'Oh, babe. Did you break up?'

'No.' I put my hand over my mouth to muffle the sobs. I didn't want Kevin and Robbie to hear me. 'Sorry.'

'Don't apologise,' she said. 'Just tell me what's going on.'

'Dad phoned me today to tell me there was a photo of Matthew with another woman in the *Sindo* mag.'

'Were they kissing?'

'They were posing for a photo together. Google it – it's the Barnardo's charity gala.'

There was silence as she did so, then a low, *Hmmm.*

'Okay,' she said. 'I hate to say this, but it doesn't look great.'

'I know,' I said. 'Do you think she's hot?'

'You're much prettier,' she said automatically. 'What did he say when you asked him?'

I didn't reply.

'Sarah. Please tell me you phoned Matthew and talked to him about this?'

'I literally just saw it, and I wanted to talk to you about it first.'

'But you're going to phone him now, right?'

The flamingos started to move on the wallpaper, flapping wings, stamping feet. I lay back down in the bed.

'Sarah?' she said.

'I don't want to nag him.'

'You're not nagging him; you're asking him a simple question.'

'This is different, Ais; he's not some loser from Dunfinnan. This is Matthew Brennan. I can't just—'

'Can't just what? Can't just have an honest conversation with him?'

'Of course I can, but it's not like we're official or anything. Do I even have the right to be upset about this?'

'Fitz, this is ridiculous. He texts you, you go to meet him wherever and whenever suits him, and then he fucks you and sends you on your way afterwards with a pat on the ass. Am I missing something here? Because it seems pretty straightforward to me.'

'Ais,' I said, 'I know it looks bad, but that's not how it is. He cares about me, I know he does. I told you what happened when I went back to his house before Christmas. This is my fault; I freaked out and now he's pushing me away. This is all my fault.'

'I don't know what to say to you.'

'Well, what do you think I should do?'

'I don't know.'

'Ais, help me. You're so good at stuff like this.'

'Sarah, I can't make these decisions for you. I have my own shit going on too, you know,' she said. 'But, for what it's worth, I think you need to talk to him.'

And I realised that I had forgotten to ask Aisling about Jamsie. I still hadn't even told her that I knew about the break-up. Fionn was right. I was a terrible friend.

'Okay,' I said. 'I'll talk to Matthew.'

I called him.

'I'm busy,' he said, his voice brusque, as if he couldn't wait to get me off the phone. 'I'll be in touch when things calm down.'

I couldn't sleep after that, scanning through screen-grabs of Millie Shaw and Florence Kavanagh that I had saved to my camera roll. At 4 a.m., I got up and turned on the light. Sitting in front of the mirror, I stared at my own face, then Millie Shaw's photo, my own face, then Florence Kavanagh. What did they have that I didn't? What would I have to do to make him love me?

I sent him photos, describing where I wanted his hands and his mouth. (And if he showed them to his friends? *She's twenty-four*, he would say to them, *and she'll do anything. I mean anything.*)

I want you, I said. *I need you inside me. I've been thinking about you while I make myself come.* And, as if by magic, he suddenly found a spare afternoon in his schedule. Funny how that worked out.

Matthew: I'm upstairs.

Matthew: Where are you? I don't have that much time, Sarah.

I didn't tell him that I had been at the hotel for over an hour already, pacing back and forth in the downstairs bathroom, practising my lines in the mirror.

Matthew. We need to talk, I imagined myself saying. *I care about you, and I think you care about me. I want to know where I stand, Matthew.*

In my head, I sounded assertive, strong. In my head, I said all the right things.

'At last,' he said, when I knocked on the door of room 63, and he pulled me inside.

'Hey,' I said. 'Before we—'

He bent down to kiss me.

'Wait, Matthew. I wanted to talk to you about what happened at Christmas. I shouldn't have left your house without—'

'That doesn't matter.'

'Are you sure? You seemed really upset. I was worried about you.'

'Sarah –' there was a half-smirk in his voice and I felt stupid for bringing it up – 'I was drunk and talking nonsense. You take things far too seriously, do you know that?'

He undressed quickly, gesturing at me to do the same, nodding in appreciation when he saw the corset I'd bought especially for today.

'Jesus,' he said, 'you look sensational.'

Did he think I wore underwear like this all the time? Did he presume I wore lace thongs and sheer bras under my work clothes, that I lounged around in French knickers on my day off?

'Matthew,' I said.

He put his hands on my shoulders, pushing me to the floor. 'Remember that text message you sent me the other day?'

I looked up at him. 'What?'

He grabbed the back of my head. 'Do what you said you wanted to do in that text,' he said. 'I've been thinking about it all week.'

That was only a fantasy, Matthew. Stop it, Matthew.

But I couldn't say that. It wouldn't be fair to lead him on.

'Fuck,' he said, leaning against the door. 'Fuck, that's good.'

I don't want to do this. I don't want—

Without warning, he came. 'You are so sexy,' he said as I made myself swallow. He let go of my hair, my scalp tingling. 'And now it's your turn. Where's this toy? The one you sent me those photos of you using?'

'I forgot it,' I lied.

Before I left the house, I'd opened the drawer that the vibrator was in. The thought of lying on the hotel bed, my legs spread so Matthew could see every part of me, made me feel so vulnerable that panic scratched its nails against my ribs.

'Ah,' he said, disappearing into the bathroom. 'That's a shame.'

I pulled my dress back on. *Matthew,* I said in my head. *Matthew, it's nearly been a year now and I think it's time we decided where we're going. Matthew, I think we should talk.*

He stepped out of the shower, towelling himself off, and got dressed. 'Right,' he said, phone already in hand. 'I had better get going. My schedule is manic today; January is always such a weird month for me.'

'Wait,' I said, and he frowned, as if unfamiliar with the concept of waiting.

'What's wrong?' he asked.

'Can we just talk for a minute?'

'Sure.' The bed dipped as he sat next to me. 'What's up?'

'Matthew,' I said, trying to remember my lines. 'Matthew, we've been seeing each other for nearly a year.'

'Has it been that long?' he said, leaning over to kiss me.

'Matthew.' I pulled away from him. 'Matthew, please. I really want to talk about this.'

'Okay,' he sighed. 'Let's do this.'

'Matthew, we've been seeing each other for nearly a year

and I thought that maybe it might be time for us to have a conversation.'

'A conversation?'

'Yes. A conversation about where things are going between us.'

'I thought things were going just fine,' he said, tracing his fingertips from my knee to my inner thigh.

'Come on,' I said, taking his hand off my leg. 'I'm being serious, here. What are we? Are we boyfriend and girl-friend?'

'I think I'm a little old to be having the boyfriend and girlfriend talk, Sarah.'

'You know what I mean.' My face was burning with embar-rassment. 'Are we properly dating?'

'*Dating?* Sarah, I thought we were on the same page, here.'

'What's the page, though?'

'Having some fun. You seemed to be as relaxed about everything as I was.' He fiddled with his cufflinks. 'You're not a robot, though; I guess I should have realised that feelings would come into it sooner or later.' He said 'feelings' as if it was a contagious disease and he was terribly sorry that I seemed to have contracted it.

'I just think we have so much fun together, and I want to spend more time with you.'

'I don't have more time to give you, Sarah. Not with work and with Harry. I thought you understood that.'

'I can't keep doing this, Matthew. It's getting too much for me.'

'Wait a minute,' Matthew said. 'Are you breaking up with me?'

'No,' I said, stroking the back of his neck. 'No, of course not. Please don't think that. But I do need to know where I stand.'

'Of course,' he said, smiling at me. 'You can't break up with me, because we were never in a real relationship in the first place, were we?'

'Yes,' I said.

'That's true, I suppose,' I said, and I got to my feet. 'I think I should probably leave.'

And he let me go. He let me go as if it was the easiest thing in the world.

I woke in the middle of the night, coughing, trying to hack the sadness out of my chest. I wanted to draw it into my mouth, like phlegm, so I could spit it out. But I couldn't. The pain sat on me, heavy, dense. I couldn't breathe with it.

My room was black and silent. I lay there, listening to my heart crack inside me.

You can't break up with me . . .

. . . because we were never . . .

. . . in a real relationship in the first place.

My face was wet. I must have been crying. Why was I crying? He hadn't promised me anything. It was always supposed to be casual. You're being ridiculous, Sarah. He wasn't your boyfriend. It wasn't a real relationship. It was nothing.

Light crept around the edges of my room. I could hear

stirring, low groaning. Doors opened and closed, the shower turned on and off. Footsteps on the stairs.

'Did you see my red shirt?'

'Nah, dude; sorry.'

'Ah, for fuck's sake. Who drank the last of my milk?'

'Sarah, you up?' Robbie said, outside my bedroom door. 'You're going to be late for work.' He said something else, too, but I couldn't hear him.

I was thinking about Matthew. He hadn't wanted to be there; he didn't want to be having that conversation. But I had to ask him. All I'd ever wanted was for him to say that I was enough. If he said it, maybe I could believe that it was actually true. I lay face down on the bed, my head buried in the pillow, telling myself I was stupid, telling myself I was overreacting. Hours passed and I needed to go to the toilet. My legs were unsteady beneath me, as if I was learning how to walk again. But I still brought my phone with me. Just in case.

'Oh,' Fionn said when he saw me. He was between his studio and his bedroom, holding a large canvas. 'I thought you had gone to work.'

The painting was beautiful: a sky broken by lightning. He was so talented, Fionn. I should have kept *Harbour Skies*. I should have done a lot of things.

'Are you okay?' he asked. I looked at him and he looked at me for the first time in months.

I closed the bathroom door behind me. 'No,' I said to the girl in the mirror. 'I am not okay.'

She was hollow eyes and flaking make-up and sticky thighs, wearing the same dress that she'd worn to that hotel. I pulled the dress off over my head and I stared at my body, wanting to see what he had seen. He had used it every way he wanted to and I had let him, telling him to do it harder, to do it faster, to do it again and again and again. Bile ate its way up my throat, spilling bitter into the sink. I turned the tap on, splashed my face with cold water.

You are acting crazy, I told myself. You weren't even in a real relationship, no matter how much you wanted to be.

I should have learned by now not to want more than I could have.

I should have turned him down the first time he asked me out.

I should have known not to get involved with a parent.

I should have kept things professional.

I should have refused to give him my number.

I should have waited longer before texting him back.

I should never have gone to meet him in that hotel.

I should have insisted that he take me for dinner first.

I should have waited until the third date to have sex with him.

I should have been more reluctant.

I should have sent shorter texts.

I should have made him chase me.

I should have been more honest.

I should have been less honest.

I should have been more like Florence.
I should have dyed my hair blonde.
I should have waited for him to text first.
I should have been less needy.
I should have been better.

It was Saturday. It was Sunday. I was still in bed. Someone had put a box of Kleenex on my bedside locker and there were balled-up tissues littering the side of the bed. Occasionally, someone would come into my room. 'Here,' they said, and they offered me a glass or a plate. 'Drink this,' they said. 'Eat this,' they said. 'It'll make you feel better.'

I held my phone in my hand like a talisman all weekend, waiting for him to call, or to text. My father phoned. Stephen phoned, wondering why I'd missed work on Friday, no doubt. Aisling phoned. I didn't answer any of them.

'Jesus Christ,' I heard Aaron say. 'Can one of you talk to her? Between the phone calls and the incessant sobbing, I don't know how much more of this I can take. What's *wrong* with her?'

The low murmur of Robbie's voice. I wished he would speak up so I could hear him. I wished someone would tell me exactly what was wrong with me so that I could fix it.

My phone ringing again. Let it be him. Let it be him.

'Sarah.' It was Aisling. It was Aisling and it was not Matthew and I felt something twisting in my gut. 'I've been trying to phone you all weekend.'

'What day is it?'

'It's Sunday evening.'

I rolled on my back.

'Sarah? Are you there?'

'Yeah.'

'Fionn texted me. He says you're in bad shape. I'll take it things didn't go well with Matthew . . . Oh, Sarah, don't cry. He's not worth it,' she said.

But he was.

'You deserve better,' she said.

But I didn't.

She stayed on the phone, telling me it was all going to be okay, telling me that these feelings wouldn't last forever. She was getting good at lying, too.

'Jesus, are you all right?' Stephen asked when I walked into the staffroom on Monday morning. 'You don't look so great.'

I knew what I looked like. I had made myself take a shower that morning, soaping my sweat-grimed body. Not standing, but swaying, leaning against the tiles to support myself. Grief had made its home in me, and it was all too comfortable there. It knew me; it had been here before. But that other grief had made sense. It was normal, expected. This one, I could not fathom. I touched it, tried to feel the shape of it, to hold it between my fingertips. The worst thing was knowing that I had done this to myself with my stupidity and my mouth taped shut and my hungry eyes and my want, my want, *my want*. After I turned off the shower, I wiped the steamed mirror clean and stood, naked, in front of it. I was thin. I was dark circles under wild eyes. I was nothing special, nothing *extraordinary*. Not like her. I wished I could throw this body to a pack of starving wolves, watch them tear it apart.

You can't break up with me, because we were never in a real relationship in the first place.

I didn't tell Aisling that Matthew said that to me. She would have been furious. *How dare he?* Aisling would have said. *How dare he say that to you?* (And, if I told her Matthew had said that, she would hate him, and we might still get

241

back together. I didn't want Aisling hating him if – when, *when* – that happened.)

'Sarah?' Stephen said, handing me a cup of tea and a KitKat.

'I'm grand,' I told him, refusing both. 'A family member died on Friday, so I had to go home for the funeral.'

'I'm sorry to hear that.'

'Yes,' I said. 'The woman had cancer. But it was quick, though. A blessed relief, everyone said.'

'Was she married? Kids?'

'Yes. A girl.'

'What age?'

'Ten.'

'Ah, that's a shocking age to lose your mother.'

'Yes,' I said. 'She'll never recover from that, will she?'

I excused myself to go to the bathroom.

She will never recover from that. She will be selfish and stupid and she will make bad choices. She will let men take her body and use it as they please. She will roll her eyes and say she doesn't care, but she does care. *She does.* She will lose him. She will realise that he was never hers to lose in the first place.

I closed the cubicle door behind me, a hand over my mouth. I tried to be as quiet as I could.

NOW

Sarah cursed as she dropped her house keys, her fingers stiff with the cold. 'Wrap up well, love,' her father had told her when she left Dunfinnan. 'It's always freezing in Dublin.'

'Hello?' she called out as she opened the front door, hoping that—

'Sarah?' His voice from their bedroom and the sinking disappointment that followed. All she had wanted was some quiet and a dark room to sit in by herself. Was that too much to ask for? Oisín stood at the top of the stairs now, looking at her as if she was a stranger.

'I thought you were staying in Killiney for Christmas?'

'I was,' he said, 'but I came back to get the house ready.'

'Ready for what?'

'I'm having a party tomorrow night. New Year's is always

such a shitshow around town, thought it would be better to have the crew here.'

'Sure,' Sarah said. 'Makes sense.'

He cracked his knuckles. 'I thought you were staying in Dunfinnan until the fifth.'

'Well,' she said, thinking of the last seven days at home. Radio One blaring constantly, *For the company,* her father said, even though she was home and she could have kept him company. An awkward dinner in Clonmel with Aisling and Ciara. *Haven't heard from you in a while,* Aisling said to Sarah, frowning as Sarah made increasingly feeble excuses. Sarah had meant to contact Aisling, she had meant to do it on too many occasions to mention. Eddie had told her two months ago that Aisling had decided to take a career break, go to Australia for a year. *She said she may as well,* Eddie had said, *since she still hasn't got her mortgage. I don't think she's met anyone else, either, and you know Jamsie is engaged to Catherine Hogan now, don't you?* Sarah had wanted to phone Aisling then, tell her how excited she was for her. *You're dead right to go, Ais,* she would say. *You'll have a ball.* But then Sarah thought of Aisling asking her about Oisín. Sarah would have to tell Aisling. She would have to tell her about how the house was too quiet now, she and Oisín barely speaking. Their relationship was disintegrating, whatever love they once shared slipping through her fingers. Sarah didn't know how to stop it happening; at this point it felt as if she would simply have to wait and see how it all played out. Sarah thought she should leave him, but where would she go if she did?

The rest of the holidays had been spent sitting in the house, her father watching TV – until yesterday, when she couldn't take it anymore. Sarah had grabbed the car keys and told her father that she was going to the graveyard.

She'd kissed two fingers and pressed them against where Nana Kathleen's name was engraved, then she sat on her mother's headstone, shivering. There were fresh flowers on the grave: white roses and holly, tied with red ribbon.

Arra, leave it alone, her father had said when Sarah asked him about the bouquet. Then, later, as they were saying goodnight, Eddie said, *I miss her too, Sarah. No matter what you might think.*

'I decided to come back early,' Sarah said to Oisín now. 'How was your Christmas?'

He hadn't phoned her on Christmas Day. Oisín always phoned her on Christmas Day. But then, Sarah hadn't phoned Oisín either.

'Good,' he said. 'Yours?'

Sarah stood there, her small suitcase at her feet, and tried to think of something to say to him. 'I think I might go out.'

'Out? Out where?'

'Just out,' she said, one hand on the doorknob already.

'But you only got back two minutes ago.'

'I need some fresh air.'

She closed the front door behind her, Oisín still protesting.

She sat down on the porch, stretching her legs out in front of her, and lit a cigarette. When that cigarette was finished, she lit another one. She waited in the cold until it was late and the hall lights went out. She waited some more, and when she felt sure that Oisín was asleep, she inched back inside, taking off her shoes and gingerly stepping upstairs. He was sprawled across the bed sheets, face down, a book on the pillow beside him. Sarah placed her hand on the back of his head, but he didn't wake up. She knew that she had loved Oisín once, and fiercely. She'd thought she would love him forever.

What was she going to do now?

THEN

'I shouldn't have forced his hand.'

'Sarah, come on.'

'I knew he was weird about commitment. I should have waited until we had been seeing each other for longer.'

'You had been having sex with the man for almost a year,' Aisling said, exasperated. 'How much more time did he need?'

'Yeah,' I said.

You can't break up with me . . .

'You're right, I suppose.' I said.

. . . Because we were never in a real relationship in the first place.

'But I shouldn't have had sex with him so soon, Ais. If I had insisted that he bring me out for dinner first, he would have respected me more.'

'Too soon? Do you really want to be with a guy who doesn't respect you because you slept with him "too soon"?'

'I bet Florence didn't sleep with him until they'd been dating for three months. She probably set an alarm on her phone to remind her of the socially acceptable time to unlock her chastity belt.'

Aisling sighed. 'You know it's not her fault, right? Florence Kavanagh has literally nothing to do with any of this.'

'She keeps Matthew on a string; if she just cut off contact with him, then he'd be able to move on properly.'

'Sarah,' Aisling said, 'she's the mother of his only child. How exactly is she supposed to cut off all contact?'

'It's still not fair. Going on holidays with him and spending Christmas with him and letting him think that he's in with a chance with her, when she's off dating someone else.'

'Isn't that kind of pathetic on Matthew's part, though?' she asked. 'Would you really want to be with someone like that, anyway?'

'It doesn't matter what I want, does it? Florence has won now.'

'Won? Won what? A sad man who has no capacity to love anyone but himself? That's some prize.'

'He has the capacity to love Florence, doesn't he? Maybe if I had been more "extraordinary", like her,' I continued, ignoring Aisling, 'then he might have—'

'Fitz, I have to go to work.'

I checked my watch. I was going to be late too, if I didn't hurry up. 'Are you mad at me?' I asked her.

'No. I'm just . . . You know I love you, right? And I want to be here for you. But I feel like we've been having the exact same conversation every day for the last six weeks. And I'm trying my hardest to be sympathetic, but Matthew Brennan is not worth all this heartache. He never was.'

Six weeks of waking up, my throat sore and my eyes burnt out. Six weeks of dragging myself out of bed, standing in front of the mirror and looking at my body, the bones rising to the surface like driftwood. Six weeks of crying in the staff bathroom between classes, despair tearing through me at the thought that he's not mine, he's not mine, he'll never be mine. Six weeks of visiting psychics, watching as they turn over their tarot cards. Death. The Tower. Nine of Swords. *Ah, you've had your heart broken,* they told me, *but it's time for you to move on. He was not the man for you.* I wondered how much money I would have to pay to make them tell me what I wanted to hear.

'I'm sorry,' I told Aisling now. 'I know it's been a lot. I'm really grateful for how good you've been to me.'

'It's nothing,' she said. 'That's what best friends are for, right?'

I didn't mention Jamsie. I could not help her when I was drowning.

'You'll have February midterms next week,' she said.

'Come home to Dunfinnan. It'll do you good to get out of the city for the week.'

'Hmm,' I said. 'Ais, listen, do you think I should text him?'

'No.'

'But I just think that if I text him and we—'

'Sarah. He hasn't texted you, has he?'

No, he had not. I woke in the morning, I showered and I brushed my teeth, and he hadn't texted me. I walked around the art room. 'That's very good, Conor,' and, 'Lighter brush strokes there, Hugh,' and, 'Did you just spit at Aodhán, Noah?' and he hadn't texted me. I went home and I listened to Joy Division on repeat, and he hadn't texted me. *Love, love will tear us apart . . . Love will tear us apart . . .* and he hadn't texted me. I could not sleep and I checked my phone and it was 1.30 a.m. and I checked my phone and it was 2.57 a.m. and I checked my phone and it was 4.33 a.m., and he hadn't texted me.

'But maybe he's just waiting for me to text first?' I said.

'Maybe,' Aisling said. 'But I doubt it.' I gasped, but she didn't apologise. 'Look, Fitz, I have to go to work.'

She hung up without saying goodbye.

Love, love will tear us apart again.
Love, love will tear us apart again.
Love, love will tear us apart again.

The earbuds were yanked away, the bed sagging as a body sat down.

'You're crushing my feet.' I kicked whomever it was off. 'And you scared me. What the fuck are you doing coming into my bedroom without knocking?'

'I did knock.'

The door was open, a sliver of light from the landing splitting the darkness. I could make out my desk and the heap of unwashed clothes on the floor, and the person sitting in front of me. It was Aaron in a T-shirt and shorts, his hair mussed.

'You didn't hear me because you're listening to that fucking song again.'

'What's your problem? I have earbuds in.'

'They're not much help when you're wailing like Björk. I'm surprised the neighbours haven't lodged an official complaint.' He rubbed his eyes. 'Fitz, we talked about this at the house meeting. I'm sorry you're going through something, but it's been two months now and the rest of us need to sleep. I thought we agreed at the meeting that—'

'Stop going on about that stupid meeting.'

It had been like some bullshit that Dr Phil would have dreamt up. I came home from work, exhausted from a day of pretending to be fine, and there they were, Fionn and Robbie and Aaron and Aaron's annoying girlfriend, sitting in the living room. *We have to talk,* Aaron said. *We're worried about you, we want to help you,* Robbie said. Fionn and Amelia stayed quiet, Fionn staring at the floor. *I'm fine,* I said.

'I still can't believe that your *girlfriend* was there,' I said now. 'As if it had anything to do with her.'

'Shh,' he said, pointing at his room, next door. 'She's in there,' he whispered. 'And this affects Amelia too. She's having a stressful time at work right now and she doesn't need to be kept awake by you singing to Joy Division five hundred times in a row.'

'If she hates it here so much, why don't you stay at her place?'

'You know her parents won't let us sleep in the same bed.'

'Well then, she should pay rent. If she wants to come to all these house meetings that you're suddenly such a big fan of, it seems fair that she contribute.'

'I don't know what you're talking about. Robbie said you still haven't paid this month; he said you owe him five hundred euro.'

'He . . .' I had forgotten that. *Do you have rent?* he'd asked me. *It's due today.* I hadn't answered him. It had seemed like too much effort.

'That's not fair, Sarah. You know that Robbie can't afford that. It's not like he's making a fortune at the gallery. Amelia said—'

'You told Amelia?'

'Of course I did,' he said. 'She's my girlfriend.'

That's what people did in proper relationships. They told their partner about their life, they asked for advice on problems they were having in work or with family or with a housemate who wouldn't get out of bed because she was too heartbroken over some guy she wasn't even going out with in the first place. They asked each other what they liked in bed, they made sure the other was sexually satisfied. They remembered their partner's birthday and what their home town was called and their father's name and their dead mother's favourite song. They treated each other with respect.

'You know,' I said, 'everyone hates Amelia.'

'What?'

'All of us. We hate her.'

253

'Fitz, come on, that's not fair.'

'It's not just me, Aaron. We *all* hate her.'

'Fitz, I'm serious—'

'That accent? Why does she sound like she's a member of the royal family, when we know she comes from Cabra? When are you ever going to come to your senses and dump the pretentious bitch? Maybe I should call a house meeting to discuss it. What do you think? Does that seem like a good idea?'

There was a whimper from the other room, so loud that Aaron and I started. A rustle of clothes. A shadow as a body blurred past us, the front door crashing open, the revving of a car engine.

'Amelia!' Aaron ran after her. '*Amelia.*'

I could hear him downstairs, leaving messages on her answering machine.

'Babe, she didn't mean it,' he said. 'Sarah is in a bad place. All the lads love you. Please phone me to let me know you got home okay . . . Amelia, did you get my message? Please phone me.'

Heavy footsteps on the stairs.

'Aaron,' I said, and he stopped outside my door. 'I'm sorry; I didn't—'

'No, Sarah.'

'Please, let me explain.'

'I don't want to hear it,' he said. 'Not from you.'

'I'm sorry,' I said, and Aaron shut his bedroom door in my face. 'I'm sorry,' I said, but Aaron left the room when I came in, pretending that I didn't exist. I apologised to his girlfriend, too, and Amelia told me that she forgave me, but she was like a shadow after that, slipping through the house without sound, leaving only traces of musky perfume and cigarette smoke behind.

'They're looking for an apartment together,' Robbie told me over breakfast. 'They've been going to viewings on their days off.'

'Oh,' I said.

'What you did was not okay,' he said. 'I don't care what you're going through right now. That was a shitty thing to do. And to bring me and Fionn into it? Sarah? What on earth possessed you?'

Fionn was barely acknowledging my existence either, preoccupied with the string of girlfriends that he paraded through the front door. Natalia was replaced by an Iseult, and then a Hannah, and now Imogen was there all the time, calling Fionn 'baby' and 'sweetie' and telling him how brilliant he was.

'My boo is so talented,' Imogen said in the kitchen, blowing a kiss at Fionn as he cooked dinner for them. 'Have you seen his new collection, Sarah? It's incredible.'

'No,' I said, even though I used to be the first person Fionn showed his work to. 'I haven't.'

I phoned Aisling at 2 a.m. when I could not sleep. 'I'm sorry to wake you, but I really want to text Matthew,' I said, and she told me not to.

'Oh, Sarah,' she said, sounding groggy. 'What good will it do?'

I phoned Aisling on the bus to work. 'I just think that maybe I should text him in case he's been waiting for me to text first.'

I phoned Aisling at small break, sequestered in the staff toilet. 'I'm going to text him.'

'You know what?' she said. 'Whatever. Go right ahead and text him.'

'Seriously?' I said, pressing my feet up against the cubicle wall. 'Do you think it's a good idea?'

'It doesn't seem to matter what I think, does it? Sarah Fitzpatrick will just do whatever Sarah Fitzpatrick wants to do.'

'What's wrong? You sound pissed off. Are you pissed off at me?'

'Why would I be pissed off? I mean, it's April now, so it's been three months since you broke up with Matthew. Three months of phoning you and texting you and listening to you and trying to be the best fucking friend that I could possibly be.'

'You've been amazing, Ais. You know how grateful I am.'

'Three months and you still haven't asked me how I'm feeling about Jamsie. You remember Jamsie, don't you? My boyfriend of seven years. I presume you heard that we broke up? That was my actual boyfriend, not like your weird, messed-up affair with a man who clearly couldn't give a shit about you. He's made that perfectly clear, hasn't he, Fitz? What else did you want him to do?'

'Ais, please—'

'But Jamsie wasn't worth mentioning, was he? Even though we were living together and I thought we were going to get married and spend the rest of our lives together and I feel like I've lost my best friend in the entire world. I could barely get out of bed for a week afterwards, Sarah. I had to move back in with my parents. Did you know that? Do you even care?'

I did. I did know. But I never asked her about it.

'Who gives a shit, though?' she continued. 'Jamsie is only some "loser from Dunfinnan", right? He treated me with respect and actually wanted to be in a relationship with me, but that doesn't count when he's from Bally-Go-Backward. Not like the all-important Matthew Brennan. Jesus, I'm so sick of hearing his name. I'm so sick of hearing you talk shit about Dunfinnan. You keep making out that it's just some hick town where no one understands fashion and we're all a bunch of farmers. You think I don't see the way you look at Ciara?'

'Ais—'

'She had post-natal depression, did you know that? She and Eoin nearly broke up because she couldn't stop crying all the time and she refused to even look at Holly for the first six months. She had to go on antidepressants. They go to Clonmel once a week for couple's counselling and Ciara's still convinced he's going to leave her.'

'How was I supposed to know that? Ciara never tells me anything.'

'She doesn't tell you anything because you've never bothered to ask her. It's always *Sarah, Sarah, Sarah*. I suppose you think Ciara was stupid getting pregnant, so typical of the idiots down the country. Well, Dunfinnan is my home, Sarah. I choose to live here. Does that make me an idiot as well? Or am I forgiven because you need someone to dump all of your shit on?'

'I don't dump all of my shit on you,' I said. 'I needed your support. That's what friends are for, right?' I listened to her breathing on the other end of the phone, just out of sync with my own.

'What about me, Fitz?' she asked. 'Did it ever occur to you that I might need some support too?'

'I'm sorry,' I said.

'You're always sorry,' she said. 'And yet nothing ever changes.'

'Ms Fitzpatrick?' It was Mrs Burke, waiting at the door of her office. Her eyes flickered down, mouth pursing.

You can't wear that skirt, Robbie had said as I rushed out of the kitchen that morning, a piece of toast stuffed between my teeth. *It has a stain on the front*, he'd shouted after me, *and it needs to be ironed.*

'Yes?' I replied, standing still as the students milled around me.

'I was hoping to have a word with you.'

'I was actually just—'

'It'll only take a few minutes, Ms Fitzpatrick. Thank you.'

I was at the DART station.

It's not good enough anymore, Ms Fitzpatrick.

I knew I should get on the DART going towards town.

I feel like I've been very patient with you.

Get on the train to Tara Street.

I'm aware you've had a bereavement, Mr Manning informed me of such.

I couldn't go home. They all hated me there.

You show up late.

I walked over to the opposite platform.

You're dishevelled, exhausted-looking.

Booterstown turned to Blackrock, turned to Dun Laoghaire.

Distracted in class.

And then Dalkey.

It's not good enough. Not *for St Finbarr's.*

I'd used Google Maps to see how long it would take to get from my house to his. *Get off at Dalkey station,* the app said. And so I did. I sat on the low metal chairs that lined the platform, holding my breath as the trains passed me. There were boys messing, pretending to fight each other as girls watched them, the way teenage girls have always watched teenage boys, staying on the sidelines and applauding feats of male bravery and daring. They laughed at the terrible jokes the boys made, close-lipped smiles to hide their braces. So young, and they were already burdened with the necessity of being beautiful.

I sat at Dalkey station for hours, the dark falling around me like rain.

'Miss?' A hand on my arm. An elderly man was sitting next to me, pristine in his tweed suit and silk pocket square. I didn't know how long he had been there.

'Yes?'

'Your phone.'

'What?'

'Your phone,' he said again. 'It's ringing.'

I rifled through my bag, my school diary and Mac lipstick and cough drops and tissues and phone charger and a copy of *Wallpaper*. 'Hello?' I said.

'Well, I'm glad you finally decided to answer your phone.' It was my father.

'I didn't hear it ringing.'

'I'm not talking about today, Sarah. You haven't picked up your phone in nearly three months.'

'I've been busy.' A train pulled into the station, the old man turning to wave goodbye. I waved back, mouthing, *Thank you*.

'Not so busy that you couldn't phone Aisling. On to her morning, noon and night, I hear.'

'Dad, just give it a rest,' I said. 'And I haven't spoken to Aisling in a week. I don't think I'll be hearing from her for a while.'

'No, I will not give it a rest,' he said. 'Just tell me. Are you in some kind of trouble?'

'What?'

'You heard me. Are you in trouble? Because if that individual doesn't take his responsibilities seriously, then he'll have me to answer to.'

He thought I was pregnant, I realised, and I gave a sharp laugh. 'No, Dad. I'm not in any trouble. And you won't have to worry about anything like that with Matthew Brennan anymore.'

'Oh, right?'

'Yeah.' My voice cracked. 'We broke up.'

My father remained silent.

'Aren't you going to say something?' I asked.

'What do you want me to say?'

'I don't know. I don't know anything anymore.' And I started to cry.

'Oh, Sarah. Please don't cry.' My father had always told me not to cry, even when I had good reason to do so. 'I know you're hurting, but you'll be glad of this in the long run. He was too old for you. You were too different,' my father said, his voice gentle.

'So, you think he was too good for me?'

'Of course I don't think that. But it would have been hard for you, Sarah. You're only twenty-four and he has a teenage child and an ex-wife and a whole lot of baggage that I'm not sure if you're ready to deal with. Not really.'

But what was the alternative? Would I stay teaching and marry someone who came from a similar background to me? Not from Dunfinnan, perhaps, but it may as well be. His home town would have the same narrow streets with a church and a pub and a small shop with an elderly woman behind the counter, on guard so the local kids don't rob penny sweets from her. I would get married and secure a mortgage for a house, and have two children, and spend my years saving for an annual holiday to the south of France, and spend my days worrying about finding the money for after-school classes and Santa presents and university fees. A small life. My husband would turn the light off at bedtime and he would pat me on the stomach, knowing better than to look for more. *Night, night,* he would say, and I would lie there after he fell asleep, fantasising about what my life would have been like, if only I had been extraordinary enough to make Matthew Brennan fall in love with me.

'I have to go, Dad,' I said.

Dad: What time will you be home on Wednesday?

Dad: The Mass is organised and everything.

Dad: You will be able to come, won't you?

Dad: I hope you'll be able to make it, anyway. Just let me know.

'I'm beginning to feel insulted,' Matthew Brennan said. 'You seem to find that phone far more interesting than me.'

'What?' I said. My father didn't believe that I would come home for 25th May, not after what had happened the year before. My father thought that my attendance for my mother's anniversary was a question now, rather than a fact. 'Sorry. Some family stuff.'

'I'll forgive your bad manners this once, but only because I'm so glad we're doing this,' Matthew said, clinking his glass against mine.

We were sitting in a booth in the Fitzwilliam Hotel bar and I couldn't believe he was here, that he wasn't a mirage that I had created out of thirst and need.

'Have a Porn Star Martini,' he'd told me, when I arrived. 'They're the best thing on the menu.'

You smell so good, I wanted to tell him. *I've missed you,* I wanted to tell him.

'I'm glad too,' I said, taking a sip. 'Jesus, that's good.'

'I told you,' he said. Matthew Brennan was always right, I should have known that by now. 'It's good to see you, Sarah. Although, I have to admit, I was surprised when I got your text. You seemed so upset the last time I saw you.'

'Well,' I said, 'that was months ago.' Four months. Four months without him. And I couldn't take it anymore. I missed him too much. I needed to see him. 'And I think it's great that we can still be friends, don't you?' Better to be friends, I reasoned. Better to have him in my life in some capacity than to lose him forever. I was tired of crying, tired of feeling sick to my stomach every time my iPhone beeped and it wasn't him. So I made a decision. An innocent text, sent two days ago, just to check in. Show him that there were no hard feelings. *So grown up of me,* I told myself. What was the harm? 'And now,' I continued, 'we can finally have a drink in public without worrying about Florence finding out about us, can't we?'

'Sarah, don't be like that.'

'Like what?' I asked. 'Another drink?'

★

'Wait. I need a second.'

'Come on,' Matthew said, pushing my skirt up.

There had been drinks and a hand placed on a knee, and a head tilted and an 'I'll sort this out'. In the lift, my face in the mirror, gaunt, eyeliner smudged. The beautiful room, a carpet in geometric purple and white squares, a balcony over-looking Stephen's Green. His mouth was on mine, and he was pushing me onto the bed. He ran his fingers in between the grooves of my jutting ribs and I waited for him to say that I was too thin.

'You are so sexy,' he said instead.

'Did you miss me?' I asked him.

'Well, I've certainly missed these,' he said as he palmed my breasts.

'Wait.' I pushed him off me. 'Wait.'

'Stop teasing, Sarah.'

'No. We need to talk.'

He lay down and groaned. 'My least favourite words in the English language.'

'I think we should talk about this,' I said, lying beside him.

'Talk about what?'

'About this. About what we're doing.'

'I think it's pretty obvious what we're doing,' he said, circling my belly button with a finger.

'I mean us. What does this mean? Like, going forward?'

'Sarah.' He sat up. 'What did you think this meant?'

'I don't know.'

I'll sort a room out, he had said downstairs. *You stay here. It's better if no one sees us going up together.* I did what I was told. He just wants to protect me, I reminded myself.

'I told you that I don't do relationships,' he said. 'I don't want to mislead you, but—'

'You haven't even tried, Matthew. *We* haven't even tried. I think we could be so good together.'

'Do you now?'

'We have so much fun together, and the sex is amazing, right?' He smiled, reaching for my breasts again. 'Then why can't you just give it a go?' I said.

'It doesn't work like that in my world, Sarah,' he said, pulling away. 'I have my work and Harry to think about; I don't have time to give you what you need. It wouldn't be fair to you.'

'I don't care about that. I just want to be with you.'

'You don't mean that, Sarah.'

'I do,' I said. 'I do mean it, Matthew. I want to take care of you.'

'You're too young to understand what that even would mean.'

'I wasn't too young for you to fuck, was I?'

'Excuse me? Let's not pretend that you're an innocent victim in all of this, Sarah.'

'I know, but . . .' My mind went blank, all of my clever arguments dissolving into nothingness.

'I'm not right for you. I'm twenty years older than you and I'm too set in my ways. I can't be the man you want me to be.'

'I never wanted you to be anything other than who you are,' I said, pressure building behind my eyes. (*I want you to be a big girl,* my father had told me before they took my mother's body away. *We need to get through the next few days; you can cry when it's all over. We don't want people thinking we can't cope.*)

'Sarah,' Matthew said. 'Sarah, come on. Don't be like this.'

'Don't be like what?' I said. 'Am I being too emotional for you? I suppose Florence would never cry in front of you, Florence would never—'

'Don't bring her into this.'

'Why not? She's moved on. She's with that guy, Daniel, now – she's happy. Maybe it's time for you to do the same thing. What'll happen when Harry goes to college? He's not going to want to spend every second weekend with you for the rest of his life. You'll be alone, Matthew. Properly alone.'

'I don't think that's any of your business, Sarah.' He got out of bed. 'I'm sorry if you had the wrong idea,' he said as he dressed. 'Truly, I am. I never meant to hurt you.'

'I saw those photos in your study, the ones of you and Florence,' I said, pulling the bed sheets up to cover my body. He stopped, his hand on the door. 'And that fucking letter. *I love you Flo. I love you more than I have ever loved anyone.* Who even writes letters anymore?'

'You went through my personal belongings?' His voice was dangerously low.

'I just—'

'You went through my things. How dare you?' he said.

269

'Florence and I were married, Sarah, we have a child together. It wasn't some meaningless shag with a stupid kid who doesn't know her ass from her elbow.'

'Don't say that; you said it wasn't just sex. You told me.'

'What did you think this was, Sarah? A fucking Disney movie? Are you completely delusional?'

'Matthew, you said it wasn't just sex between us. You said—'

'And that gave you permission to snoop, did it?'

'I'm sorry. I didn't think; we had both had so much wine that night and those cocktails and I—'

'I don't think we should see each other anymore.'

'Matthew,' I was begging now, desperate, 'I'm sorry; I shouldn't have done that. I know that now. It was a mistake. You've made mistakes too, right? We've both done things we shouldn't have.'

'I've been nothing but straight with you about what I wanted from this,' he said. 'Do not contact me again, do you understand me?'

'I'm sorry.' I kneeled on the bed, trying to reach out to him. 'Please don't be mad at me, I made a mistake. I just wanted to know you better, to understand you. Is that so wrong?'

'Oh, Jesus, would you ever just shut up?' he said, his face twisting in disgust.

'Please, Matthew. I'm begging you. I only ever wanted you to—'

'I couldn't care less about what you want,' he said.

It was dark in Fionn's room. I took off my shoes, crawling in the bed beside him. The sheets smelled different than they did before, a floral scent mixing in with the oil paints. Imogen, I supposed. I didn't like it. He was supposed to smell of him, only him. He jerked awake, sighing my name as if he had expected me to be here.

'Where have you been, Sarah?' he asked me.

'I was with Matthew. He said . . . He said . . .'

I didn't know how I'd got home. I couldn't remember leaving the hotel room or getting a taxi or opening the front door or walking upstairs, although I must have done all of those things. All I knew was that I was here now, with Fionn.

He put his hand on my face. 'You're crying.'

'I'm sorry,' I said. 'I need you to forgive me. I need you,

Fionn.'

He didn't speak for a long time. The silence was heavy, a dark mouth, closing its teeth around us both.

'You really hurt me, Fitz. That painting . . . It was us. It was you and me.'

'I'm sorry,' I said again. 'I'm so sorry.'

'I know you are.'

'I fucked up with you and now I've fucked up with Matthew. You should have seen his face, Fionn. What he *said*.'

'He's a dickhead.'

'He looked like he hated me.'

'Fitz . . .'

He stroked my hair, waiting for me to say something. Until, finally –

'Matthew doesn't love me, does he?'

'No.'

'And he never will, will he?'

'I don't think so, no.'

I sat up, trying to catch my breath. I breathed in and I lived. I breathed out and I lived. I thought of all the things I let him do to me.

And he still didn't love me.

NOW

'But where am I going to get a taxi at this hour on New Year's Eve?'

'Go home,' Oisín said as he closed the door on the last guest, a friend of his from UCD, who was holding out a wrap of coke and telling Oisín he was 'minus craic'. His name was Lorcan or Cillian. Sarah could never tell the difference; they all looked the same, with their soft hands and bland faces.

'Oh,' Oisín said, when he turned to find Sarah sitting on the bottom stair. 'I didn't realise you were there.'

'Well, I am.'

'Did you have a fun night?'

'It would have been better if I had known someone here,' she said.

'You could have asked anyone you wanted to,' he said,

walking away from her and into the kitchen. He had been walking away from her all night.

'With a day's notice?' she said as she followed him. She had been following him all night too. 'Everyone already had plans.'

Fionn was going to a party that his newest girlfriend, Zoe, was DJ'ing at. 'It'll be terrible,' he said. 'Some rich wanker who bought too many Graham Knuttel paintings during the boom and can't offload them now.' Robbie and Kevin had rented a cottage on the Beara Peninsula so they could spend 'quality time' with their dog, George Michael. Sarah had asked Aisling to come, 'But you can't tell Ciara, okay?' Aisling had refused to lie, her voice cold on the phone. 'You're putting me in an awkward position, Sarah,' she said.

So, Sarah had decided to treat the New Year's Eve party as Oisín's, but it didn't take her long to regret that decision.

'Oh my God, you went to Dublin Art College,' a friend of Oisín's from university slurred. 'You must know Bebhinn Rafferty then; she would have totally been in your year.'

Sarah shook her head.

'Or what about Faye Kilroy? Like, everyone knows Faye?'

I don't know Faye and I don't know Bebhinn because I didn't make any real friends at DAC besides Fionn, Sarah felt like screaming at her. *I don't know them because everyone was so much cooler than I was and made me feel so utterly inadequate that I sat in that damp flat on Thomas Street, listening to my iPod by myself, wishing I could go back to Dunfinnan, but knowing,*

if I went home, I would have failed. I would have to admit that
I was the same as the rest of them, after all.

'Hello?' Oisín's friend (Sorcha? Siún?) had said, waving her hand in front of Sarah's face, almost singeing Sarah's eyelashes with her cigarette. 'Anyone there?'

'I thought you were going to be in Dunfinnan,' Oisín said now. 'I didn't deliberately try and ruin your New Year's, as much as you want to think that I did.'

The kitchen was destroyed: wine spilled, particles of broken glass glittering in the grooves between the floor tiles, overflowing ashtrays and empty bottles scattered on the countertop.

'You didn't even tell me you were having a party.'

'Sarah, I've told you a million times that—'

'And look at the state of this place,' she said. 'It's trashed.'

'Who cares? The cleaners are coming tomorrow; they'll sort it out. Why are you getting so worked up?'

'Oh, sorry, I forgot about the cleaners, Your Majesty. Aren't you so lucky to have such faithful servants who can take care of your mess?'

Oisín leaned against the sink. 'Why are you being like this?'

'I'm surprised you even care,' Sarah said. 'You seemed to spend the entire night trying to avoid me.'

'No, I wasn't,' he said, but his ears were turning red. Oisín had always been a terrible liar. 'I was catching up with some old mates.'

'Don't worry, I saw you "catching up" with Aifric.'

'Aifric is my friend, Sarah. And she would like to be your friend too, if you'd let her.'

'Oh, so when you were huddled in a corner with her for two hours tonight, all you were talking about was Aifric's burning ambition to be my best friend, right?'

He pulled a chair out from the dining table and slumped onto it. 'I can't—'

'Can't what?'

He looked up at her. 'Is it always going to be like this?'

'Is it always going to be like what?'

Would you ever leave me? Sarah had asked him during those first few months of lust-sickness, when she and Oisín barely left his bedroom. *Would you leave me if I got really sick?* (She thought of her mother, her skin turning yellow, then grey, her voice flickering like a faulty light bulb at the end. And then she thought of Matthew, leaving her alone in that hotel room without a second thought. She couldn't go through that again.) And Oisín had promised Sarah he would stay.

'What if I had a one-night stand with someone else?' she asked. 'If I gained a lot of weight? If I had a fight with your parents and they told you it was them or me? Would you stay, Oisín? Would you choose me?'

'Yes,' he said. 'Yes, yes, yes. I would always choose you, Sarah. I would never leave you.'

She had believed him. She had been unravelling when she was with Matthew, slowly, slowly, then falling apart all at once. Oisín had seemed so solid in comparison, like someone she could rely on to put her back together, piece by piece.

Oisín cracked his knuckles. Sarah hated it when he did that. Why did he insist on doing that when he knew how much it irritated her? 'Maybe we should . . .'

'Maybe we should what?' Sarah asked.

'Maybe we should break up.'

Sarah held a hand out to touch the island countertop, the marble cool beneath her hand. 'I don't understand.'

'I don't think I love you anymore,' he said.

'You don't mean that. Oisín. Don't say that. You can't just say that. Oisín,' she said, kneeling beside his chair, trying not to let her panic show. 'Oisín, come on. Don't be like this. I'm sorry, okay? I know I've been difficult—'

He snorted.

'Okay, I've been a nightmare. But I can change. Please, Oisín. We can work this out.'

His face was tired. 'Can we?'

Do you remember when we first started dating, Oisín? Do you remember the night we met?

It had been Sarah's twenty-fifth birthday that July, and Fionn had insisted that they go out to celebrate. Their friendship had seemed to heal after that night she went to his bedroom, crying over Matthew, but the recovery was a broken, limping thing. Sometimes it felt as if everything was fine, that they were back to normal, and then Fionn would go quiet for days, 'forget' to return Sarah's phone calls, spend more time with whatever girl he was currently dating. Their friendship had always been the one thing that Sarah was sure she couldn't break, and yet she had managed to do it, anyway.

On the morning of her birthday, Fionn came into her room. 'We're going to get trashed,' he said. 'It's not every day that you turn a quarter of a century.' That made twenty-five sound old, and she had felt old recently, as if everything that had happened with Matthew had aged her in some indefinable way. In the last two months, it had taken Sarah longer to get out of bed in the morning; it was more of an effort to get dressed, to smile, to act normally. She missed him. Or maybe she missed being chosen by him, and how special that had made her feel. And now, while it didn't hurt as much as it did before – she was no longer on fire with the pain – somehow it was not a relief. Instead, everything had fallen flat. She was alone without him, and, worse, she was ordinary. How had she never realised how ordinary she was before she met Matthew Brennan? Grey. She was breathing dullness in like smoke, into her hollow lungs and hollow stomach. Hollow heart.

And it was her birthday that day and, even though it was stupid, even though she knew Matthew wouldn't remember, she kept checking her phone. Just in case.

'I've asked Aisling to come up,' Fionn told her.

'Ais and I are fighting,' Sarah said. 'We haven't talked in months.'

'I don't know anything about that,' Fionn replied, 'but she's coming, anyway.'

Aisling arrived three hours later, a small overnight bag in one hand, a bottle of Prosecco in the other.

'You look so thin,' Sarah said, trying not to sound jealous.

'I know,' Aisling replied. 'I'm fucking miserable.' She hugged Sarah.

'I'm sorry about Jamsie,' Sarah whispered into her ear.

'So am I,' Aisling said.

They opened the bottle of Prosecco, Sarah searching for cheap flutes she had bought in Dunnes. Where were they, for fuck's sake?

'Matthew hated Prosecco,' Sarah said. 'He was such a snob about it. He would only drink champagne, and it had to be good champagne, you know?'

Aisling excused herself to go to the bathroom, and Sarah could hear giggling and 'Shhhh! She'll hear you,' and then the door to the kitchen opened and it was Fionn, holding out a chocolate sponge cake, singing 'Happy Birthday'. It was as if nothing had happened and Fionn still loved her.

'Make a wish,' Aisling said as Sarah blew the candles out.

And she wished for *him* to change his mind.

'Matthew loves sponge, but it has to be raspberry and cream,' Sarah said, and Fionn slammed the knife down.

'No,' he said. 'You are not going to spend tonight talking about that arsehole.'

Sarah nodded. She had to be careful with Fionn, these days. 'Fine,' she said. 'I won't talk about him. I promise.'

Later, when the Prosecco was gone, Sarah asked, 'Do you have anything?'

'Of course,' Fionn said, returning with a small enamel box. It was like Matthew's cigar box, she thought, the one— She stopped herself. She wasn't going to think about that. 'Do you want Special K?' he asked. 'Coke?'

'No, not coke. Not tonight.' Sarah wanted to feel happy tonight. 'Have you pills?' she asked him.

'I have this,' he replied, giving her a clear plastic baggie of MDMA and a packet of Rizla. He watched as she tore a sheet of paper in two, sprinkling the crystals in and twisting the top to seal it. 'Only one,' he said. 'This shit is strong.'

She handed a bomb to him, putting the other in her bag. 'Better wait until we're inside the club to take them, then,' she said.

Aisling refused. 'Things are bad enough,' she said. 'I don't need to be dealing with a comedown on top of it.'

'So,' Sarah said, as Fionn ordered a taxi, 'where are we going?'

'On a Tuesday night in Dublin?' he replied. 'You know where we're going, girl.'

Harcourt Street. 'I shouldn't have worn a dress,' Sarah said, as they arrived, 'not to Copper's. I may as well be wearing a sign saying "*Sexually assault me, please*".'

Fionn paid for the three of them to get in. Shots at the bar. Fending off advances from sweaty men in checked shirts. Smiling politely, afraid their faces would turn vicious if she told them to stop. *Fuck you, you fat fucking bitch,* they always said when Sarah decided she was not in the mood to play. *I didn't fancy you anyway.*

Fionn had dropped his MDMA, his pupils bleeding black. 'I want things to be okay with us, Sarah. I love you, Sarah,' he said, hugging her. 'I've always loved you.'

'Mind him, will you? He's off his face,' she told Aisling, laughing. 'I have to go to the toilet to take mine.'

A hand on her shoulder. 'I'm sorry,' the man said. He was handsome and tall, almost as tall as Matthew. His teeth were very white under the lights, his afro cut short to his head. 'I didn't mean to bother you,' he said, 'but I wanted to say hello.'

'Right,' Sarah replied. 'Well, hello.'

'What's a nice girl like you doing in a place like this?'

'Who said I was a nice girl?' she replied.

'Ha,' he said, blushing. 'I'm here for a colleague's going-away party,' he continued. 'I don't normally come to Copper's on a Tuesday night.'

'Neither do I,' Sarah said. 'It's my birthday today.'

'Happy birthday,' he said, insisting on buying her a drink to celebrate. There were more drinks, their bodies moving closer, Sarah quickly texting Aisling to let her know she was okay.

'It's so loud in here, I can't hear you,' she whispered in his ear, his mouth so near to hers.

A rushed taxi drive back to his apartment in the IFSC: an airy loft, views over the docks, and vast canvases on the walls.

'Is that an Oonagh MacManus?' she said in disbelief.

'Yes,' he said, kissing her again, pushing her onto the couch, both of them stripping off their clothes as fast as they could.

'Come to bed,' he said afterwards, and she curled into the foetal position away from him under the covers. He spooned her, a hand between her legs. She was almost asleep when she found herself coming, trembling silently. Later, she would think about that, about the ease with which Oisín had been able to make her orgasm, but she had been so relaxed that night. She wasn't thinking about what she looked like or what effect she was having on the man with her. She was just *present*.

'Good?' he asked her.

She waited, breathing into the pleasure. Then she turned to look at him. She knew this man was different. And she knew, somehow, that she would be different with him. She wanted to be different. She wanted it so much.

'Hello,' Sarah said.

'Hello,' Oisín said back.

Classes started back after Christmas, then it was February midterm break. ('Are you and Oisín doing anything nice?' her father asked on the phone, and Sarah lied and told him they were. 'A city break,' she said. No need to worry Eddie about this. Not yet.) The Easter holidays came and went, and then, somehow, summer was in sight again, Sarah's exam students dragging their wan faces and nail-bitten fingers to class. They trusted Sarah, looked to her for answers, for advice on their coursework, or their portfolios, if they were applying to art college. 'You're doing a great job, Sarah,' the principal told her. 'I'm so glad that you joined us here at Sacred Heart.'

Sarah wanted to tell Oisín (*'A great job,' Ms Loughnan said. Isn't that brilliant?*), but he wasn't there. He never seemed to be there anymore. He left for work in the morning before Sarah woke up, arrived home when it was time to go to bed.

'Where were you, Oisín?' she asked, and he would always shrug.

'Out,' he replied.

Sarah didn't question him further. She was on her best behaviour after what had happened on New Year's; she couldn't give him another opportunity to say he didn't love her anymore. She smiled at Oisín, she asked him how his day was; she didn't snap at him or yell. They were polite to each other, unfailingly so, until it began to feel as if they were roommates who had found themselves living together by accident. Lodgers, not lovers.

Some days, it didn't even feel as if they were friends. If Sarah had learned anything after her mother had died, it was how a house could feel utterly empty with two people still living there. And here she was again, with Oisín this time, noticing how quiet the house became, despite the cacophony of noise that made up their day – the toaster popping, the kettle seething, a slurp of tea, the television on while the two of them sat side by side on the sofa, nearly touching but not quite. Breathing in unison, but never looking at one another, they stared at the screen for something to focus on.

'Is everything okay?' Oonagh asked her. Sarah and Oisín were at the Killiney house for Oonagh's birthday. ('You don't have to come if you don't want to,' Oisín had said earlier. 'Don't you want me to come?' Sarah asked him. 'I didn't say that, did I?' he replied.) It was a warm day, so the rest of the family were sitting on the patio overlooking the bay, sipping sangria. Sarah was helping Oonagh clear the table, rinsing the plates before stacking them in the dishwasher.

'What?' Sarah said. 'Sorry, yes, I'm having a lovely day. It's roasting for May, isn't it?'

'Well, it's June tomorrow, I guess,' Oonagh said. 'And how are you, after your mother's anniversary? Did you go home last week?'

'Yes. Thank you for the Mass card – Dad was delighted with it.'

'Oisín didn't go down with you?'

'He couldn't get the time off work, apparently.'

Oonagh opened the fridge, took the jug of sangria out and poured Sarah a glass. 'There,' she said. 'You look like you need it.'

'It's been a lovely day,' Sarah said again, placing the glass down on the counter. She was trying to drink less, these days. 'And such great news about Domhnall and Eimear.'

Domhnall and Eimear had arrived at the party, Eimear's hand outstretched, a large diamond sparkling in the sunshine. Screams of joy and hugs and, 'You'll be my best man, Ois, won't you?' Sarah's gripping fear that someone would ask Oisín when he was planning on making an honest woman of his own girlfriend. What would his reaction be? Sarah didn't want it to happen; the thought of marrying Oisín terrified her, but the thought of Oisín not wanting to marry her either, broke Sarah. Oisín was supposed to want her. He was supposed to love her forever.

'Yes, I'm delighted,' Oonagh said. 'But I was asking if everything was all right with you and Oisín. You've barely said a word to each other all day.'

Sarah felt unable to move. *We're fine,* she was going to say, but she couldn't get her lips to form the words.

'I don't know,' Sarah said instead. And Oonagh reached out and held her hand.

And then, it was June. 'Anything planned for the afternoon?' the maths teacher asked Sarah as they left the convent at the same time. 'I might go to the beach,' Sarah replied, 'since it's such a nice day.'

When Sarah reached Sandycove, she sat on the wall at the side of the tiny beach. It had been a year since she was last here, a year since she had seen Matthew, but she knew she was safe today. He wouldn't be going for his walk until Saturday, because he was a creature of habit; he didn't like anything or anyone to disturb his daily routine.

Children were building sandcastles, screaming with tears when the older kids ran across them, scattering their creations to the wind. Sarah remembered her first time at the seaside. She was young, so young, and her mother was still there.

'We're going to the beach,' Helen had told her. 'Are you excited, my lovely Sarah?'

Sarah wondered how her mother would have felt about Matthew. Would Helen have been disappointed in her? Or would she have sympathised? Maybe she would have had a similar tale to tell, a youthful misdemeanour, nights spent weeping herself to sleep over a man who had promised her so little and who had given her even less. Maybe that was why Helen had settled for Eddie, a man so much less attractive than she was. Had she thought that Eddie would be a safe option, that he wouldn't hurt her? And then he had, anyway, whether he meant to or not. Perhaps no man was ever a safe option. Loving someone only gave them the opportunity to break your heart. *Like mother, like daughter,* Helen might have said when Sarah came home crying over Matthew. Wasn't that every woman's fate? To turn into her mother? To see her mother's features appearing on her face, her mother's voice cracking out of her throat?

How would Sarah have explained her infatuation with Matthew to Helen? Would she have admitted that she had seen how Matthew's money made him powerful, and that power had, in turn, made him untouchable? No one could dismiss Matthew Brennan; his status had given him automatic access to places that Sarah knew she could not dream of going alone. The only power Sarah ever had with Matthew was when she took off her clothes and watched his eyes turn dark with desire, and even that was taken from her when he forced her to her knees.

She had been stupid; she could see that now. Matthew had always been so clear about what he wanted from her, and still, still Sarah had hoped. In the days that passed after that ill-fated encounter in the Fitzwilliam Hotel, Sarah couldn't understand that hope. She became so familiar with her own tears, with the precise anatomy of her sobs. A double gasp, inhale, inhale, inhale, and she couldn't find the way to push the breath out of her mouth as she rocked back and forward, keening, pain ripping through her. Sometimes she almost felt bored with herself. Sarah knew she didn't own this sadness, not like she had when her mother had died. That grief was alive, pulsing in her throat, and it had been hers; she had been entitled to it. With Matthew, Sarah was a thief, robbing someone else of their heartbreak, stolen moments of sorrow that she should apologise for taking. They didn't belong to her.

Sarah pulled her knees into her chest, staring at the sea. Why had she been so distraught? She didn't even know Matthew, not really. She had made a collage out of scraps of imagination and flights of fancy, imbuing him with qualities that he probably did not possess. Did all women take half-truths and implied promises and side glances and smiles and weave them together to create a narrative, the way she had done? Did those women write their own bedtime stories too, recite them out loud for comfort? Or did they just move on, relegating their unpleasant experiences to the footnotes in their romantic history? Matthew had used her, yes, he had taken what he could from her, but maybe it was time to admit that Sarah had used him too, in her own way. She thought of that night in his house when he had reached out to her, when he had tried to be vulnerable, and how repellent she had found it. She hadn't wanted Matthew to be a real person with real needs. She had wanted him to remain a mystery that she could go insane trying to untangle.

Sarah stood up, brushing sand off her jeans. And then, her heartbeat slowing, she thought she saw him.

But it wasn't Matthew. It had never been Matthew.

'How was work?' Sarah asked Oisín that evening.

He opened the fridge and drank orange juice straight from the carton. He put the empty container back in the fridge instead of in the recycling bin, as if daring her to start a fight.

'Grand,' he said.

'Anything exciting happen?'

'Nah.'

'Where did you go for lunch?'

'Dunne and Crescenzi, with Richard.'

Sarah didn't know who Richard was. Oisín always went for lunch with Cooper, and they always went to Lemon, Cooper making fun of Oisín because he ordered the exact same crêpe every time. Who was Richard? When did he start working at Bryant? Was he a client adviser too?

'I made that four-cheese lasagne,' she said. 'I haven't made it in ages and I know it's your favourite.'

'I'm not hungry.'

'You can have it tomorrow evening, then. If you want.'

'I'm going out with the UCD lads tomorrow night.' Oisín walked into the living room and switched on the TV.

'That sounds fun,' Sarah said, following him.

'Yeah.' He turned the volume up.

'I could come?'

'It's just the lads.'

'Oh,' she said. 'Okay.'

She stood there, watching Oisín watch the TV. But he didn't say any more.

'Oh, God,' Oisín said as he nearly fell out of the bed, pulling the duvet with him.

'Good night, then, I'll take it?' Sarah asked. She wasn't accusing him of anything; she wasn't nagging or causing an argument. It was a simple question.

'What time is it?' He buried his head under the pillow. 'Is it always this bright in here?'

'It's half ten.'

Sarah had tried to stay awake until Oisín came home last night, dozing in front of reruns of some terrible reality show on Channel 4. She wanted to tell him about her last day at school, how two second years, Fiadh Mooney and Sadie Scanlon, had almost come to blows at lunchtime. As their year head, Sarah had taken the girls into an empty classroom and attempted to mediate a truce.

'You don't understand,' Sadie had said, crying. 'I was only broken up with Luca for, like, five minutes, when Fiadh got with him.'

Fiadh bristled at this, about to retort when Sarah gave her a stern look, telling them that friendship was far too important and that they shouldn't allow any boy to come between them. 'Chicks before . . .' and she broke off, both girls collapsing in laughter when they realised what Sarah had been about to say.

'You're cool, miss,' Fiadh had said; high praise indeed from a fifteen-year-old girl.

Last year, Oisín would have laughed at that anecdote. Everything had been different last year.

After work, Sarah had waved off requests from the other teachers to come for drinks to mark the summer holidays, walking alone to Oonagh's house in Booterstown (our house, she told herself; it's our house). She made dinner. She watched TV. And she waited for Oisín to come home. That's what women did, she thought. That's what she had watched her mother do for years. Helen had sat at the kitchen table, waiting for her life to begin. And then, she couldn't wait anymore.

Sarah had made herself go to bed at midnight, drifting into the uneasy sleep of someone who knew that they would be disturbed at any minute, jolting awake when she heard the front door open. Oisín had crashed beside her, fully clothed.

'Oisín,' she had said. 'Oisín, do you want to get changed?' But he didn't move.

Sarah couldn't fall back to sleep after that. She reminded herself of all the ways in which Oisín was perfect for her, all the things he had done for her, how good and kind he was to her. She counted the reasons why she couldn't leave him. She counted the reasons why she couldn't allow him to leave her either.

'Do you want me to get you something to eat?' Sarah asked Oisín now, as he turned over. The latticed bed linen had etched its pattern on his forehead; his eyes were bloodshot. 'Or something to drink? I'll make you Dioralyte, put some Solpadeine in it too. That'll help.'

Oisín's suit jacket and shoes were in a heap at the bottom of the staircase. Sarah picked them up, leaving the shoes in the rack by the front door, hanging the jacket on a chair in the kitchen. She fished his phone out of his pocket and placed it on the tray. He needs me, Sarah said to herself as she tipped two eggs into a saucepan of boiling water. Her phone rang as she waited for them to cook. It was her father.

Hi Dad, Sarah imagined herself saying. *How are you?* And when he asked her the same, she would tell him that she wasn't doing too great. She would tell him that Oisín was about to break up with her, it was obvious. *It's gotten so quiet in this house, Dad,* she would say, *but the two of us would know all about that, wouldn't we?* Eddie would ask her what went wrong, and what could Sarah say? That she had loved Oisín, and he had loved her. She had thought that he was The One, and that this was the relationship that would finally make her forget everything that had happened before. Sarah had thought she was happy, she had certainly felt happy at times, and yet she still hadn't been able to stop thinking about Matthew. Matthew, who was petty and vain and self-obsessed; Matthew, who was too old for her; Matthew, who treated her as if she was worthless. Matthew. Why did it always come back to Matthew Brennan?

Oisín had offered Sarah unconditional love and security; shouldn't that have been enough for her? But their life together had become mundane so quickly (*Did you take the bins out? Did you oil the gate, like I asked you? Why do you always leave your dirty dishes in the sink? Why do you have to slurp your tea? I don't want to see that movie; I'm tired of watching grown men run around in Lycra costumes. Why do we have to go out with your friends again? Are you listening to me? Oisín, I asked if you were listening to me . . .*) and Sarah felt too young to be bored. Matthew had never bored her; not with the nerves she fought as she took the hotel elevator to room 63, the churning anticipation as she checked her phone to see if there was a message, the ferocious, falling relief when he finally decided to contact her. Oisín had been straightforward – he texted regularly, he phoned when he said he would, he said 'I love you' first, smiling, as if it was safe – and, because of that, Sarah knew she hadn't valued his love, or Oisín himself. Recently, Sarah had been thinking that Oisín might simply have been ready to fall in love when she met him – that she had been in the right place at the right time. Any girl in Copper's that night would have done; it could have been Aisling standing in this kitchen instead of Sarah. And while Sarah agreed with what Aisling told her – that Matthew was a fuckboy, that he was afraid of commitment, that his issues went deeper than Sarah could even begin to comprehend– there was a part of her which still believed that Matthew would only fall in love with someone who was truly deserving of him, and he had decided that Sarah was not. Sometimes, Sarah felt as if she could spend the rest of her life fighting to make him change his mind, that only when Matthew gave in and said he loved her would she ever find any kind of peace.

Oisín's phone beeped and, without thinking, Sarah unlocked it.

'Does Oisín have your passcode too?' Aisling had asked when she saw Sarah do this, and Sarah had laughed.

'No, of course not,' she said.

Aisling didn't comment, although it was obvious she wanted to. She liked them as a couple. 'You're calmer with Oisín,' she told Sarah. 'You were always so wound up when you were with . . .' She stopped herself, changing the subject. They never said Matthew's name aloud anymore.

Aifric: You put me in a really awkward position tonight. I know you and Sarah are having some problems, but she's a nice girl and I like her. I'm not covering for you anymore, so grow up.

Sarah sat on a kitchen stool. She checked Oisín's other unopened texts. There was one from JJ at 3 a.m., asking where Oisín had gone to, and then –

Cliona: Tonight was amazing. I can't wait to do it again.

xxxxxx

Sarah scrolled up through the conversation. They had been texting for a while, Cliona's inability to differentiate between 'their' and 'they're' not proving to be a deal-breaker for Oisín. *You're so funny, Cliona,* Oisín texted her, although Sarah couldn't see much evidence of wit in these messages.

'Very funny,' Matthew used to say to her. 'Very funny, for a girl.'

Maybe men didn't want women to be funny, not the women they were having sex with, anyway. Sarah suspected that men wanted a girlfriend to be 'fun', which seemed to mean she should find them funny and laugh at their jokes, never making any of her own.

Sarah inhaled sharply when she saw that Oisín called this other woman *sugar-bum*, something he had christened Sarah when they started dating. The language he used was interchangeable; he could have copied and pasted his texts to Sarah from two years ago and no one would have been able to tell the difference.

Cliona had texted him on Thursday, saying that she and Aifric would be out on Friday night after their *shoot for*

Virginia Macari, and that she hoped Oisín was going to come too. Not just a boys' night out, then, Sarah thought. Why hadn't Oisín changed his passcode? Was there a part of him that wanted Sarah to see these texts? If this had been last year, she would have run up the stairs in fury and thrown the phone at Oisín's face. *You bastard,* she would have shouted at him. *How could you do this to me?*

Sarah didn't do that today. It was as if she had been waiting for this to happen. She wanted to talk to someone, but who would she phone? She hadn't spoken to Aisling since Christmas; Fionn was always working. She had an urge to ask Oonagh for advice, but she wasn't sure if she would like what Oonagh had to say. She put the phone into the chest pocket of her pyjamas, then stared at her hands, wondering why they weren't shaking. She felt so calm.

She buttered the toast and made a strong pot of tea, the way she used to for her father when he was still drinking, holding his hangover between his fingers like a hand grenade, looking for someone to throw it at. Sarah had hoped Eddie would say that she was a great girl, that tea and toast was just what he needed. *Thank you, Sarah,* she'd imagined him saying. *What would I do without you?* But he never did. He would take two sips and return to bed for the day, leaving Sarah alone again, planning new ways to make her father happy.

'Here you go, now,' Sarah said, nudging the door to their bedroom open with her foot. 'Breakfast is served.' She rested the tray on Oisín's outstretched legs. 'Poached eggs,' she said. 'Just the way you like them.'

When he finished eating, Sarah put the tray on the floor and sat next to him. 'Good?'

'Yes,' he replied, swallowing back the Solpadeine with a grimace. 'Thank you.'

'No bother,' she said. She pulled his phone out of her pocket and handed it to him. 'You left this downstairs.'

He took it from her, wincing as he scrolled through his now-opened messages. He lifted his head, his eyes fearful.

'Sarah, I—'

She kissed him, silencing him. He hesitated, but then he kissed her back. Sarah knelt, moving over to straddle him, grinding her hips against his until she felt him get hard, almost despite himself.

'Sarah . . .'

'Remember,' she said, resting her forehead against his. 'Remember that first night?' She pulled him closer, slipping her hand between them, easing Oisín into her. 'Oisín,' she said, repeating his name as if she was casting a spell to bring him back to her, to make him belong to her once more. Sarah was close to coming when she began to cry. She tried to stay quiet, to allow Oisín to enjoy himself, but it was impossible, her breath dissolving into sobs.

'Sarah,' he said. She could feel his erection soften inside her and she felt as if she should apologise. She should probably apologise for a lot of things. 'Please, Sarah. Please don't cry.'

She drew back so that she could see his face. She saw in him the future they could have had together, if they had been different people, if they had each been able to give the other what they needed. And then it was gone.

'I'm sorry,' Sarah said.

'I know you are,' Oisín replied, touching his fingers to her heart for one last time. 'I'm sorry too.'

'Is this all you have, pet?' Eddie asked Sarah when he picked her up at Clonmel station. The bus had arrived early, so she sat on a bench outside, two duffel bags at her feet, waiting for Eddie's jeep to pull up.

'Yes.'

When Sarah had left Dunfinnan for art college, Eddie had driven her to Dublin, her clothes and shoes shoved in black plastic bags, her books and art supplies and her port-folio in cardboard boxes, crammed into the back of the jeep. But when she packed up her life in Booterstown, she found that nothing there belonged to her. She walked through the rooms, then stood in front of a framed photo of her and Oisín on the mantelpiece, one that was taken when they had been hopeful. She didn't take it with her. Sarah closed the front door behind her and put her house keys through the letter box, marvelling at the ease with which a life together could be dismantled. She had moved into the spare bedroom for a couple of days, staying in bed until Oisín left for work in the morning, sneaking upstairs when he returned in the evening. All it took was a phone call to Eddie to tell him that she would be coming home, and it was over. Sarah had sent Oonagh a text message too, explaining that she and Oisín had broken up, but that she would always be grateful for their time together. Oonagh had texted back one sentence: *I'm proud of you, Sarah,* she said.

'And guess what?' Eddie said, as he opened the back door, kicking a set of wellies out of the way. The kitchen was immaculate and smelled strongly of bleach. Sarah bit her lip to stop herself from laughing. 'I got the shower in the main bathroom fixed for you yesterday. Dan O'Mahony said the pressure should be much better now.'

'Ah, Dad, you shouldn't have gone to any hassle.'

'Not a bit of it,' he said, as he went into the hall to throw her duffel bags at the foot of the stairs. 'It made more sense, what with you being home for the summer and all.'

'Okay,' Sarah said. Home for the summer. I'm home for the summer. 'Thanks, Dad.'

She was suddenly exhausted. She wanted nothing more than to crawl into bed, pull the duvet over her head and fall asleep for one hundred years.

'So,' Eddie said, as they sat at the table to have some tea.

Sarah stirred milk into hers, flecks of white skimming

the surface. It must be going off, she thought. I should tell him.

But she didn't. She sat there and drank it anyway.

'So,' she repeated.

'What are your plans for the summer?' he asked, opening a tin of USA biscuits and handing Sarah the pink wafer, her favourite.

'I'm not sure,' she said, dunking the biscuit into her tea. 'Thanks for having me, though; I appreciate it.'

'Don't be daft,' he said. 'This is your home. It always will be.' He stirred another teaspoon of sugar into his tea.

Sarah knew she should tell him that sugar was bad for him, that it caused diabetes, increased the risk of dying from heart disease, cancer. But she didn't do that either.

'Would you . . . ?' Eddie began.

'Would I what?'

'Well, now that you have some time, would you think about doing a bit of painting?'

'What?'

'Only if you felt like it,' Eddie rushed on. 'Now that you have some time, I mean. I cleaned out the shed for you, in case you got the notion. Oonagh said—'

'Oonagh? Oonagh MacManus?'

'Yes.'

'Why were you talking to Oonagh MacManus, Dad? How do you even have her number?'

'She gave it to me after that barbeque in your house last

year. We had a bit of a debate about the Irish language; you know I think it's a waste of taxpayers' money to—'

'But why are you in touch with her now? It doesn't make any sense.'

'Why wouldn't I be in touch with her?'

'Well, like, I can't imagine what you and Oonagh Mac-Manus would have in common.'

'Sarah,' her father said, 'people are just people, you know.'

'True, I guess,' Sarah said, staring out the window. There were mounds of silage in black sheeting in the main field, cows being herded down the lane to the milking parlour by one of the farmhands. The front garden, which had been the preserve of Nana Kathleen – and Sarah's mother, before her – was overgrown, the roses lining the narrow path up to the front door choked in a tangled mess of weeds. Mrs Morrison would be horrified, she thought to herself. What would happen when Oisín's new girlfriend moved into the house in Booterstown? Would Mrs Morrison call Clíona 'Áine' as well?

'Silage has been cut,' Sarah said, reaching out to take another pink wafer from the biscuit tin.

'What?' Eddie said, looking out the window too. 'Yes. We have a new guy helping us. He's young. Around your age.'

'Oh, God – don't, Dad.'

'Don't what?'

'Don't try to matchmake; it's weird.'

'I wasn't trying to matchmake,' Eddie protested. 'I just

thought it might be nice for you to have some company. I doubt you'll want to hang out with a man in his sixties for the summer.' He poured more tea into his cup. 'Have you texted Aisling at all? Does she know you're home?'

'Not yet.'

'She's off to Brisbane in a couple of weeks, Sarah; don't be hanging around, now.'

'I don't know if she wants to hear from me,' Sarah said. 'I haven't spoken to her since Christmas.'

'Of course she wants to hear from you.'

'I don't think I've been a very good friend to her, this last year.' Sarah looked out the window again, one last dawdling cow disappearing out of sight. 'I don't think I was a very good girlfriend, either.'

Eddie shifted in his seat. 'Ah, well.'

'I just wish . . .' She swallowed hard. 'I wish I had done things differently.'

'Sarah –' Eddie stopped, choosing his words carefully – 'we all have regrets. That's part of being an adult, I'm afraid. You think that I don't have regrets? You think that I don't have things I would do differently, if I had my time over? If you had any idea what I . . .' He sighed. 'Well. I think we both know that I made mistakes. But sometimes you just have to get on with things, don't you?'

'Get on with things,' she repeated.

'Yes,' her father said. 'Get on with things. There's no going back anyway, now, is there?' He stood up, pressing

306

his hands against his knees for leverage, wincing as his joints cracked. 'I'm getting old,' he said.

'You work too hard, Dad. You should just sell the farm; it's not like I'm going to be taking it over, now, is it?'

'Sure, what would I do with myself then?' he said, bending over to gather up a stack of newspapers by the fireplace. 'I don't know why I keep buying these; they take up most of the recycling.' He walked towards the door, newspapers in hand, and said, with his back turned, 'Your friend was in the *Sunday Independent* this weekend.'

'My friend?'

'Your man, Brennan,' Eddie said, as he came back to the table. 'He was at some ball, all dickied up.'

'Really.'

'He'd go to the opening of an envelope, that fella.' Eddie cleared his throat. 'His life seems lonely, if you ask me.'

Sarah met Eddie's gaze and they both half-smiled. Maybe Eddie was right. Maybe Matthew's life was lonely. Maybe he did feel unfulfilled. Whatever it was, it had nothing to do with her anymore. Sarah had enough problems of her own. Why had they never seemed as important for her to fix as Matthew's issues had?

'I think I'll go upstairs and take a nap,' Sarah said. 'I'm wrecked.'

'Okay,' her father said. 'I'll call you when it's time for dinner.'

The wooden cabinet by the door was grimy with dust,

but the photo was still there, trapped behind the glass pane: the photo Sarah had used as inspiration for her Leaving Cert art project. Sarah and her mother and father, walking on Tramore beach. Sarah and Helen hand in hand, Helen smiling down at Sarah, Eddie trailing behind them.

'That was a good day, wasn't it?' her father said.

'It was.'

'We could go to Tramore again this summer, if the weather is good enough? Maybe for your birthday?'

She would be twenty-eight this year. Twenty-eight and single and living back at home with her father.

'Sarah?' Eddie said. 'Would you like that?'

'Sure.'

Sarah could hear her father get up and move closer, until he was hovering behind her.

'It was such a hot summer, that year,' he said. 'And you were so small. Your mam had you covered in suncream, head to toe, and that sunhat too, even though you hated it. Remember? You kept saying it was too tight.'

'She was a good mother.'

'She was,' Eddie said. 'That she was. Do you remember when she went to get ice creams?' he asked.

Yes, Sarah thought. You gave out about the price of them, telling Mam they were cheaper in SuperValu in Clonmel, and could we not just buy them there. Mam told you not to be miserly, that it was my first day at the beach, and that we were all going to have ice creams, whether you liked it or not.

'And when she had gone to the ice-cream van, you ran away from me.' He snorted. 'Never thought I'd see the day when I would be outrun by a four-year-old, but there you go. You headed straight for the sea. No fear. Nothing. A little warrior, even then.'

A warrior? Sarah thought. That seemed unlikely. She felt as if she had spent her whole life trying to outrun her fears. But she couldn't run anymore.

'And then this wave crashed on top of you, knocking you clean over. Christ Jesus, my heart.'

I don't remember that.

'And you bawled your eyes out; sure, you were only a tot at that stage. And I picked you up and held you in my arms, and I had to sing that song from that godawful TV show you used to insist on watching. Ah, here, what was it called again? The one with the dinosaur? I had to keep singing until you stopped crying.'

Her father reached out and touched her shoulder, so gently she could have imagined it.

'Do you remember that, Sarah?' he asked her, his voice almost pleading.

'Yes, Dad,' she said. She was lying, but maybe that didn't matter, in the end. 'I remember.'

ACKNOWLEDGEMENTS

My parents, Marie and Michael O'Neill. Thank you for taking such good care of me; for all the sports psychology (Dad, obviously) and the elaborate plans to hunt down online trolls and report them to the guards/their parents (Mom, these fools don't know who they're dealing with). I have no words to describe how much I love you both, and I'm supposed to be the writer in the family.

Thank you to my endlessly encouraging sister, Michelle O'Neill, whose confidence in me means so much. Thanks also to my wonderful aunt, Anne Murphy, my beloved Granny Murphy, and the extended Murphy/O'Neill clan. You can't pick your family but if I could, you would still be the ones I chose.

Rachel Conway, my agent/friend/therapist/cheerleader. I don't know how you remain so patient but your seemingly inexhaustible reserves of support have kept me sane. Thank you for always being there for me, both professionally and personally. You are a star.

Thank you to my editor, Niamh Mulvey, for pushing me to make this book the very best that it could possibly be. Your notes are always incisive, sharp and extraordinarily perceptive.

Thank you to Rose Tomaszewska for her constructive thoughts on the first draft. Thanks also to Jon Riley and Rich Arcus at riverrun, to Hannah Robinson, Bethan Ferguson, Alainna Hadjigeorgiou, and everyone at Quercus and Hachette Ireland who work so hard on my behalf. I am very grateful.

Thanks to Geraldine O'Sullivan for taking the time to give me an in-depth tour of her studio, and answering all my inane questions about the life of an artist. Thanks to Claire Tracey for her advice on parent–teacher meetings and school timetables, and Laura Hickey, for saving half my manuscript.

Thank you, Marian Keyes, for reading that PDF so quickly and reassuring me that I wasn't the Worst Writer in the Entire World™. You and Tony have been unbelievably generous to me, and I am lucky to call you my friends/adoptive parents.

Many thanks to my early readers – Cat Doyle (who brainstormed the initial plot outline with me, and then patiently read every new draft. *Almost Love* wouldn't exist without you), Cecelia Ahern (sorry there were no mermaids!), Sarah Perry (your email made me cry with joy), Aine Loughnan (who was gracious enough to pretend this book was as important as her two human children), Traolach O'Buachalla (you just get it, T), Rachel Wright (your feedback was as wise and honest as you are), and the very lovely Susan Cahill.

Special thanks to Grace O'Sullivan, my Trinity Bitches (Suzanne Curley, Lorna English, Jenn Flewett, Roisin Kelly, Caroline Meade and Emma Sisk), Vicky Landers, Ann McCarrick, Orlagh Quinlan, Niamh Ni Dhomnaill, Katie Grant, Jackie Emerson, Catherine Deasy, Irene Kelleher and Aoife Murray. And to the rest of my incredible friends, especially my writer pals – there are too many to list here but you know who you are. Your love has kept me afloat during the last couple of years.

Thank you to Vickie Maye, my editor at the *Irish Examiner*, for taking a chance on me. Thanks to Adrienne Becker for her tireless championing of *Only Ever Yours*, Pamela Drynan for her kindness during the making of the *Asking For It?* documentary, and Brian Cliff, who won an auction in aid of the CLIC Sargent charity to have a character named after his daughter, Maura Cliff.

Thank you to the booksellers who backed my novels from the very beginning, and finally, the biggest thanks must go to the readers. You make all of this worthwhile.